THE MISTRESS CONTRACT

FILTHY BILLIONAIRES

EVELYN AUSTIN

SILVER GRIFFON ASSOCIATES
ORANGE, CA, USA

Silver Griffon Associates
P.O. Box 7383
Orange, CA 92863

Publisher's Note: This is a work of fiction. Names, characters, places, and incidents are a product of the author's imagination. Locales and public names are sometimes used for atmospheric purposes. Any resemblance to actual people, living or dead, or to businesses, companies, events, institutions, or locales is completely coincidental.

Trademarked names appear throughout this book. Rather than use a trademark symbol with every occurrence of a trademarked name, names are used in an editorial fashion, with no intention of infringement of the respective owner's trademark.

Book Layout ©2022 BookDesignTemplates.com
Cover Art ©2022 Kristie Vanilla Lilly Designs Co.

The Mistress Contract / Evelyn Austin. – 1st ed.
ISBN 978-1-940951-30-0

www.EvelynAustin.com

CHAPTER 1
THE INTERVIEW

SO TODAY IS THE BIG INTERVIEW. I JUST FOUND OUT ABOUT it, and already my expectations are soaring. This could change *everything*, and though I'm fighting hard to keep from getting my hopes up, it's hard. I'm already imagining a hundred different outcomes, each with me succeeding wildly at changing my stars.

God knows, I need to change my stars. And *quickly*.

So I try my best to ignore the fact that it's raining during this not-so-lovely spring morning in Los Angeles as I push through the fancy chrome-bedecked entrance of the Montage Beverly Hills.

Whoa, talk about snob central.

I abruptly shorten my stride as the soles of my sensible—but very wet—heels slip across the perfectly polished marble. I pause, catching my breath and swallowing the lump in my throat. I need this. No one here needs it more than me.

And I'm smart. *You've got this, girl!*

My roommate Sam's voice echoes in my head again with her usually cheery upbeat encouragement. I *do* have this. Or if I don't have it *yet,* I'll grab it with both hands and never let it go. I'm *determined.*

But the only details I have are that this is for a personal assistant position and the pay is omigod fantastic. That was more than enough to pique my interest. Strangely, she'd only shrugged when I'd pressed her for more info.

The lobby of the Montage, Beverly Hills is done all in dark teak wood and stylish colored glass. Luxurious and modern in a trendy, Craftsman-inspired way. As a tuition-poor student of a private university, I'd rarely seen inside a place like this unless working a night job cleaning rooms or manning the reservation desk. I check the notes Sam scribbled out for me—a secretary would meet me at the entrance to one of the hotel's restaurants to handle my intake. Unusual, yes. Maybe this is for a high-speed start-up with low initial overhead?

But…in Beverly Hills?

I glance at the time on my phone. Shit. I'm late, *really* late. Damn rain.

As I approach a table manned by two women in very fashionable business attire, I pull my application out of the folder in which I'd been carrying it.

One of the women smiles, revealing perfect white teeth. "Your name?"

"Madeline Swanson," I answer. "I have a two o'clock interview." Hopefully she won't notice it's almost two thirty. But her eyebrows rise as she glances at her gold wristwatch.

"I, uh, I got a little lost," I add.

"No problem." With a tight smile, she hands me a form on a clipboard with a pen attached. "Fill these out and wait right here." She indicates the row of seated women to her right. "It'll just be a few minutes."

I take the forms and walk to the only available seat. It doesn't miss my attention that every woman here is beautiful, and I suddenly fear I've stepped into the wrong interview. They know this is for an assistant position, right? Not a modeling gig? This is Southern California, after all, but sheesh, *someone* should be plain-looking.... Maybe that was what I was here to do. To fulfill that quota.

I suddenly feel self-conscious in my black cardigan and flowered pencil skirt, a hand-me-down from one of my roommates, Gwen, who wears a size smaller than me. It's too tight and doesn't exactly scream professional assistant, but it's literally the only skirt I own.

I glance down at the form the woman gave me. It's all medical questions, which I answer pretty quickly, checking off *no* for nearly every question. The second form is a non-disclosure agreement. I fill in my name and sign without reading the details.

Once done, I take a minute to size up my competition. If they're hiring on looks alone, then my chances are pretty dismal. Every woman here looks like an out-of-work actress—tight, thin bodies, carefully manicured nails, perfect makeup and smooth, flawless hair, designer bags. They don't even bother to return my curious glances. With my hair up in a ponytail and my discount clothing, I'm clearly no competition.

After a few minutes, the woman calls me up and points toward an elevator. "Take that all the way up to the top floor, penthouse."

I blink at that little bit of information she'd so casually delivered. Why they'd secure the penthouse for something as trivial as assistant interviews, I could never guess. Maybe the company wanted to make a good first impression? I'm not even sure what company this is for anyway. I'd noticed no logo on the application forms. But I'm so desperate, I hardly care.

As I walk toward the bank of elevators, my insides begin to shake, my heart hammering hard against my ribs. I feel a little faint. But I manage to keep it together as I push the button for the penthouse.

The elevator sweeps upward with maximum velocity, and I lose my stomach around the third floor. By the time the elevator doors whoosh open, my knees are practically knocking together in an attempt to hold me up. As I step through, my heels sink into plush pink carpeting and I look around. It's a small receiving area, and to my left there's only one door. It's cracked open, but I knock anyway.

I hear a brusque, "Come in," and push the door open.

Blinking as I step in, I fight the urge to gasp. The suite is extraordinary—huge, for one thing. It's at least one hundred times the size of my tiny shared room in student housing. And the place is drenched in luxury. The furniture is all glass and chrome—sleek, but in the classic style. Windows line the entire far wall, looking out over the spectacular skyline of downtown Los Angeles.

The sunken living room is ringed by a raised platform all around, which butts up against the floor-to-ceiling windows.

Suddenly, I realize I'm out of my element. This is all a big mistake. Sam must have gotten her wires crossed. Whatever these people are looking for, it's definitely not me.

Slowly, I turn to leave when someone enters the room through an interior doorway.

"Enter. *This* way," the man says, his deep, accented voice stopping me cold.

Turning somewhat sheepishly, I try to school my features. I don't want him to see my fear, my uncertainty, so I plaster on a shaky smile, lifting my eyes to meet his. He stands beside the window on the raised platform. Sucking in a sharp breath, I freeze, my heart thumping wildly. I'm stunned—actually *stunned*—by his beauty.

At least six foot three, he's young with dark brown hair and blue, blue eyes. He's *hot.* Like, crazy hot. It takes everything for me not to squeak and run out of the room, which I would do, if I weren't rooted to the spot.

He smiles and holds out his hand. "I'm Evan." His smooth, British accent trickles down my spine and makes me feel a little light-headed. I blink, struggling to regain my faculties.

Then I totter up to him like a newborn foal, managing to climb down into the sunken living room, cross it and climb the two steps up to the platform to him. Quickly licking my lips and working moisture into my mouth, I take his proffered hand.

"Madeline," I say in a strangled voice.

His grip is strong, and a weird jolt of energy rushes through me at the contact. I jerk my hand back. My cheeks flush hot, and I'm suddenly embarrassed, though he doesn't seem to notice. Or maybe he just doesn't care.

His spicy scent surrounds me as he pulls his hand back and slips both in his pockets. His smell is heavenly. I draw in a quick breath. What the hell is wrong with me? I've never been this affected by a stranger before.

His eyes then travel—*slowly*—from my neck, down across my chest, my waist, lingering for a moment on my hips, till they hit my legs and the hideous skirt, skittering away immediately. I suddenly wish I was seated or cringing behind a table or desk somewhere, with at least a few furnished barriers between us.

Throughout this attentive inspection, his impossibly handsome features have remained impassive. That strange gleam in his blue eyes makes him appear conflicted until finally an almost bored look crosses his features.

Obviously he's not much impressed with what he sees. Given my competition waiting downstairs, it's not difficult to understand why.

Best to get this over with, then. My stomach sinks. All those wonderful hopes I'd entered the building with are now circling the drain.

I hold out my application and medical form to him. "I'm sorry, I don't have my resume with me. My printer jammed this morning."

A lie. The truth is I can't afford the ink, so it now sits on my desk, a useless paperweight.

He eyes me, lids narrowing slightly before taking the proper paperwork and holding it near the window for the light in order to read the paper.

I lace my fingers together and mentally will myself to keep from fidgeting. How I wish he'd invited me to sit, damnit.

He shifts, and with each movement, I get another whiff of that smell and it gives me this weird sort of rush. Nonplussed, I resolve to try and breathe through my mouth for the rest of the interview.

God, this is awkward. But he is all cool confidence as he stands before me, large, designer-bedecked feet planted a wide shoulders-width apart. He shifts the focus of those baby-blues on me again with laser intensity, and I suddenly find it hard to breathe. "Tell me about yourself."

I take a deep breath. This is always the part I hate. I'm more comfortable talking about other people, their lives, and their interests. I have no desire, whatsoever, to talk about myself.

"Well, I go to school at Caltech full-time. And I currently work in the campus coffee shop whenever I can get the hours."

Interest lights in his eyes as he tilts his head suddenly. His gaze rakes over me, from head to foot, as though he can't believe I'm a Caltech student. I get that a lot. "What do you study?"

"Engineering and Applied Science, specifically Aerospace."

His eyes narrow, and he touches a finger to his chin. "And have you ever done work of this nature before?"

I'm too embarrassed to admit that I have no idea what the job description even is, so I do what any girl would do in my position. I bluff. "Not exactly," I mumble. That stern, assessing gaze unnerves me. "But—but I'm a fast learner, and I'm confident I can do the work."

He laughs, his gaze still lingering on me, heating my skin in all the places it touches. "Well, we'll see about that."

I frown, puzzled. Did I say something amusing? It's clear by his reaction that I'd botched this already. Suddenly, I can't wait to get out of here. This is clearly a waste of both our time.

My hands start to sweat, and I resist the urge to wipe them across my thighs over my skirt, as he again glances through my paperwork.

"It doesn't say here whether or not you're on birth control." He glances up at me, expecting an answer.

My eyes widen as my jaw drops "I, um..." I'm searching for an answer. I'd deliberately skipped that question. It isn't any of their business, anyway. "Is that even relevant?" Or for that matter, legal to ask?

His beautiful features harden. "Of course, it's relevant. I insist on birth control."

I blink. Wow, control freak central. Is he really *that* against paying for maternity leave? In my case it isn't even an issue. I don't have a boyfriend, let alone a sex life.

I'm now looking at him like he's grown hooves, genuinely baffled. "Uh…*why?*"

Now he's looking at *me* like *I'm* an idiot. "I think that should be obvious, no?"

I frown, but don't reply. Best not to even press the discussion. This interview was over thirty seconds—at the most—after it began.

His gaze is on me again, hot, intense, and I'm paralyzed by his brilliant aquamarine stare. I almost have to remind myself to breathe.

His mouth opens slightly, and the papers crackle as his fist tightens at his side. "You may remove your clothes now."

I blink, hesitating for a slight moment before even comprehending what he's asking. I feel like I'm under some sort of strange spell that slows all my reactions.

"Um. *What?*"

Chapter 2
On Your Knees

HE SPEAKS AGAIN, HIS WORDS SLOW AND DELIBERATE, edged with that erotic, almost otherworldly accent. "No need to be shy, Miss Swanson. If you get the contract, we'll be fucking, after all."

His words have a strange affect on me—confusion is at the forefront, followed by yet more confusion. Had I heard him correctly or was I having some type of aural hallucination? Or was this man just a douchebag?

"*What?*" As in—What. The. Everliving. *Fuck.*

He seems mildly amused by my confusion. "You'll have to get used to my language, as well. I speak plainly. The contract is for a mistress—a regular sexual partner. There *will* be fucking…and *a lot* of it." He concludes with a grin and then a nod. Again, his eyes fix on the top buttons of my blouse, as if waiting for me to rip it open for him.

But the words *contract* and *fucking* and *mistress* shock me, and I gape at him, horrified.

What the *hell* have I walked into?

I step back abruptly, my knees knocking together and my heels slipping across the glossy stone floor. He follows me, still maintaining a distance, but it pushes me to take another step away from him.

Except this time, my foot comes down on air—I've hit the steps into the sunken living room without realizing. Losing my balance, I feel myself go over—probably destined to splat and bang my head on the glass coffee table. *That's all she wrote.*

But the man—Evan's—reflexes are lightning fast, and through a blur, I see him move quick enough to hook a powerful arm around my waist and save me from what would probably have been severe injury—or at least severe humiliation.

He jerks my body back up, against his, and for the first time I'm aware—though I'd suspected—that his body is rock hard beneath that suit.

He holds me tight against him for long moments, and those stunning eyes capture my own. Everything is still. There is silence all around us—a silence so loud that it roars. All I can hear are my own rushed breaths and the wildly beating heart in my throat and at my temple.

"Thank—thank—"

He shushes me, placing a large finger against my lips. "Are you alright?" he asks, and with his finger against my lips, all I can do is nod, wide-eyed, like a child.

His eyes hold mine captive as he tilts his finger slightly, using it to outline my lips. His touch is electric, burning me like fire. My lips tingle under his touch, quivering against his finger. His eyes leave mine, only to follow where his finger is going as, quickly, he changes from his index finger to his thumb, tracing my mouth again.

And I'm melting beneath his touch as if he's casting a spell on me. His thumb flexes, tugging at my lower lip, as if asking permission, and without even thinking, I open my mouth. As I knew it would, his thumb pushes inside, first to the knuckle, then entering completely. At the same time, he's redirecting us, putting my back against the full length window—although whether it's for support to help me stand or to trap me there, I couldn't know.

His thumb pushes deeper inside my mouth, all the way to the lower knuckle. The tip touches the back of my throat. And though he doesn't say a word, when his eyes change, so subtly, I know exactly what he wants.

My lips close around the thumb, my tongue caressing it as I start to suck. His breath hitches, and slowly—so painfully slowly—he withdraws his thumb from my mouth, pulling against my suction. Without warning, he pushes in again and repeats the cycle, simulating the sex act with his thumb penetrating my mouth.

His eyes lock on mine, his face moving in closer, and there's this connection—so intense it's physical—beyond where he's lightly pumping his thumb into my mouth and dragging it out again. I adjust my jaw as he pushes in as deep as he can go and when he pulls out, my teeth scrape lightly against the length of his thumb.

Raw animal desire flames in those ocean-blue eyes. And I'm seared by their heat. Looking into them is like looking into the sun, but I can't pull my gaze away. He's captured me.

His body presses against mine, his breathing labored now. I feel his cock swell—a thick and heavy bulge against my hip—and give a small whimper in response. He growls, pushing his thumb all the way in again so that I'm fighting off my gag reflex. His eyes are fierce now, scorching. Gazing down at me with hunger and ownership.

Suddenly I can picture the act that this is substituting for—as clearly as if it's happening in front of me. I see his large, masculine body, naked, hard and sculpted perfectly in every way. It's pressed to mine, lying on top of me in a bed as he flexes his trim hips and pushes that hard cock into my body, over and over again. I swallow, imagining the feel of him pressing into my entrance between my legs until he's seated there deeper than where his thumb presses against the back of my throat.

My body floods with heat and need, craving, raw thirst.

I want him in every way that he could impose himself on me. Whether it's his thumb in my mouth, his mouth on my mouth, his body on my body, his swollen cock sliding inside of me.

I don't just want it. I *need* it.

And I am seconds away from falling to my knees and giving myself to him in each and every one of those ways.

But when he speaks, the spell is broken.

"I want you on your knees."

I stiffen, protest rising in my body. Strange, that... I was seconds away from sinking to my knees for him of my own accord. Seconds away from unzipping his fly and taking his stiff cock in my hand, into my mouth. But his command splashes across my awareness like ice-cold water.

He feels my resistance, his eyes growing wary and his features lined with mild alarm. In response, he pushes his thumb in again to the back of my throat. When I pull my head back, it comes up against the glass behind me and I cannot avoid him as he sinks into me again. He repeats his demand and keeps his thumb in place, preventing me from moving.

So I do the only thing I can think of.

I clamp my jaw closed as hard as I possibly can. His mouth opens and he lets out nothing more than a gasp—no yelp or scream—though I'm biting hard enough to draw blood.

In fact, I can taste a metallic tang now as I tighten my jaw even more, channeling my inner pit bull.

He pulls his hand free, blowing out a breath, and when he does, I bolt for the door.

In two long strides, he catches up with me. Placing a firm grip on my elbow, he pulls me to stop.

I spin toward him, jerking my arm out of his grip. "This was a mistake."

It's all I can get out. He pins me down with those damn eyes and that *GQ* face. Heat rushes through me, and my nipples tighten.

If *fucking* is what he really wants, I have to admit I want it, too. I swallow in a tight throat at the thought of his strong hands and sensual mouth moving over my body. It's been far too long since I've felt a man inside me, filling me. But I don't want it like *this,* and not with some random stranger—no matter how beautiful!

And for that matter—what kind of sick bastard conducts *interviews* for a mistress? A flash of memory assails me—all those gorgeous model-wannabes in the lobby downstairs. They're all vying for that position!

"We're not finished here," he murmurs, but releases my elbow.

My eyebrow arches up. "We *are.* I'm leaving and you can get back to interviewing prostitutes."

His shoulders tighten and a tick starts in his jaw. I've managed to piss him off, but I couldn't care less. He thought I was a *hooker* and that's more than I can handle.

He says nothing, and I don't wait for an answer. Seconds later, I'm in the hallway, finally able to breathe again. I punch the down button, glancing nervously behind me, afraid he is going to come out after me. The elevator takes its own sweet time in arriving so I dart for the stairs, taking them two at a time. I reach the bottom floor in record speed, completely out of breath and covered with sweat as I stumble through the door.

How could I be so stupid? Who accidentally interviews for a "mistress position?" *Me*, of course. I'd jumped at the opportunity when Sam had told me yesterday, not bothering to research the "company" at all. That was my second mistake. My first mistake had been trusting Sam—the girl had some serious *cajones* to pull this practical joke on me. I'd begin plotting my revenge as soon as I'd finished ripping her a new one.

CHAPTER 3
BRILLIANT AND BEAUTIFUL

I GET TO WORK FIVE MINUTES BEFORE MY SHIFT STARTS, still steaming mad. The smell of ground coffee permeates the air as I grab my apron off the hook in the backroom. Spotting Sam as she looks over the weekly work schedule, I make a beeline for her.

"*Seriously*, Sam?"

She looks up at me, smiling. Her blond hair is twisted up into a messy top bun. Somehow it still manages to look perfect. "Oh, hey." She winks. "How'd the *interview* go?"

I huff at her. I'm still wearing the clothes I'd interviewed in, so when I stomp my foot, the sound of my heel echoes on the white linoleum tile. I glance around to ensure we aren't overheard. "Are you aware that you sent me for an interview to become some random guy's *mistress?*"

Infuriated doesn't even begin to cover what I'm feeling. Along with disgusted, indignant, angry.

"Don't be angry, Maddy. It's a sweet deal. A car, a house, all paid expenses. And the guy is so damn *hot!*"

I remember the way he'd looked at me—with those crystal-blue eyes and that wicked grin—and heat rushes through me. I don't bother denying it. "See, this is the difference between you and me. You see a sweet deal, and all I see is a guy trying to buy sex. Who *is* he, anyway?"

He'd introduced himself as Evan without giving his last name. I'd never bothered to ask and by the time I'd realized what he wanted, I was too busy scrambling out of there to care.

Sam blinks at me like I'm an idiot. "For real? You don't know?"

I blink right back at her. "*Should* I know?"

Sam flashes me a you're-hopeless look. "You study astronomy and you don't know who Evan Kohl is?"

Holy crap! "It's aerospace," I correct, almost automatically. "And I know who Evan Kohl is. What's that got to do with—wait," I glance at her again. "You're saying *that* was Evan Kohl? Bullshit. Evan Kohl is some old guy."

He's the founder of XVerse, the absolute leader in space exploration, as a matter of fact. The sexy guy at the hotel was far too young to be one of the most brilliant minds of our time.

He'd introduced himself to me as Evan, but there is no way he's *that* Evan.

"You're joking. Who is this guy, *really?*"

Sam sighs and appears to fight rolling her eyes. "My cousin's office was asked to coordinate the interviews. No name was ever given, but I did a little digging and found out for myself. It's the one and only Evan Kohl."

And, still faced with my skeptical stare, she whips out her iPhone and types a command into Google. Then she flashes the phone in front of my face. "That's the guy you met, right?"

My mouth drops as I look at the phone, a picture of the mystery man in dark slacks and a button-down blue shirt standing beside a sign with the stylized silver X, for XVerse Space Technologies. Holy. Everliving. Fuck.

"Earth to Maddy." She snaps in front of my face. I blink and shake off the shock. She slips her phone into the back pocket of her jeans.

Then she gives a slight shrug. "I thought you'd be perfect for the job."

I make a face at her. "If it's such a 'perfect job,' then why didn't *you* go interview for it?"

She raises her brow at me. "Um, because I have a boyfriend who might object to me sleeping with a hot billionaire—at least I *think* he'd object." She looks off into the distance, thinking. "Maybe if it was worth his while…"

I make a sound of disgust, throw up my hands and walk away. "You're hopeless, Sam."

***

For the next week, I manage to forget about that awkward encounter with the beautiful Mr. Kohl and focus completely on my studies. In a few weeks, the new term will start, and soon I'll be taking my qualifying exams to become a doctoral candidate. I'll have to stand up in front of two professors and present my case to convince them I'm worthy of the rigorous PhD program. Half the students who take the exam fail every year, and I could easily be one of them. It's the institute's way of weeding out the weak—university Darwinism at its finest.

Just the thought of facing my qualifying exam makes me want to plant my ass at a bar and drink myself into oblivion—but I've vowed to live like a sequestered monk until exams are over. I have too much riding on this.

Though, even if I do pass the exam, I still have no idea how I'm going to pay next semester's tuition. Even living in off-campus housing with five other girls in partially scholarship-subsidized housing, my paltry contribution to the rent is a week late. I'm living off ramen noodles and two-day-old pizza. And so far I haven't heard a word back regarding the scholarships I'd applied for.

There is one last resort, but I refuse to even consider it. I'd sworn to myself that I wouldn't run to my father for help. Not after what that bastard did to my mom. I'm on my own, for better or for worse. This program is my shot at making something of my future, and I can't screw it up. Not for anything.

I'm sitting on the floor of our huge shared living room, open books surrounding me, when Sam pushes through the front door. "Hey." She shuts the door and immediately strips off her T-shirt. "Don't you have class in ten?"

"Oh, shit." I glance up at the orange retro clock above the fireplace. It's almost two o'clock. I've been staring at these books for *four* hours and I've almost forgotten about the special lecture. "I must have lost track of time."

"Don't forget we have a shift this afternoon. Now get your ass to class, young lady."

"Ma'am, yes, ma'am." I wave a mock salute at her.

My hair is a mess so I hurriedly yank it into a ponytail. With no time to slap on any makeup, I smear some gloss on my lips, grab my notebook and fly out the door with an airy wave at Sam.

The house is just a block from campus, and I make it to the lecture hall three minutes before class starts. Since I'm late, of course, the only seats available are up front. With a resigned sigh, I drop into one.

This isn't our usual classroom but a bigger hall to accommodate extra students for a guest lecture. I haven't even checked who it would be today but I enjoy these, so I flip open my Moleskine notebook and pull the cap off my pen, hurriedly scribbling down the date.

Silence falls over the lecture hall as Professor Naveri steps up to the podium to introduce the speaker.

"Good afternoon, everyone. Thank you for coming. Unfortunately, our afternoon speaker had to cancel, but we were fortunate enough to secure Mr. Evan Kohl, founder and CEO of XVerse Space Technologies, as a last-minute replacement."

My pen freezes mid-stroke, hovering inches above the blank page. Everything goes out of focus for a millisecond, and I can feel the blood drain from my face.

Did he just say *Evan Kohl?*

CHAPTER 4
PERK N' GRIND

THE LECTURE HALL ERUPTS INTO ENTHUSIASTIC applause as I struggle to understand what the fuck Evan Kohl is doing here without previous announcement or fanfare. Professor Naveri goes on to list Kohl's numerous accomplishments, but I'm too shocked to hear anything but the frantic beat of my own heart.

My eyes dart to the exits, which are too far away. If I try to run for it, everyone would see me, including Kohl. I'm trapped. I slide down into my wooden seat and pray he doesn't see me, instead.

Evan Kohl takes the podium, looking every bit as gorgeous as I remember. He's wearing a designer suit and crisp, white shirt to contrast his dark hair. And an aquamarine tie that matches the color of his eyes. Holy crap. It should be illegal to be that good-looking.

His eyes coolly scan the audience of the lecture hall—some two hundred undergraduates or so—before resting on me. For one heartbeat, two, I freeze, unable to do even the most basic thing I want to do—look away. I'm frozen like an animal in the sights of its most feared predator. I register recognition on his features but no other emotion. He doesn't smile, frown, or scowl.

And he most definitely does not appear as surprised to see me as I am to see him.

Has he come here to see *me*? But just as the thought forms, I snicker at myself for even considering it. There's no way he'd even know which classes I take. Not to mention that the idea of him coming all this way to see me is more than a little ridiculous. Kohl is revered on this campus and they'd jump at a chance to take him as a lecturer.

I jerk my eyes away from him and stare at the blank page in front of me and for lack of anything better to do, press my pen against the paper and begin doodling in an effort to appear deeply interested in whatever I'm doing. I'm most certainly *not* breathing quickly, fighting the tightness in my throat and my palms are most definitely *not* sweaty. Not after I rub them across my jeans, anyway.

When I look up again, he's speaking, projecting toward the back of the hall and falling easily into an interesting presentation about the innovation of the rotating detonation rocket engine that will allow upper-stage rockets to become lighter, faster and more efficient.

I can't help but scribble down some notes. It doesn't matter that the guy who's speaking is a scumbag who screens women and sets them up in a fuckpad for his own personal use. He's still one of the most brilliant and innovative minds working in the field today.

And…he is fucking hot, I'll admit. Like…wet panties hot.

My eyes wander up to him, finally, after he's been speaking for about ten minutes, engaging the crowd, asking questions, advancing slides, even making a few jokes. He's at ease in front of large groups of people, pausing for effect, smiling and revealing those perfect, white teeth. I clamp down on my jaw and cross my legs. The movement catches his eye and he turns his gaze back to me again. And…

I can't breathe. Suddenly, it's an almost impossible task to accomplish. Heat floods through me, pooling at the base of my spine and at the juncture of my thighs. I squeeze my legs together tighter, and a jolt of pleasure zings through me. The look we share is like a thing alive, like a physical connection. Though I don't know him well, I think I imagine some discomfort in his expression as that string of tension between us is pulled taut to almost breaking.

He finally yanks his eyes away, clears his throat and continues. I never look down again, but his eyes avoid mine. I find myself watching his every move, every tick, every adjustment of his posture. He studiously moves his eyes everywhere but in my direction as he continues to take questions from the audience.

When the session ends, I quickly gather up my notebook and pen, then glance at my phone to check the time. I have to be at work in less than ten minutes. People are pouring down the steps to make their way out the main entrance, where Kohl is standing shaking hands with students as they exit. There is no way I'm walking that close to him and shaking his hand. But it appears unavoidable for anyone going out that main door.

So I do what any ingenious student avoiding the unreasonably handsome guest lecturer whom she'd met under the most embarrassing of circumstances would do. I bolt the opposite way, up the steps of the lecture hall and shoot one glance down toward the bottom doorway.

His gaze collides with mine, narrowing slightly as he notes my escape.

I smirk and head out the back door, feeling cheeky. I've outsmarted one of the most brilliant minds of our time.

***

I make a beeline straight to the Perk N' Grind. It's a small campus, so everything is within five minutes' walking distance. Breezing through the back door, I clock in and pull on my familiar red apron.

There is a long line waiting for me. As it's between classes and the biggest study week of the semester, caffeine is in high demand. Three o'clock isn't usually the busy shift any other time of the year.

Keith moves aside, relinquishing the cash register so I can relieve him. "You're in luck," he quips. "It just got hella busy."

"Great." I sigh.

He laughs, then winks at me. "Have fun."

As soon as he is out of hearing range, Sam sidles up to me. "Keith's still totally into you, I see," she whispers. I shoot her a glare but don't respond. The guy in front of me is already rattling off his order.

Fifteen minutes later, we have the line under control. I'm steaming milk for a double latte, when Sam reaches over and grabs my wrist. Milk sloshes over the lip of the metal frothing pitcher. "Sam—" I snap, annoyed, wiping up the spilled milk.

"Oh, my God," she hisses. "Don't look now, but he's here."

My rag stills on the counter, and I look up at Sam. "*Who's* here?"

Her blue eyes are wide, lips pressed together, as if barely able to contain her excitement. She's still clutching my wrist, completely mute, which is a first for her.

A sick sort of feeling gathers in my stomach. I have a feeling I know who *he* is, given her reaction and the fact that I've just seen him in the lecture hall a half hour prior. To confirm my theory, I peek over the silver-plated espresso machine in front of me.

Then I suck in a sharp gasp, immediately wishing I hadn't.

CHAPTER 5
HUNGRY LIKE THE WOLF

EVAN KOHL IS SITTING AT ONE OF THE ROUND WOODEN tables in the coffee shop where I work. He stands out like a timber wolf in a herd of sheep, relaxed and easy in his dark-gray, tailored suit and expensive shoes. On campus, the normal dress code is strictly California casual. This guy looks anything *but* casual. He is all class and sophistication, and I can't pull my gaze away.

He looks up from his fancy phone and his gaze collides with mine, just as it had in the lecture hall. Like a coward, I immediately duck behind the espresso machine, like it's a shield. Then I squeeze my eyes shut. The awkward situation in the lecture hall has just multiplied times ten.

Sam hauls me up by the elbow. "What the hell are you doing? Go talk to him. He's obviously here for you."

I roll my eyes. Sam has no idea he'd just been leading my seminar lecture. Had he followed me over here? Or was it just a weird coincidence—*again*?

"He's *not* here for me. He's probably here to meet with one of the professors…or something."

Faculty have coffee meetings here all the time. It's a regular occurrence. He's probably here to discuss his presentation or funding for a research project or anything besides what Sam is thinking.

"Uh-huh. That's why he's staring at you like a hungry wolf."

I scrunch my nose, mildly alarmed by her picking up an illusion that had just occurred to me, too. "A *wolf*, really?"

"What?" Her strawberry brow twitches. "Wolves are sexy."

"They're also predatory. They rip flesh from bone with their bare teeth. The last thing I need in my life is a hungry *anything*." I push out a breath. "Can we just drop it? He isn't here for me."

She has a million questions written on her face, but she seems afraid of pushing me too far. She opens her mouth and then shuts it again.

"Yeah, sure…whatever."

For thirty minutes, I tell myself he isn't there anymore. He isn't staring at me as I make coffee, watching my every move. My skin prickles with the thought of his eyes on me and my body flushes with the memory of his arm around me, holding me to him. Of him pushing his thumb into my mouth. Of that look in his eyes and that command. *I want you on your knees.* Despite myself, the memory of that encounter makes me ache. And every time that thought flashes into my mind, I force it out again by thinking of a difficult equation to block out everything else.

Finally, when I can't take it any longer, I turn to Sam. "Will you go over there and ask him what he wants?"

By now it's clear he's not here to meet anyone. He hasn't even ordered coffee. He is just staring, patiently waiting. For what, I don't know.

She beams. "Sure."

She walks over to him confidently, her long, slender legs peeking out from beneath her shorts and apron. She lowers herself onto the seat next to him and plasters on a flirty smile. When she bites her lip and flicks her red-golden hair twice, three times, I know she's crushing on him. And why wouldn't she? He is beautiful. I try not to notice how his suit jacket stretches across his broad chest, or how perfectly his hair is combed back from his angular face.

I go about my business wiping down the counter as they talk, trying to look casual and unaffected—all the while cataloging every gesture and facial expression. The wait is agonizing. I'm desperate to know what he wants and why he is here.

A few minutes later, Sam returns with a huge grin on her face.

"Well? What does he want?" I ask.

Her eyes light up. "He wants a double cappuccino." She taps me on the nose. "And *you.*"

The breath sucks out of me at that little tidbit. *Me?* No way. I told him I wasn't going to be a mistress—and I made it very clear how insulting I'd found it—and *him.* Maybe he's afraid I'll sue him for harassment or something, and he's here to buy my silence. Rich guys do that. They shove money at everything, or withhold it like a parent with a forbidden toy. A tool of *control.* I should know about that, *all* too well.

"Fine, get him the cappuccino, but tell him *I'm* not for sale."

Leaning against the counter, she flashes me a grin. "Why don't you tell him yourself?"

I sneer at her. "You are enjoying this way too much."

"Are you kidding? I've been your roommate for three years, and I've never seen you with a guy. Ever. There's a point where it's just sad."

Sad. I swallow past a tight throat. I know she doesn't mean to be hurtful, but the words sting anyway. After the breakup with Jason, there was just no time—or desire—to hook up with anyone else. My studies always come first, and everything else is a distant—*very* distant—second.

I clear my throat and say, "Fine. I'll take him the damn cappuccino."

"Go talk to him now." She glance at her watch. "It's time for your first break, anyway. I'll make him his drink and take it over."

I reach up and untie my apron, shoving it at Sam. "Fine—if it gets rid of him, then I'll talk to him. Jeez."

I take a deep breath, steeling myself. I feel like a lamb about to step into a lion's—or *wolf's*—den. I walk over to the table and stand awkwardly on the opposite side of it from him. "Um. Hi."

He stands up. "Hello, Madeline." With that rich British accent, he sounds as oddly formal as he looks. How the hell old is he, anyway? Early thirties is my guess. I'd studiously avoided looking him up on the internet since finding out is identity. It would come to no good to look at pictures of him and reinforce just how awe-inspiring, gorgeous, brilliant and downright fucking *perfect* he is. I don't need to read about that. He's still the skeeve who *hires* his girlfriends.

He gestures to the chair next to him. "Won't you sit down?"

I fold my arms across my chest. "No, thanks. This won't take long."

He raises a brow. "I'd like to talk, if you have a moment. Sam said you're on your break."

I clench my jaw. Nice, Sam. Telling him I'm on a break, then suggesting I take one. If I didn't know better, I'd say she was working for the enemy. I'd deal with her later.

"What do you want?" I bite out.

He reaches to the front of his suit jacket and buttons it. "Can we take a short walk?"

I eye him for a minute. The university's large botanical gardens are close and we'd have privacy there. But do I really want to be alone with this guy? Especially after our weird encounter the week before. On the other hand, do I really want to chance my co-workers overhearing the rehash of that embarrassing incident? It would be best to get this over with as quickly as possible.

"Fine. You have five minutes."

His brow twitches up. "I thought your break was fifteen minutes?"

I arch my brow at him. "Yes, but you only get five of them."

His face splits in that same wicked smile I'd seen from him that first day, and my heart literally palpitates. It actually hurts. I take a deep breath and look away, irritated with myself. It's been too long…since Jason. But I've never really had the desire since then. I've never thought of myself as a romantic, but my heart has never wanted to go there since it had been broken so cleanly and thoroughly once before.

But we aren't dealing with anything to do with the heart here. This is all physical. A chemical reaction to gorgeous, cutting blue eyes, a perfect, square jaw, broad shoulders. He leads us toward the front door and leans forward to push it open for me.

My arms are still folded tightly across my chest as I slip through the doorway and lead the way, along the sidewalk toward the nearest entrance to the garden.

Kohl is by my side in seconds, matching his long-legged stride with mine. I'm only five-five so he towers over me by almost a foot and that, together with his cold, business-like persona, is more than a little intimidating.

I stop at the gate, lifting the wrought-iron clasp to enter. He follows after me, and I immediately determine that this is a bad idea. At this hour the place is deserted. Flat out empty.

And here I am, alone with a handsome stranger who wants a mistress. But clearly, given the fact that he'd interviewed half of Hollywood's most gorgeous women, he couldn't be approaching me as anything more than a cover-his-ass type of gesture.

"So…" he begins. I clear my throat but don't speak. *He* wants to talk, after all. He must know exactly what he wants to say. "We got off on the wrong foot last week."

King of the Understatement. I expel a laugh. "You could say that."

He grins. "I just did."

I throw a sidelong glance at him and then look away. "So what do you want?"

He fixes his gaze on me. "Not *what*. Who."

I blink, suddenly afraid to look at him. He's playing with me, clearly.

"I'm not sure what to say in response to that. Or if I even understand what you are implying. For that matter, why does a man like you need to screen women to hook up with? Wouldn't they be more than easy to come by?"

"A 'man like me'?" A dark brow arches up, and if anything, it only makes him look sexier. "Dare I ask what that means?"

I suddenly feel uncomfortable and give a stiff shrug. "Uh…well, successful, obviously very busy. Rich…and um, good-looking."

His eyes flicker away from mine and follow the path in front of us as we make our way toward a rose arbor and the small brick pathway that leads through it.

"I have particular needs. I'm looking for someone who…is willing and able to fulfill them—and enthusiastically. Someone strong, smart. Someone who has compatible needs that I, in turn, can fulfill."

I frown. He just said a whole lot of nothing.

"What *needs*?"

We're in the narrow arbor now, walking side by side but close enough that we occasionally brush against each other on the narrow path. Each time we do, it's like an electric shock all through my body. Cold thrills travel up my arm, or my leg wherever my body has brushed against his. And I try to remind myself that it's my imagination, that it's merely a chemical reaction, my heart starts racing in response nevertheless.

He stops, suddenly, and turns to me to answer my question. We're in the shady, dappled sunlight, and his voice is low, rumbling in his broad chest. Sexy.

"I have a substantial appetite, and my tastes tend toward the darker end of the spectrum."

Darker. My heartbeat doubles in pace, thrumming at my throat. But is this fear? Or excitement? It doesn't take me long to realize that it's *both.* "Like?" I hear myself ask. Damn, I don't want to hear this! Why did I ask that?

He steps closer to me, touches a long finger to my chin. I have to fight to keep myself from jumping back and away from him. *Never let them smell your fear,* the random piece of advice pops into my head. I can feel my insides begin to tremble, but I fight to keep that action under control, to not let him see my fear as his intent eyes bore into mine, pinning them down.

His voice is a low and steady rumble in his broad chest. "When I possess a woman, I possess her completely. She is mine to cherish. To protect. To spoil. To pleasure. To dominate. To *own*. She is *mine* in every way. And the physical acts between us reflect that. They involve the complete body and the mind as well. And thus, the interplay between us takes a pleasurable act and raises it to a completely new plane of ecstasy."

Ecstasy. I gulp. I'm sure even he can hear it. My heartbeat is triple-timing now. While he's been talking, his finger has traced the edge of my jaw, slipped down to my neck, traced my carotid artery down the side of my throat and is now tickling the edge of my V-neck T-shirt. My breath is so shallow, it's practically coming in pants.

"And—and h-how do you achieve that…that, um, whole new plane of ecstasy?"

He leans closer and speaks in little more than a whisper. "With the exchange of pleasure, pain, and power."

My eyes close, and suddenly I'm seeing another vivid picture. Me, kneeling before him, my hands tied behind my back as he looms over me, a stern, commanding look on his face. A rush of desire floods through me. A desire to please him. A flush of satisfaction and pleasure at the thought that he wants me to.

Out of all those women…he wants me? My thoughts swim as if under hundreds of feet of water. The world wavers and rights itself, and I suddenly remember how to breathe.

Taking a quick step back, I gulp for air, breaking the moment. What the fuck is this man doing to me? And why am I letting him do it?

Something flashes in his eyes for a brief moment. His head tilts, as if he's studying me, suddenly his tongue slips out and wets his bottom lip as if he's that hungry wolf fantasizing about his next meal. *And I'm it...*

"I, uh, I should be getting back."

His features harden, but he nods, holding out his hand as if to point out the way we had just come. I follow his direction and he falls into step just behind me. *Closely* behind me.

"Have dinner with me. When your shift is over."

I shoot a glance at him, my step faltering. "Um. I don't think that's a good idea."

"Because?"

"Well...your mistress search and all. With all those gorgeous candidates I saw, you have a lot of sifting to do. Unless you've finished your search and found one."

I can feel his eyes on me, but I don't dare return the look. "I did, in fact."

My breath stutters. Either he's talking about me and I'm freaked. *Or*, he's *not* talking about me and I'm...experiencing some type of sick feeling congealing in my gut.

Such a weird mixture of emotions.

The thought of him with one of those starlets or models makes me inexplicably angry. My hands work into fists at my side, and he follows me as I continue to walk slowly in silence.

"You aren't curious to know who it is?"

I stop at the closed gate through which we entered.

"I didn't think it was my place to ask." I glance up at him, and he's standing in the sunlight, so I have to squint. And I can't see the look on his face.

"Let me make it clear to you, then," he responds in a strangely dark voice. And before I can respond, he has captured my wrist and steps a fraction closer, trapping me between the wall and his lean, powerful body.

"What are you—" is all I get out while I watch, stunned, as his head descends on mine, pinning me to the wall.

Just before our mouths meet, he utters in a harsh whisper., "Madeline."

The hand holding my wrist pushes it against the wall, and as his mouth crushes against mine, I feel his other hand gently grasp my throat, his thumb stroking the sensitive skin there.

I can't think, feel, smell, taste or see anything else but him. My heart is trying to club its way out of my chest. I haven't felt this kind of excitement near a man since—well—ever.

Heat rushes through me, flooding every cell of my body, making me feel dizzy and drugged as his lips crush against mine.

CHAPTER 6
BASIC AND PRIMAL

FIRE IGNITES INSIDE OF ME, STEAMING AND WRITHING LIKE lava inside a volcano. As Kohl's mouth moves against mine, the pressure inside me—*everywhere* inside me—intensifies exponentially.

And suddenly I'm aching, *throbbing*, with the need for more.

His mouth greedily takes from me with confidence and without hesitation. There is no gentle asking for permission. Evan Kohl is here to conquer—*veni, vidi, vici*—and that's exactly what he's doing. All too quickly.

Oh, God. More quickly than I ever could have imagined. His tongue brushes against my bottom lip, a silent command to open for him, and in spite of myself, I don't hesitate.

Threading his hand through my hair, he deepens the kiss, pulling me tighter against him. I go willingly, too intoxicated by him to pull away. Heat rushes through me, zinging through my veins like lightning. I expel a small whimper, unable to get enough. Every sweep of his tongue, every nip of his teeth, sends my heart racing into overdrive.

With my back still pressed against the smooth garden wall, his hand drifts down to my waist, over my hip, cupping the globe of my ass possessively.

Somewhere in the back of my mind, I know this is insane. I've only just met this guy—and I detest him, right? But I don't seem to care. Right now, there is only him and me and this crazy, breathless moment.

I've *never* felt this before—this intoxicating reaction. I've been kissed, sure—I've even been in a long-term relationship before. But this is something else.

In spite of these doubts running through my mind, my hands grip the lapels of his suit jacket. I pull him a fraction closer, and his hands on me tighten reflexively. This thing between us is electric, rushing through me like a drug. I want more—everywhere. I want to feel the heat of his bare skin against mine, our sticky, sweaty bodies pressed together. I want his lips on me *everywhere*, his tongue tasting every inch of me.

He lets loose a quiet groan. "God, Madeline. Give yourself to me." His breath whispers across my lips as he presses his erection against my hip. "Feel how hard you make me. How much I want to fuck you."

His words trickle over me, and I slowly come out of my daze.

Sex. That is all this is to him.

Of course, what do I expect from a man who hires his girlfriends?

I pull away—as much as I can in this small space between his hard body and the cold wall. His hands fall to his sides. We're both out of breath, huffing for air as if we'd just finished a marathon.

I swallow and glance up into his eyes. What I see is my own hunger reflected back at me. "Why are you here? What do you want from me?" I ask in a voice that is shamefully breathless.

I'm genuinely confused. Evan Kohl is rich, successful and so damn hot it hurts. He can have any woman he wants. But he's here with me—*kissing* me, telling me how much he wants me.

Head tilting down, he places his hands on the wall behind me, on either side of my head—effectively trapping me where I stand. He appears to be choosing his words. When he meets my gaze again and speaks, his voice is a low, sexy growl. "I want to fuck you, Madeline. Two bodies coming together in the most basic and primal way. In *every* imaginable way."

A shiver of awareness skips down my spine, but I work hard to suppress it. Kohl has a raw, masculine magnetism that could ensnare any female with a pulse—but I can't allow myself to succumb to it. I know from past experience that when I fall for a guy, I fall hard—and Kohl doesn't seem like the type to catch me before I hit rock bottom.

"There were a dozen gorgeous women lined up at that hotel, eager to jump your bones. Why *me?*"

He shrugs, but there's something in his eyes—a dark vulnerability that slices right through me. "Maybe...I see something in you. A strength in your resistance. A resilience. A rare intelligence.... And..." He moves a hand to touch my bottom lip still swollen from his fierce possession. "The most gorgeous set of lips I've ever tasted."

His words are like a narcotic, lulling me into a dreamy haze, filling my blood and soothing every doubt I've ever had about myself. I'm practically carried away by it. He's wooing me—and wooing hard. But for what?

He wants my body. He wants to get inside me. Inside my body—and maybe, too, inside my head.

"No." I whisper. With every bit of resistance I can muster, it's the only thing I can bring myself to say. Because right now, my entire body is shouting *yes, yes, yes!*

But he only smiles that same cocky smile. "I love a good challenge, Madeline. You'll definitely give it to me."

I blink at his response, which strikes me like a slap on the face. I suddenly understand. It's not me he wants. It's the thrill of the chase. I've seen his type before—most notably in my own father. All that matters is the hunt. My father took several mistresses while he was still married to my mom—and it had damn near destroyed her. There's no way I'd *ever* do that to someone else.

Suddenly I hold my arm out, straightening it. With my hand I push firmly against his hard chest. "I'm not for sale, Mr. Kohl," I say tightly. "And your five minutes were up five minutes ago."

Just as I turn to walk through the gate, he reaches out and grabs my wrist, stopping me. Like before, his touch practically burns me. My heart thuds violently in my chest as I turn back around to face him.

His eyes are hard and laser-focused on me. "I'll tell you this only once, Madeline. I'm not a man who gives up easily." And I can tell from the determination in those azure eyes—the way they bore into me. The way they already presume to claim me. I know that I haven't seen the last of Evan Kohl.

Chapter 7
A God on Campus

"What happened? Don't leave anything out. Tell me *everything*." Sam claps her hands together, the words rushing out in an excited high-pitched stream. "Does he want to whisk you away to one of his mansions in the Caribbean?"

I walk behind the counter and pull on my red apron. "Nothing happened," I lie. "He just wanted to apologize for the other day, that's all."

"Right." Sam places a hand on her hip and fixes me with a you-don't-think-I'm-going-to-believe-that stare. "A sexy gazillionare took time out of his busy schedule to come down here and say he was *sorry*. No fucking way. He wants you. I know sexual frustration when I see it."

He definitely wants me, but that isn't what unnerves me. It's my own response to him—that raw, clawing desire—that shakes me to my very core. Never before have I felt such a powerful connection to anyone—not even Jason. Though I'll never admit it to anyone else, I'm afraid of what that might mean.

I shrug, trying my best to appear nonchalant. "Maybe he just wanted to make sure I wasn't going to sue him or something. I don't know. Can we just drop it?"

"*Sure*, Maddy-bear." She winks at me. "But you'll spill eventually—even if I have to get you drunk to do it."

Unsteadily I turn from her and try to get the smell and feel of Evan Kohl out of my memory. That shaky feeling in my legs is still there even hours after he has left. And when I lay in bed that night—all I can think about his touch, his kiss, the thrill of his nearness. And how much those feelings make me want to touch myself. And I'm tempted—*so* tempted—to get myself off while fantasizing about him, but somewhere behind all that desire is cold fear. I'm afraid of what it will do. I'm afraid it will give him power over me.

Even more power than he's already starting to have.

It takes me hours to finally fall asleep.

***

For two days, I try to forget about Evan Kohl. Much easier said than done, unfortunately. Every time I close my eyes, he's there—that sexy, enigmatic smile and those blue, blue eyes.

I'm sitting in a lecture when my phone dings, indicating I've received an email. I check quickly and almost choke when I see the name in the *from* field.

Kohl.

Of course. He'd warned me he didn't give up easily, hadn't he?

How did he even get my email address? Then I remember—I gave him all my contact information on the "assistant" application at the interview. I blow out a breath, and open the email, studiously ignoring my professor, who's now explaining a complicated equation on the whiteboard—an equation that will be on the finals. But curiosity burns at me, and before I can resist, I open the email.

> *From: Kohl, Evan*
> *To: Swanson, Madeline*
> *Subject: Negotiations*
>
> *Madeline,*
>
> *Think of this as a jumping-off point for negotiations.*
>
> *Evan*
>
> *P.S. I can still taste you on my tongue.*

Heat rushes to my cheeks and through my entire body. I glance around nervously, making sure no one is peeking over my shoulder. No one is, of course—it's just my own paranoia. But Evan Kohl is a god on this campus, and if anyone catches wind of him kissing me—and continuing to pursue me—there'll be no end to the questions and snotty comments.

A file is attached to the email, but I don't dare open it. What would be the point? I already know what it is, anyway. If the subject line hasn't tipped me off, the file name, *Mistress Contract* certainly would. Hello, Captain Obvious.

I itch to grab my laptop from my backpack and open the attachment. Instead, I turn off my phone and drop it into my bag. No good would come from opening that file, and the sooner I forget about it, the better.

I sail through the next two lectures, managing to keep my thoughts focused on my subjects and *not* the enigmatic Mr. Kohl.

When I get back to the house, three of my housemates, Sam, Avery and Cassie, are all sitting in the living room, studying. Sam looks up and pulls out her earbuds as I walk through the door.

"Hey, how was class?"

I blow out a breath. "Great, until I got an email from Kohl," I say. "That guy just doesn't give up. I'm beginning to understand why he graduated high school at fourteen."

Avery and Cassie immediately perk up.

"Whoa, wait, is this the sexy billionaire you were telling us about?" Cassie asks Sam. There are absolutely *no* secrets in this house—one downside to sharing a house with five other girls.

Sam ignores her. "Holy shit. He emailed you? About what?"

I drop my backpack next to the door and plop down onto the couch. "He emailed me the *mistress* contract." I can't keep the disgust out of my voice.

Cassie's hazel eyes widen. "Did you open it?"

"Why would I? There's no way I'm going to be Kohl's *mistress*." God, every time I think of the word, I want to gag.

Sam jumps up and joins me on the couch. "Open it. I'm dying to see what it says. Maybe he'll give you a Jag or a yacht!"

I roll my eyes. "It doesn't matter. There's no way in hell I'm doing it."

"Never say never, girlfriend. Come on…we can at least *read* the contract. What's the harm in that? He doesn't even need to know. Aren't you the least bit curious?"

I huff. She has a point. Reading it doesn't commit me to anything. I don't have to sign it. Besides, I know Sam will pester me until she gets a look. And to be honest, I'm more than a little curious. I may as well get it over with…

With a pointed eye roll, I grab my bag and pull my laptop out, then open it. Sam sits up with a shriek and claps her hands. Avery and Cassie join us on the couch, crowding around me. I shoot them a dirty look while I wait for the connection to kick in and the email to download.

"Jeez, you'd think it was *you* getting the contract or something. Ugh. I don't even know if I can read this out loud. It might make me want to vomit."

"Let me do it, then!" Sam holds out her arms making grabby-hands, and with a resigned sigh, I pass her the laptop. She bends over it, focusing on opening the file. Then she scans it quickly, her eyes sliding down the screen.

"Okay so…a lot of legalese. 'This agreement is entered into by Evan William Kohl, hereinafter referred to as 'the contractor,' and Madeline Elizabeth Swanson, hereinafter referred to as 'the mistress.'"

Her eyes goggle and already I'm feeling nauseous. "Ugh, don't go on with that…"

But Sam isn't even paying attention, her eyes skimming down the page, absorbing it all, her face, in turn, alight with curiosity, surprise or even glee. "Holy shit, Maddy…he's thought of everything."

That really doesn't surprise me. I fold my arms tightly against my chest and tilt my head at her without verbally asking the question.

"He'll provide housing—full rent at a house he owns near campus, a car, an account for clothing and other living expenses as well as covering the cost of schooling and all supplies for the duration of the agreement."

My stomach drops. I start running calculations in my head at how much that would possibly be. For that cost, he could get a high-class call girl to blow him every day of the week and twice on Tuesdays.

"Jeezus, he could just spend that money on prostitutes and save himself the trouble," I mutter.

Cassie laughs. "Apparently he doesn't want a prostitute. He wants *you*."

Yeah...but he isn't going to get me. My jaw clenches in resolve, refusing to even entertain the idea.

Nope. It was *so* not happening.

CHAPTER 8
A MUTUALLY CONVENIENT RELATIONSHIP

SAM IS STILL LISTING OUT THE PARTICULARS OF KOHL'S SICK *contract* and having a marvelous time doing it, with apparently no concern for my reactions to it.

My throat tightens with that same weird thrill-fear I felt the other day in his presence. "God knows why he'd prefer me to a prostitute. I'm not...uh...'skilled' at that type of 'labor.'"

Sam shrugs. "Maybe that's not what he's looking for."

I shake my head. "This is ridiculous, Sam. You of all people know I will never be anyone's *mistress* and why I have a very strong reason not to be."

Sam looks up from the screen and studies me for a long moment, true sympathy in her eyes. "Mads...this isn't like what your dad did. There's a clause in here that specifically covers outside sexual relationships."

I perk up. "Oh?"

"Yes, in that it forbids them...he can't see anyone else romantically or sexually and neither can you. It's exclusive. So it's not like you'd be supplanting a spouse or a girlfriend. There are no children involved. It's not even the same thing as your dad.

He might be calling you a 'mistress' but you wouldn't really be one in *that* sense of the word."

I huff out a breath. "Let's be clear here, okay? I won't be one in *any* sense of the word."

She sighs and returns her attention to the screen. "So what is your big hang up about this, besides the mistress label?"

I scrunch my brow. "It's prostitution. He's trading sex for…for…"

"He's setting up a mutually convenient relationship. You'd be available to him for social outings, special events and sex."

"Whenever he wants it?"

She shrugs. "It's not clear. I think he's leaving that open to negotiation."

I let out a long, weary sigh. "God, this is so effing weird. Let's just stop talking about it."

Sam straightens and quietly closes the computer, leaning back against the couch. "So just for argument's sake…" she starts.

I raise a brow but say nothing, reaching down to fiddle with a loose string on one of the threadbare throw pillows.

"You haven't had sex for like…*years*, right?"

I shrug, failing to meet her gaze—or any of my other roommates. They, at least, have dates from time to time—or even more regularly than that. They all know damn well the answer to that question, anyway. "And…you found him attractive?"

I resist shooting her a glare. That's the stupidest question ever. An inert rock would find him attractive.

"Did he get your lady parts warm and juicy?" Cassie chimes in.

"Shut up, Cassie," Sam snaps. The two of them haven't been getting along very well of late, and this conversation seems to be bringing that out.

"Yeah, Cass *and* Sam. Leave Maddy alone," Avery says. At least I have *one* person on my side.

Cassie stands, grabbing a couple books that are sitting on the coffee table. "I'd love to stay, but I've got a class in ten minutes."

Avery glances up at the clock. "Oh, shit. Me too." She jumps up and snatches her backpack as well. "Good luck, Mads. You know, I'm on your side."

"Thanks," I say, watching them both leave.

Once Sam and I are alone, she turns back to me, her tone softening. "Maddy...consider this for a second. It could be an amazing opportunity for you. For one thing, you are broke as hell and about to have to pony up for one ginormous chunk of change for your doctorate tuition. Plus, you've been subsisting on ramen noodles for months and still owe me three hundred and forty bucks."

I look up and she holds up a hand. "*Not* that I'm expecting you to cough up. I'm just sayin'.... Didn't we have a conversation about a month ago about how you might have to eat crow and go to your dad for money? How you found that idea the most abhorrent thing ever? I mean you haven't spoken to him since you were thirteen when he walked out on you and your mom. Not even when he presented you with that fat trust fund on your eighteenth birthday—"

I flinch. "I don't need his fucking guilt money."

Sam's face grows completely stone serious. "Maddy, quit lying to yourself. You *do* need that money. Sometime in the next month, you are going to have to pick up that phone and call daddy dearest and sweetly ask him for the trust fund money that you so vehemently rejected five years ago."

Hell. *No.* That will never happen.

Sam stares at me for a few moments longer. "*Or* you can take *this*"—she taps the top of the closed laptop—"as the windfall that it is. A convenient and *pleasant* setup that you can *enjoy.* And maybe it's been a long time and you need some reminding, but sex *is* fun and very enjoyable with the right partner—"

I wave her off. "Quit talking to me like I'm some blushing virgin before my wedding night. I had a boyfriend all through high school and part of college."

She leans forward. "Mads, listen to yourself. You've only been with one guy—*ever*—a callous little shit who dumped you because he was threatened by your brilliance."

Sucking in air as if she had just punched me in the stomach, I lean away from her. "Wow, that was low."

"Is it not the truth?"

I look away but refuse to tell her that she's right. Jason had, indeed, been extremely jealous of my full ride scholarship to Caltech when the best he could do was the local state school. He'd put on the brave face temporarily but had hooked up with someone else within weeks of me leaving town. I'd had no idea until I got home for Christmas break and found out he was marrying her because he'd gotten her pregnant.

"But Mads…you *are* brilliant! Just own that. You are at the top of your class. And I know you think a lot of guys are intimidated by that and that's why they stay away but others avoid you because you give off the 'don't even ask' vibes. But score another one for Evan Kohl because though you are brilliant, well, he's in a whole other league, right? There's probably no chance he's going to feel intimidated by you. Probably exactly the opposite."

I frowned. "What do you mean?"

"I'm saying that in spite of him interviewing the most gorgeous models and starlets that SoCal has to offer—he wants *you*. He knows you are smart. He's attracted to your brains as well as your looks. Maybe he's not just in this for the physical part of things."

I scoff at her, remembering Kohl's own words to me. *I want to fuck you, Madeline. Two bodies coming together in the most primal way...* It *is* all about the physical. I fan my face as it flames with renewed heat at those words, which scorch me clear down to the core. Yeah, I'm turned on by the memory of it, of *him* in the garden. I'm sinfully attracted to him...but did I really want it to be like *this*?

"Why doesn't he just want to date, though? Why the weird contract?"

Sam shrugs. "He did say this was a jumping-off point. Maybe you should ask him."

I glare at her for a long moment before reaching out my hand, asking for the laptop back. I spend the next couple hours reading and re-reading the so-called mistress contract until I'm so tired, I can't see straight.

I quickly change into yoga pants and a tank top and brush my teeth. When I peek into Sam's room, she is still hunched over her computer, typing away furiously.

"You going to sleep?" I ask.

"Yeah, in a sec. I just need to finish this email."

She's half smiling, biting her bottom lip as her fingers fly over the keys. I'm instantly suspicious. Sam only bites her lip when she's flirting.

I scurry over to Sam's bed. But she's quicker than I am, and snaps her laptop closed before I can catch a glimpse of her screen.

"Who are you emailing?" I ask in a singsong voice.

"No one," she says quickly, but she can't keep the smile off her face.

"It's a guy! I *knew* it. Who is he?" I snap my fingers. "I bet it's that cute little undergrad who follows you around all the time."

"It's *no one*." She shoves me off her bed, and I plop back down onto my own mattress. "I was just emailing my professor, geez!"

"Oh! The really hot one?"

"Oh my God, Maddy." She laughs. "His hotness is completely irrelevant."

"Since when is hotness ever irrelevant?"

"Since it was my advisor." She laughs. "He's off limits."

I turn off the Hello Kitty light between our beds and pull the covers over me. "Sure, whatever you say."

Off limits. Yeah, I know that feeling. Like for me, Evan Kohl is off limits. Without question.

But even as I state it firmly in my mind, as I drift off into sleep, I still can't forget the heat and promise of pleasure at his hands all wrapped up in the most amazing kiss I've ever experienced.

CHAPTER 9
NEGOTIATIONS

THAT NIGHT, I DRIFT TO SLEEP AND MY THOUGHTS center on Evan Kohl. And apparently, my imagination is delighted with the opportunity to run wild.

I'm in a dark room, my hands tied together in front of me, naked. A dark figure looms over me. I can't see his face, but somehow I know it's Kohl. He says nothing as he leans over me, his breath brushing across my sensitive skin. I'm not sure what he plans to do, and it doesn't matter. With my hands tied, I couldn't stop him anyway. I feel vulnerable, and yet excitement trips through me. None of this makes sense, but it all feels so familiar, natural.

"Kneel for me, Madeline," comes the rough, echoed voice in my mind. Harsh. Grating. It's dark and I'm scared, trembling with fear and...a deep, deep longing.

When I wake up, it's morning, and Sam is already gone. I try to shake off the dream, but even as I grab a bowl of stale Cheerios and plop down in front of my laptop, the heaviness in my chest lingers.

To distract myself, I browse the internet idly for a while, watching random cat videos, before ending up on Kohl's Wikipedia page. I skim through his numerous accomplishments and business ventures until I find what I'm looking for. His personal life is only two paragraphs long, and covers everything from his political affiliation to the type of cars he drives. But what interests me most is his romantic life. My heart thumps in my chest as I read through the list of models he's dated. Two are Victoria's Secret angels, for God's sake.

Shit. I shouldn't have looked.

Now all I can think about is what the fuck he would want with *me*—a nobody from Missouri who would rather assemble solar sails than shop for heels.

I open my email program and decide to reply to his email with no idea, really, of what I'm actually going to say.

From: Swanson, Madeline
To: Kohl, Evan
Subject: re: Negotiations

Mr. Kohl,

I've read through your paperwork, and I have a few questions.

First, how is The Mistress guaranteed that you wouldn't change your mind and discontinue the relationship once it has begun, leaving her to fend for herself financially?

Second, what other safeguards are in place? For example, you have not delineated your requirements for how often The Mistress should be "available" to you and what "services" would be required to fulfill the contract. What if she doesn't feel like it one night—is she still obligated to see you? What agency does The Mistress have in this contracted relationship?

Also, what if you and The Mistress are incompatible? Is there a trial period?

I'm sure whomever you choose will negotiate these terms to the satisfaction of both parties, but I felt compelled to mention them nonetheless.

Best of luck with your search.

Sincerely,

Madeline Swanson

I lean back in my chair and re-read the words a dozen times, tweaking here and there, before I decide they're business-like enough and hit *send*. I laugh a little at the irony. How many people would kill for Evan Kohl's personal email address? A month ago, I definitely would have. But now that I have it, all I want is for him to *stop* emailing me.

Maybe it's because Sam is right. What he's offering is a pretty sweet deal, if I could just ignore the mistress label. But I'm not sure I can.

Minutes later, my computer dings to notify me that I've received an email.

From: Kohl, Evan
To: Swanson, Madeline
Subject: re: Negotiations

Madeline,

It's time to drop the pretense. You want this as much as I do. Any woman who kisses a man like you kissed me in that garden is begging to be fucked, plain and simple.

E

I blink at the words. *Begging to be fucked.*

My thoughts are cast back to that dream, and I'm instantly turned on all over again. I can still feel his lips pressed to mine, the heat of his breath, the taste of him on my tongue. I *do* want him. In fact, I'd like nothing more than to strip that tailored suit off his lean body and ride his cock like a cowgirl. But if it means degrading myself by signing up to be his mistress, then I'll pass.

I reply immediately.

From: Swanson, Madeline
To: Kohl, Evan
Subject: re: Negotiations

Mr. Kohl,

There's no pretense, and I can assure you I'm not begging for anything. Though I've noticed you haven't answered my questions.

M

From: Kohl, Evan
To: Swanson, Madeline
Subject: re: Negotiations

Have dinner with me, and I'll answer anything. Tonight, 8:00 p.m.
E

From: Swanson, Madeline
To: Kohl, Evan
Subject: re: Negotiations

I'm not that curious.
M

I close my laptop and check the time. Ten o'clock. I need to be at work in thirty minutes, and I haven't even showered yet. I jump into the shower quickly, throw on some jeans and head out the door. I don't have any classes until two o'clock, so I'll get a solid three hours on my time card, which will help come payday.

As I walk into the coffee shop and grab my apron, I see Keith at the cash register. He turns as soon as I walk in. "Hey," he says, lifting his chin.

I glance around the small sitting area. It's empty. "Has it been this quiet all morning?"

Keith leans against the counter, and crosses his arms over his chest. "Yep. Everyone must be studying for exams."

Which is exactly what I should be doing. Fortunately, I brought my books. Until exams are over, they'll go everywhere with me.

"My exam is next week." A knot forms in my stomach at the thought. I've been studying for weeks, but I still don't feel prepared. "Do you think you could give me some pointers?"

Keith is a second year aerospace student, and passed his quals last year with flying colors. He's one of the smartest guys I know, and at Caltech, that's saying something. He'll be in the same lab with me next year, provided I pass. We have the same advisor.

An hour into my shift, Keith and I are hunched over my fluid mechanics textbook on the back counter when someone clears his throat behind us. Shit...a customer.

I whip around. "Sorry, didn't hear you come in," I say, lifting my eyes.

It's Kohl.

Hands in his pockets, he glances up at me, and I swear to God, my heart stops beating for a second. He's wearing a black, long-sleeved polo, unbuttoned at the neck, and dark-blue jeans. He looks sleek, powerful, and so goddamn delicious I almost groan. And here I am wearing an old baby tee, no bra, no makeup, and my hair is pulled up into a messy bun. *Fuck*. Of course.

His blue eyes narrow on Keith's back for a split second before they drift back to me.

"What are you doing here?" I ask.

He smiles at me—that sexy, enigmatic smile that turns me inside out. This guy is no good for me. All it takes is a smile, and I'm already wet and ready for him.

"Would you believe I was thirsty?"

I shake my head and wait. He fixes that steady, unsettling gaze on me again and that flash is there...that determination.

So this is him not giving up. And not taking the firm "no" in my last email for an answer.

"You didn't answer my email," he said.

"Wrong. I *did* answer your email."

His smile deepens. "It wasn't the answer I wanted."

Is this guy serious?

I have a few choice words for him, but I hold them in, *barely.* First and foremost, the entire world does not fall at his feet. He may be a god on this campus, but that doesn't mean I'll bow to his every command—or *kneel* to it. Not. Happening. And second, what good would dinner do? I'm not interested in his proposition, *period.*

"You want a different answer, ask a different girl," I say, quoting *Working Girl,* one of my favorite movies. "Now, if you'll excuse me, I'm busy."

"Madeline." My name rolls off his tongue with that beautiful accent, and I can't help it, I melt a little inside. "Have dinner with me." He lifts a brow. "Unless you're afraid."

Annoyance pricks at me. I *am* afraid. I'm afraid of how he makes me feel. I'm afraid of how much I want him. But most of all, I'm afraid of opening up to someone, only to get hurt again. And while this might just be a business arrangement for him, I'm not sure I can make that same promise.

"My answer is still *no,* Mr. Kohl." He opens his mouth to say something, but I don't give him the chance. I pull off my apron and move around the counter. "I'm going on break," I call to Keith.

I head toward the short hallway that leads from the coffee shop into the bookstore. There's a women's restroom there, and I make a beeline for it. The only way to deal with Kohl is retreat. Men like him don't give up, and I'm not about to go toe-to-toe with him in the middle of the campus coffee shop.

The second I push through the bathroom door, I release the breath I'd been holding for what seems like hours. I glance in the mirror and groan. It's worse than I thought. Not only am I completely makeup free, but there are dark circles under my eyes that give me a charming zombie-like appearance. Great.

Seconds later, Kohl pushes through the door. I whip around to face him, my breath caught in my throat, barely able to believe his audacity. I open my mouth to say something, but I'm shocked speechless. I watch him shut and lock the main bathroom door and turn toward me. The look he gives me is hard, predatory, and it makes my nipples harden.

I'm trapped in here with him, and fuck if that doesn't both excite and terrify me.   This time, I don't know if I have it in me to say *no*.

And that hungry wolf look in his eyes is clear—no isn't going to be an answer he'll accept, anyway.

Chapter 10
Trapped

I swallow nervously as Kohl's hot gaze rakes over my body, before settling on my hard nipples. Fuck. I curse the fact that I went braless today. This tee is thin and—when covered by the apron—perfectly modest. But through it, he can see everything. He licks his lips, lifting them into a sexy half-smile, and he advances on me. I'm a cornered animal, briefly contemplating a mad dash to one of the stalls. But I discard that idea. My instinct is to step back, but I hold my ground. I'm not going to let him intimidate me.

Once he's close, I smell him again. And I'm instantly reminded of that feeling in his penthouse hotel room, in the garden when he was looming over me. That cold, electric thrill. That frenzied excitement stirring in my blood. He reaches out to brush his thumb across my cheek, and my eyes flutter closed, my breath stuttering. I crave his touch. I crave the feel of his skin gliding across mine. I hate how desperate he makes me feel, but try as I might, I can't block those feelings.

Threading his arm around my waist, he pulls me against his body. Muscles flex beneath his shirt, and it feels so damn good, I moan.

The finger that was on my cheek drops, and suddenly he's toying with my nipple through the thin shirt. It tightens even more, into an erect, painful bud. The pleasure from that touch zings through my entire body, weakening my legs.

Without warning, his head bends, lips colliding with mine in a rough, passionate kiss. His tongue sweeps into my mouth, and I'm swept away by him. His lips, his tongue, claim me with savagery. If he's holding anything back, I can't tell what it might be, because he's coming at me with the full force of his will, pinning me down.

With his lips still connected to mine, he presses me roughly up against the wall, grasping my wrists in his hands. He brings them up above my head, cinching them together and securing them in the large, tight grip of one hand, pressed high against the wall. I can't catch my breath. I'm trapped, completely at his mercy, and a flush of arousal boils inside of me.

Without tearing his eyes from mine, he uses his free hand to find the hem of my baby tee and roughly pushes beneath the fabric. His skin is hot against mine, sending a shiver of awareness down my spine. That rough hand skims the soft skin of my stomach to firmly palm my bare breast. His deep-blue eyes darken but never leave mine and his breath is coming fast. He's as turned on as I am.

My throat is tight and I can't swallow, and now he's running his thumb over my bare nipple. I shriek, almost coming right then and there. He brings his face in close, lips just millimeters from mine. He turns his head, smells my neck and sucks on my skin at the base, sending fire crackling in my veins. Then he pinches my nipple between his two fingers and the exquisite pain is more than I can take. With a groan, I squeeze my eyes shut, biting my lower lip to keep from crying out again.

"You like that, Madeline?"

I don't answer. I can't. My entire body is lit up from the inside. I'm on fire, rubbing against him, my body shamelessly begging for more as he rolls the tip of my nipple between his thumb and forefinger, tugging it over and over again. I open my eyes, and I find myself trapped again by his hard, hungry gaze.

With a low growl, he gropes for the edge of my T-shirt again, and yanks it up, over my head, pushing it into his other hand, which still holds my suspended wrists. Cold air rushes over my skin, and the tiled wall at my back feels like ice.

His head lowers, his hot mouth finding my nipple with unwavering intent. He sucks me, *hard.* I feel the pull of my nipple into his mouth all over my body—in the prickling in my scalp, the loopy rhythm of my heartbeat, the ache in my core, the throbbing of my clit.

Without the use of my hands, all I can do is arch into him, pressing my breast more firmly against his mouth. My jaw drops and all breath escapes me, all *thought* escapes me. All there is, all I can feel are his hands on me, his mouth on my nipple, licking and sucking it—grazing it with his teeth. I whimper like a child, shivering against him. His free hand is now at the small of my back pressing me to him, and I willingly go, abandoning thought and reason and that small warning at the back of my head that tells me, *This man is danger.*

I'm panting now. I have no control over my own breathing, the wordless sounds of animal pleasure escaping my lips. I want him to bite me, I want more pain, but I can't seem to find the words to tell him.

His head moves to my other breast, fastening over it with powerful suction. The nipple he has just left wet and hard feels ice-cold hitting the cool bathroom air. His grip around my wrists tightens as if he can't control his own excitement. And my hands start to go numb. Without breaking from the attention to my nipple, his large, calloused hand slides over my ribs until he reaches the waistband of my jeans. Flicking the button open and making quick work of the fly, he growls and dips his large hand inside my panties.

Slowly his fingers prod toward my entrance, gliding over my swollen clit, and I jump, electrified. His head pulls away from my breast without letting up on the suction, pulling it with him roughly as he jerks away. I can see his face now, inches from my own, his own breathing hoarse and labored. A muscle ticks in his jaw, as though he's trying to hold himself back. I can feel the tension in his arms.

"Christ, you are so wet," he groans. "I want to push my cock inside you and fuck you *hard* against this wall right now."

And God, I could almost tear off my own jeans and let him do just that. I really want to. I feel the large bulge of his cock pressed against my side and I can think of nothing else but what it would feel like to have him anchored and moving inside me. As if echoing my thoughts, his finger pushes into me, probing my channel, murmuring about how tight and good I feel. He presses deeper, and my eyes close again, my head falling slack to the side.

The sweet, icy ache between my thighs is building, spreading through my entire body. Any second, I'm going to shatter.

"Tell me, *right now*, that you are coming to dinner with me tonight."

I...*what?*

His finger pushes deeper into me, his thumb brushing across my clit in a slow circular motion. I try to hold back my moan, but it's useless. I have no control over what's coming out of my mouth or any thought beyond the sheer, hypnotic pleasure of his hands and mouth on my body. I let out a low, tormented moan that echos off the white tile walls.

Fuck, he's good at this. *Too good.*

His tone grows more insistent. "Say it, Madeline. Say *yes,* you will."

His finger continues to move inside me, hard, deep thrusts, taking me to the very edge. My hips grind against his hand, searching for release. I'm so close to coming, I can fucking taste it.

And his hand slows, ever so slightly, as if sensing my oncoming crisis and wanting to prolong it. As if proving to me that he is the one in control—that I won't come until *he* allows it.

"Yes. God, yes, whatever you want," I gasp, breathless. "*Please* make me come."

The second the words leave my mouth, he pulls out of me. To my utter humiliation, I actually whimper a little. I was close. So damn close, and the fucking bastard knew it and pulled away! Who does that?

A man who always gets his way no matter what, that's who. I stare at him, wide-eyed, wishing I could knee him in the balls when he releases my wrists and steps just out of my reach. His lips curve into a wicked smile.

"Excellent. I'll be at your place at eight. You will be ready for me."

And before I can say a word, he's gone.

CHAPTER 11
I DON'T BITE...

"No." Sam scrunches her nose and shakes her head. "It makes your hips look too wide."

"Ugh, *thanks,*" I say sarcastically, peeling the purple cocktail dress off my body. I turn back toward the closet and rifle through the rest of Sam's dresses. They're all at least one size too small for me. "You really need to think about eating a cheeseburger once in a while. Don't you have anything in a bigger size?"

Sam springs off the bed and pushes me aside. She sorts through the closet for a minute, before pulling out a seashell pink strapless dress from the back. It's cute, actually, gathered in the front, with a sash around the waist, the skirt falling to just above the knees. Simple. Elegant. But would it fit? I don't want to get my hopes up.

I eye her. "What size is it?"

Sam shrugs. "I bought it three years ago for my cousin's wedding. I'd just broken up with a guy and I'd gained a few pounds."

With a scowl, I snatch the dress from her hands and slip it on. She zips me up, and thank God, it fits. I turn to the side, inspecting it from that angle.

"I won't be able to wear a bra with this."

She shrugs, handing me some strappy silver heels. "You don't need one."

They're absolutely gorgeous heeled sandals. But I reluctantly put them on. I hardly ever wear heels, and will likely end up falling flat on my face. But this dress doesn't exactly go with flip-flops, so I don't really have a choice. And these shoes go so well with the elegant dress that I'm starting to feel like Cinderella.

Standing in front of the full-length mirror, I gape at myself. I look…different, to say the least. Hair pulled up into an elegant knot and my makeup done, Sam has transformed me into someone else.

"You have any nice underwear?" she asks, inspecting me in the mirror over my shoulder. "Something lacy?"

I shoot her a look. "No one's seeing my underwear but me."

She raises a brow as if she hardly believes me. "Wait, I have a few nice pairs I picked up but haven't worn yet. Silky black lace. Nice and sexy."

"Don't bother. My granny panties hold everything in."

She shakes her head, bending to dig through her bottom drawer. "The underwear is for *you*. To give you confidence. Here," she says, yanking off a Victoria's Secret tag and handing them to me.

They are beautiful, skimpy. I sigh.

Hands on her hips, Sam shakes her head at me. "So, tell me, why are you getting all dressed up for a guy you don't even *like?*"

I shrug. "I like him, actually." Maybe a little *too* much. "Just because I won't be his mistress doesn't mean I don't like the idea of a gorgeous man lusting after me. I'm still a woman."

I glance at the clock. Seven fifty-six. I hurriedly slip off my underwear and pull on the new panties. It's strange, but she's right…with the underwear, the glamorous updo, the strappy heels and the cute dress, I feel more confident, more feminine, more powerful.

Sam hands me a matching silver clutch into which I drop my keys, my phone and a five-dollar bill. She shoots me a look and I shrug. If he gets too grabby, I might need bus fare to get home. Hopefully not, because that five is the last one I own until payday.

I literally jump a foot when there's a knock at the door at exactly 8:01. Fuck.

Sam laughs and rushes for the door, beating me there with a smug grin. She whips it open and he's standing in the doorway, his face serene, the expression one of expectancy. He glances from Sam to me and back, flashing her his winning smile. I take that moment to give him a once-over, devouring him with my eyes. His tall frame is dressed in a sleek, black evening suit, snowy-white shirt and a dark-gray tie. Every stitch is tailored to perfection and hugs his powerful frame perfectly. Suddenly I can't swallow in my tight throat, my heart thudding dangerously.

I want to back out here and now. I'm terrified, like a cornered hare facing down the fox. I reach up to put my hand on the door, almost giving in to the urge to slam it in his face, to run and hide inside my closet, curled up in the corner, like I used to when I was little—when my parents fought.

His gaze meets mine and he seems to sense that fight-or-flight instinct tensing in every muscle of my body. He places a hand on the door to prevent me from shutting it. "Good evening, Madeline."

"Uh," I manage.

Sam gets behind me and shoves me. "Have fun, you two! I *won't* wait up…"

I shoot her an evil look over my shoulder as I step timidly toward him. He stands aside, his eyes gliding down over my form, catching on the strapless neckline of my dress and then again on my legs.

"Well," he purrs as he steps back, placing a hand at the small of my back to guide me alongside him. "You certainly clean up nicely."

I throw him a quick look, my eyes landing on that broad chest before skating away. "So do you."

As we walk along to the car he has waiting for us on the curb, I become hyperaware of that hand on the small of my back, the warmth of it through the slick fabric of my dress. The pressure is just enough to be firm, guiding me to walk where he wants me to go, but not enough to feel overbearing. But there was no ignoring it, either.

My poor, unsatisfied body is fixating on every nuance of that touch, the outline of his large hand and every square millimeter of contact. As tempted as I'd been to stay in the bathroom and finish what he'd started this morning, I'd reassembled myself and marched back out to the counter as if nothing had happened. Kohl had disappeared and Keith had thrown me curious glances but didn't ask me a thing.

And I'd been left to replay those hyper-pleasurable few minutes over and over in my mind and remind myself of my throbbing, enlarged clit that protested its neglect every time I turned and rubbed it the wrong way in my jeans.

My body is still reeling from lack of fulfillment. I dart Kohl a dark look. It's probably how he'd planned it. I swallow, my heartbeat suddenly beating that tempo in my throat again. He guides me to a dark town car up ahead.

A driver gets out as we approach and whips around to the passenger side to open the door for us. Evan indicates that I should enter the limo before him, and I scoot over as far as I can, afraid to sit too close to him. As I glide across the sleek leather seat, my senses are bombarded by that fresh new car smell. By the time he enters, I'm practically plastered to the far window. He throws me a glance and then looks away, a smile curving his sexy mouth.

"I don't bite, Madeline—at least not yet."

That same heat floods me at his words, and I'm reminded of how much I'd wanted him to bite my nipple when he'd had his hot mouth wrapped around it earlier. And that quote of his, about that higher plane of ecstasy achieved by "exchange of pleasure, pain and power." I can't stop thinking—and *wondering*—what he means by that. I realize that I'm way naive and inexperienced compared to him.

As if remembering that molten pleasure of their own accord, my nipples immediately tighten under my dress and I'm thankful that the satin of the bodice is too thick to reveal that to him. But when his gaze settles on my chest, I realize that my own quick breathing has given me away. Heat crawls up my neck—another dead giveaway, damnit.

Instead of trying anything, though, he simply takes my hand and pulls it into his lap. Turning it upward, he traces an idle pattern into my palm. It tingles, sensitive to his touch.

"Have you been thinking about me, Madeline?" he asks, his tone low and sexy with that British accent that heats my blood. "I've been thinking about you. I had a board meeting today and all I could think about was the delicious taste of your soft nipples."

He's hard. I can see his erection straining eagerly against the crotch of his pants.

He turns his head and presses his hot mouth to my ear. "There's so much more to taste. I'm sure it will be every bit as delicious as the sampling I've already had. *More* so…"

Then he brushes his lips across my forehead. "I'm very much looking forward to spending the evening with you. Who knows what we'll get up to?"

CHAPTER 12
EXETER HOUSE

HIS WORDS ECHO IN MY MIND.

Who knows what we'll get up to?

Nothing! is my silent answer. But even as my mind protests, my body is warming to him in every way. As if those few minutes with his mouth on my breasts and his hand down my panties was enough to imprint his touch on me.

The car slows, and I glance out the window. I see that we're by the beach, Malibu maybe, with all the chic shops and elegant bistros. We pull to a stop in front of a sprawling, beach-front hotel. Exeter House, one of the most exclusive social clubs in Southern California. Attached to the classy, white-shuttered building is a restaurant, right on the beach.

I turn to Kohl, wide-eyed. "You're a member of Exeter House?" Even the most elite, the top one percent of the top one percent, can only *dream* of becoming a member of this ultra-exclusive club. *Presidents* have applied and been declined.

Exclusive isn't just an expression with them. I swallow, studying the sign again.

Fuck. This is unreal.

Kohl just smiles and shrugs one shoulder. "I have a place here," he says nonchalantly, as if he's talking about the YMCA. "But we're not going there tonight."

I nod slowly, a little relieved and a little disappointed. Catching a glimpse of the *inside* of Exeter House would be a once-in-a-lifetime thing. But even the attached restaurant, though not part of the required membership, is incredibly exclusive—a mecca for actors and billionaires. A place to be *seen*.

The restaurant is elegant, gorgeous fixtures, and dim lighting. The glamorously dressed hostess smiles and greets him as Monsieur Kohl, escorting us to a private room in the back of the restaurant. It's quiet here, with the faint strains of a live quartet reaching us in our little alcove from the main dining room. I'm suddenly very aware that we are alone and it's quiet. For lack of anything better to do and because my nerves are pulled so taut they might snap, I snatch up the menu.

But when the server comes, Evan orders for us. In French. He carries on a conversation with the woman in fluent French. She laughs and rests her hand on his shoulder, leaning into him flirtatiously.

Wow, I'm sitting *right here*.

He smiles at her, and the sound of that language coming out if his sexy mouth is enough to shred whatever resistance I have been holding onto. And I remember something from the online research I did about him—his mother was a French native so he probably grew up speaking it.

I remember to shut my mouth about two seconds before the server turns to collect my menu. She hasn't even asked me what I want or even greeted me. Evan seems to notice my discomfort. "You like filet mignon?"

I nod.

"Medium rare?" He's right again. I blink. Is that just a lucky guess or has he been studying up on me? And how exactly would he even get that information? It's not like I've had the money to order a steak at any half-decent eating establishment in the last two years.

He smiles. "You seem a little on edge. I ordered us a nice bottle of Cabernet Sauvignon. That should help you relax."

But his eyes hold a mischievous glint in them, like he knows exactly why I'm on edge. *He's* the reason I'm on edge—him and his hands and his mouth and the sinful, hot things he's done to my body—without bringing anything to fruition. I'm frustrated as hell and he knows it.

I wonder if being his lover will always be like that. I also wonder if he was so commanding in bed that his partner wouldn't be able to climax without his express permission. I frown. He notices because he's watching. Like a hawk.

"You may as well ask, Madeline. That's why we are here, isn't it?"

I shake my head. "Why a *mistress* and why a *contract*? Why not have a normal relationship? Or just a short-term affair?" My eyes slide down his chest, across his broad shoulders, to his powerful hands resting on the table in front of him, calmly folded. A short-term affair might be just what I need to get this man out of my system. Like binging on chocolate cake and then not wanting it again for months.

I remember his searing mouth suckling my nipples to aching points, his thumb deftly circling my clit. My panties instantly soak at the memory and I swallow. I'm in deep, deep shit if I can't get any more control of myself than *this.*

He laces his fingers together. "For one thing, I do not do relationships. I've been there, done that. Does not work for me. Period. As for an affair…is that what *you'd* prefer?"

Negotiations, eh? I know how to do this. Growing up, my dad had been an expert at negotiating, and I learned just from watching him, when I was small and he still lived with us. "I propose a one-night stand."

A dimple forms just below his mouth as he smiles, licks his bottom lip. He sits back and looks at me for a moment between narrowed eyes. "One night?" His eyes slowly rove to my mouth, down my neck to settle at the top of my dress. Those eyes touch me like firm, strong hands, scorching me. "One night with you will not be enough for me. That taste will only make me want more. And I'm not someone who tolerates being kept wanting."

His blue eyes twinkle, and I scowl at the cruel irony of his words. He's kept me in a state of wanting since this morning. I'm *wanting* so much it's practically painful.

I steeple my fingers over my place setting. "That's my offer. Take it or leave it."

"What is it about the contract that you dislike?"

The sommelier arrives with the wine and uncorks it in front of us, pouring a small portion into Evan's glass and asking him to taste. He swirls the burgundy liquid, gives it a sniff and then takes a sip, pausing for a moment, his sensual lips pursing, his eyes losing the focus of deep concentration.

"*C'est bon, merci,*" he says.

And the sommelier turns to fill our glasses before setting the bottle on the table, leaving the cork off. Evan nods to him and he leaves. I wish I could get up and go with him.

I fiddle with the stem of my glass, determined not to drink any of it. This man has already addled my wits quite handily without adding alcohol to the equation.

But he hasn't forgotten that he asked me a question and I left the answer hanging in the air between us. There's a tense, silent few minutes while he just stares at me with those deep-blue eyes, pinning me down.

I clear my throat, focusing on the wine glass. "I despise the word *mistress* and I don't see the need for a contract."

"The contract is there to protect both parties. And as for the word mistress, it need never be mentioned again."

My eyebrows raise. "Then what would you call it?"

He looks like he's about to laugh but decides against it. "Does it matter? How about just 'the contract?'"

I blink. "And how does it protect *me*, for example?"

"Aside from listing how you'll be provided for—"

"See, that's just it…. If I were to displace myself to a residence for your *convenience*," I say the word with a hint of disdain, "who's to say how my life could be upended should you change your mind?"

"The contractor—" He cuts himself off when I shake my head.

"No, don't use that crap language. At least use the correct pronouns. If this is what you are trying to set up, then own it. '*I want…*'" I modeled for him.

Something flashes in his azure eyes, though I can't tell whether it's irritation or intrigue. "*I* would be responsible for *your* care and living expenses for one full year should *I* choose to end the agreement between *us*." He raises his brows at me as if to ask, *Was that satisfactory?*

I swallow. "And what if *I* choose to end it?"

His gaze flicks away for a moment, and he takes a small sip of his wine before speaking. "I'd have two weeks to find a suitable replacement."

"Oh? And during those two weeks...?"

"The physical relationship would continue. But at the end of the day, after those two weeks, the final decision is yours."

I blink. Two weeks' notice, just like with a regular job. Would he require me to punch a timecard, too? Which gets me thinking...

"And am I obligated to see you whenever you want me?"

He looks confused. "I'm not requiring you to give up your life."

"But what if you want to see me and I have other plans? Would your desire to see me supplant that?"

"I'd like to be given favorable consideration, at least. If you have something important, of course, like school or some family event, that's one thing. But I would rank at the top of the priority list."

"Hmm." I put my hand to my chin as if thinking about it. "What about advance notice? One week."

His eyes harden. "No."

I pause, waiting for him to come up with his terms, but he doesn't. He's onto me, apparently. In any negotiation, you are supposed to play hard ball and wait for the other party to come back to you with softer terms. I swallow.

"What do you like then?" I ask.

He swirls the wine in his half-drunk glass, staring into it for a moment. "Twenty-four hours."

"A day? No way. Seventy-two."

He pins me down, a knowing glint in his eyes. "Twenty-four hours."

I pause, watch as he downs the rest of his wine and then places the glass on the table, running a long finger up and down the stem—the same finger that was buried deep inside me this morning. I lick my lips, my mouth suddenly dry.

"So how does the contract protect *you?*" I ask, mostly to change the subject but partly because I'm dying to pin him down on something. A guy this brilliant, this gorgeous, this fantastically rich, must be a whackadoo to want a contracted bedmate, or girlfriend or whatever you'd call it.

"Well, aside from your continued discretion, of course, the contract sets up…boundaries. Boundaries which are important—*essential*—to me. It's a physical relationship. A camaraderie. Even a friendship."

A smile dances on my mouth. "But love isn't allowed?"

He's not smiling anymore. "There will be no talk of love at all."

I raise my brows, surprised. "Save for the fact that you are banning it. And you think signing a paper would prevent this?"

His head tilted slightly, his eyes somber. "I think that you have a brilliant head on your shoulders, Madeline, and are unlikely to let your heart get carried away by silly fancies. Am I right?"

I swallow and look away, briefly thinking of Jason, my ex. Did I even have a heart left after he had so callously shattered it?

"I have a feeling you and I are of the same mind on the subject of love," he says.

The server brings us our dinner, and we begin to eat in silence for several long minutes. I heartily cut into my steak, and when I put the first bite in my mouth, I can't help but groan. It melts in my mouth and tastes amazing.

Evan watches me with hooded eyes. "You haven't touched your wine. Are you afraid you won't trust yourself?"

I take a deep breath. "You could say that."

I don't trust myself one little bit, as a matter of fact. His words from the car still ring in my head, *Who knows what we'll get up to tonight?*

I know what my body wants us to get up to, so I have to rely on my wits and my sharp mind to keep me out of trouble. That means that wine is definitely out…

Because I need every resource I have available to me to keep up with Mr. Evan Kohl.

CHAPTER 13
FIRM BOUNDARIES

"JUST SO WE ARE CLEAR," I SAY AFTER A FEW MORE MINUTES of enjoying the amazing steak, "we don't get to do anything until after I sign this contract?"

He swallows, wipes his mouth. "That is correct."

"Well, that's putting a lot of faith in my *skills*. How do you know that it would even work between us in the bedroom?"

This time he does laugh. "Oh, I've had enough women. I think I'm a fair judge of when the chemistry is there. And I'd say that it is indeed there for us."

Suddenly my mouth is dry, and I can't catch my breath. "But what if…what if I don't agree? If I sign that contract and we go to bed. Am I stuck continuing with it for two weeks because of the notice?"

A dark brow arches. "What do you want, a grace period?"

I brighten. "Yes, that's exactly what I'd like, um, one month…"

"One week."

"Three weeks," I persist.

His eyes harden. "*One* week," he repeats.

This is getting frustrating. The more we talk about this, the more I can imagine those strong hands on my body again, touching me the way he'd touched me in the coffee shop bathroom. Kissing me everywhere. Pushing himself into me.

I take a deep breath and suddenly reach for the wine, sucking down half the glass before setting it down.

"How many times a week am I required—"

His brow furrows. "There's no requirement. But after the first time, I think you'll be willing whenever I can break away to see you."

I arch a brow. "You have a lot of confidence in *your* skills."

He smiles. He's so goddamn fucking gorgeous that my already-soaked panties grow even wetter. "I've had a lot of practice."

I clear my throat. "Well, I haven't." I figure it's best to throw that out there now and let him chew on it. Let him know that I'm not some party girl who knows all the kinky tricks. "I mean...I'm not a virgin or anything. But I've only been with one guy. My high school boyfriend. We were together for years and we first did it when I was fifteen, but—"

He waves a hand, a brief scowl passing over his beautiful features. "No need to give me a play-by-play, Madeline. I get that you're nervous about your lack of experience. But I don't care about that, because teaching you *my* preferences will be all the more enjoyable."

"Well," I hedge, "I do have a few firm boundaries."

His brow lifts. "Such as?"

I swallow, suddenly uncomfortable. I don't usually talk about my sexual preferences with strangers. "No group sex, no videotaping, and no anal."

His beautiful eyes narrow, and I swear I can feel the intensity of his gaze on me. "Have you ever tried anal?"

I swallow. "No, of course not. I'd never degrade myself like that."

He leans forward, his gaze hungry and intense. "I am telling you now, Madeline, I *will* own every inch of you. I will dominate you in every way imaginable. There can be no boundaries between us."

I gulp. Literally *gulp* as a million images fly through my mind, picturing whatever it is he'd like us to do. And to my shock and horror, every single one of those possibilities excites me. I'm on a rush, like that thrill you get when speeding downhill at sixty miles per hour on a roller coaster or dangling from the end of a bungee cord or sitting front and center at a slashfest mashup of *Nightmare on Elm Street* and *Halloween*.

I'm surfing a wave of pure adrenaline. And it feels *amazing,* electrifying. I feel alive for the first time in years.

Not long after, we finish our meal and Evan signs the check. He rises and comes around to pull out my chair for me as I stand. Very old world and gentlemanly. When he draws near me, I can smell his cologne, that fresh windswept ocean scent of his. I swallow, turn my head away. It's still early, not even ten, so I wonder what else is in store for us on what has to go down in the books as the world's weirdest date.

"I have a suite booked, but I thought we could take a drive along the coast first," he says.

I blink. That was presumptuous of him. "Why would you need to book a suite? I thought the members all had apartments at Exeter House?" I ask.

"I do have a penthouse here," he says. "But it's private, and I don't bring guests to my private residence."

"Not even your *mistresses?*" I ask, using that word I hate.

His lips curl up into a half-smile. "Especially not mistresses."

That strikes me as really strange. We're talking about sex in the most primal ways, but he can't take me to his penthouse, because it's *private*? I'm *almost* offended by that, but I remind myself he's very high-profile. Maybe women have burned him in the past by exposing his personal information? That's my only guess, and I go with it.

He keeps his hand on the curve of my back again as he guides me out to the valet where the driver is already waiting for us, the door propped open. I assume the staff alerted the driver that we were on our way out.

I slide back into the limo. The wine and conversation at dinner have relaxed me a little and so I don't make a beeline for the other door, like I did before. When Evan enters, his long, hard leg brushes briefly against mine and I feel it like a shock. The air darts out of my lungs, and I pull my leg away.

"Just drive for a bit, will you, please?" Evan asks as the driver slides behind the wheel. At his reply, Evan pushes the button to close the partition between us and the driver. He doesn't say anything, until the car starts moving.

"Was there anything else you wanted to cover that we didn't go over at dinner?" he finally asks in a quiet voice.

I frown for a moment, thinking, then shake my head. "I think that was pretty much all of it."

"I have a question for you, then."

I look up. "What?"

But I never get a chance to finish what I'm saying because his hand hooks around the back of my neck, pulling my head to his, his mouth landing on mine in a firm, sure kiss. His mouth savages mine, ferociously as if he's devouring me. He's overwhelming me, his tongue plunging into my mouth, pillaging everywhere it touches.

His other hand is on my breast, rubbing against the satin material, making my nipple tighten in seconds. I groan and he does not let up. He's softening me up again. But though I can tell myself this in my head, my body is literally overwhelmed by him. His body, bigger, more imposing, stronger, his arm like iron is latching around my waist pulling me tightly against him. I can tell that he's seconds away from unzipping my dress and God, I want him to.

"There are things I want to know, too." He breathes, his hot mouth pressed against my neck, his hand trailing its way to my knee and up under my skirt, caressing my thigh. "I want to know what it feels like to have your hard nipples pressed against my bare chest when you are underneath me. I want to know what you sound like when you come. I want to know what the inside of your thighs taste like." He traps my ear in his mouth, running his tongue over the lobe, sending lightning straight down to my center. "I want to know what it feels like when you come on my cock."

The air rushes out of my lungs. I'm not even sure if it's possible for me to be more turned on than I am at this moment. I'm about ready to lie down right here and open my legs for him. But he pulls back to look into my face and then I can see that I've affected him, too. He's flushed, breathing hard, his blue eyes dilated so that they are almost black.

He wants me. He wants to *fuck* me.

And I want him to.

"What's it to be, Madeline?" he finally says. "Do I tell the driver to take you home right now? Or will you come back with me to Exeter House and sign the contract?"

I lick my lips, falling back against the seat. It's clear that nothing will happen between us if I don't sign and I want him so badly I can hardly think straight. I swallow and stare into those beautiful eyes. I can see the flecks of white and gray around the irises and they mesmerize me like a child's kaleidoscope.

And in this moment I realize…I have no idea how I'm going to answer him.

CHAPTER 14
SAY YES

"*WHAT'S IT TO BE, MADELINE?*" HE'S ASKED ME THE question and the air between us is thick with tension. And desire. He clearly wants this as much as I do.

Leaning back against the town car's leather seat, he regards me with those stunning blue eyes, patiently awaiting my response. His lips are still red from our kiss, his dark hair slightly mussed. He wants me to sign a contract. He wants me to be his *mistress*.

I suck in a deep breath. I can't believe I'm going to say this. Seriously, something must be wrong with me. Sign a contract just so I can sleep with a guy? But for every objection I've raised, Evan has had a logical, completely sound response. And the contract itself sounds less and less crazy the more we've discussed it.

I swallow past the tightness in my throat, and look him square in the eyes. "Let's go to the hotel."

A faint smile touches the edges of his lips before he leans over and flicks the switch to lower the tinted glass partition between the driver and us. "Take us back to Exeter House."

"Yes, sir."

The partition rises, and we're alone again. He settles back against the seat and stares out the window, one powerful hand working against his thigh. We spend the next ten minutes in expectant silence, tension eating up the space between us.

I'm dying to ask him what comes next, but I don't want to break the silence. Instead, I watch him as he looks out the window, shadows passing over his beautiful face.

He's going to fuck me. This man will be deep inside me soon. I can't help but wonder what he will be like. To hear him talk, he is a very skilled lover. I've never been with someone like that. And the realization that I'm now giving him consent to "possess me completely" sends a shiver of anticipation coursing through me.

It's been so long since I've felt a man's touch, his weight on me. I've played it safe for so long, been the good girl for so long that I'd almost atrophied into some sort of unfeeling automaton. But something about him, the way he talks, the way he looks at me. The way he touches me. It makes me feel alive—and *happy* to be so. Even if this ends up being a short-term affair, a wild few months of pure carnal pleasure, I can't help but feel that even that would be worth it.

Finally, the limo pulls to a stop, and I glance out the window at a lineup of small beach cottages alongside the bigger Exeter House. They sit on the sand, right on the beach. Though it's dark, the rhythmic, primal pounding of the surf on the beach provides an apt backdrop for this night.

He holds the door for me as I get out and then takes my hand and leads me up a walkway, past a small fishpond. In the dark, it's hard to see, but the little cottage is beautiful, rustic looking. Quiet. And completely isolated.

I draw in a shaky breath as we reach the small porch and he pulls out a card key, waving it in front of the lock. We enter, stepping past the foyer and into the large, elegant living room. The furnishings are a bold navy-blue and white, a nautical theme accented by dark mahogany wood. It's gorgeous in its simplicity. And though elegant, also homey.

I immediately feel myself relax—just a little bit.

Without a word, Kohl strides over to the dining table, reaches into his coat pocket and extracts some folded papers. Unfolding them, he lays them flat. It's the contract. I walk over to where he's bent over it to get a look at what he's doing. He flips through the pages, making quick notations and handwritten amendments to the points we discussed over dinner. Then, on the last page, he signs where it denotes the "contractor" to sign. He scratches out the word "mistress" under the line next to it, writing instead "contractee." Then, he lays down the pen and straightens. He steps aside to make room for me, and while I read through his amendments, he's removing his jacket and tie, draping them over a chair.

Nervously, I bend to take the pen, tucking an escaped strand of dark hair back behind my ear. Aside from his amendments, the contract is identical to the document he emailed to me days ago. I initial next to each of his notations and then flip to the last page, signing on the dotted line.

I swallow, laying down the pen. It's done. *I'm his.*

With a harsh expulsion of breath, he's at my side in seconds, pressing me against the table as if he couldn't wait a second longer. His mouth comes down, capturing mine in a hungry kiss. His tongue sweeps into my mouth, taking possession, taking control. Telling me now with his body the exact same thing his contract states in writing. *I belong to him.*

He tastes like the expensive wine we had at dinner, and I drink him in eagerly, opening my mouth to his invasion. Now that the contract is signed, there's no reason for me to hold back.

His hot mouth breaks away from my lips as he grips me, one hand reaching up to pull down my dark brown hair, running his fingers through it repeatedly until it obeys his command and is now sweeping past my shoulders. At the nape of my neck, he grabs a handful of it, his fingers tightening so that it pulls painfully at my scalp, forcing me to look up into his face.

"Beautiful," he growls, fastening his lips to my throat. Then he lifts me so that I'm seated on the table. It's an elegant table made of a solid slab of thick, smooth marble. It's icy and hard beneath me. "Now I'm going to taste your sweet little pussy."

His words are like a drug, and I'm mesmerized. *Oh, God yes.* The sound of his deep baritone vibrates through me, and I moan. I need his mouth on me, sucking me until I come.

In one quick motion, he pulls my legs apart, placing himself between my knees that hang over the table. He catches the hem of my dress and pushes it up, up my thighs hitching it past my waist so that I'm exposed to him—wet black lace panties and all. Slowly, his eyes still pinned on mine, he trails his hand up my inner thigh and then slips a finger up the length of my entrance through my drenched panties. His breathing is labored now, but he's still not watching what he's doing. He's watching my face.

He nudges the black lace aside and pushes at my entrance with his long fingers.

"So fucking wet. For me."

I lean back on my arms to look up at him. My eyes close as his fingers continue to explore my exposed entrance. "Yes," I moan. "I've been wet all night."

He growls, low in his throat, his eyes burning with lust. "You've just signed yourself to me. Do you understand?"

I nod, licking my lips.

"You agree to obey me…" His fingers prod harder. "Yes?"

Then he hovers over me, pushing against my shoulder and forcing me to lie back on the table. I watch as, tight-featured, he shoves my skirt up farther, then grabs the crotch of my panties and rips it open with a fierce jerk, exposing me completely.

"Say yes, Madeline. You've agreed to obey me."

"Yes," I breathe as he sinks two fingers inside me, stretching me, forcing me to release a cry of pleasure.

"Fuck. I can't wait to bury myself in this tight pussy. Jesus, Madeline. You were made for me to enjoy. And I plan on doing just that tonight. I'll take pleasure in every inch of you. And you won't hold back. Will you, my sweet?"

"No," I squeeze my eyes closed as his fingers start to pump in and out of me in a slow, torturous rhythm. It feels so good that I shamelessly grind my hips against him, moaning, begging wordlessly for more.

"Open your legs for me, Madeline. Open wide." And as I said I would do, I obey.

Without warning, his hand stills. Then he ducks, burying his head between my thighs, and I'm lost. His hot breath bathes the sensitive skin above my inner thighs and I jump when his tongue connects with my clit. It feels like an electric shock on the most sensitive spot on my body.

He licks my clit, over and over again—alternating between flicking it harshly with the blade of his tongue and lapping slowly, languorously. There is fire in my belly, warm and raw pleasure seeping down my thighs. Then, he plunges his tongue deep inside my swollen channel.

"Evan!" I moan. "Oh, God." My legs instinctively tighten, and he shoves a leg aside.

"I said *open*, Madeline. Obey me."

My eyes squeeze tight and I comply. He continues to lick and suck my clit. The pleasure is wild, intense; it sends me hurtling toward the edge in record speed. I grip the table as he continues to devour me, taking me to the very brink. His tongue is a divine gift, his lips surrounding me, demanding my compliance to their demands. Every muscle in my body tightens, preparing for shuddering release.

My back arches, and he pushes me down again, flat on the table, holding me immobile with the steady, relentless rhythm of his lips and tongue. *Fuck*, it feels so good, and I'm mindless with pleasure as I push up and over the edge at last, coming apart beneath his mouth. Instinctively I clamp my legs around his head, but his hands come up and spread me wide again, firmly pushing my knees back against the table.

Pulses from my orgasm are still washing over me, my eyes rolling back into my head. When I open them I notice that he is looking down at me, watching me closely with fire and hunger in those blue, blue eyes.

He starts to unbutton his shirt. "Sit up, Madeline."

Slowly I struggle to a sitting position as I continue to watch him. With his shirt now unbuttoned, I get my first glimpse of the man underneath. His body is beautiful, every muscle well-defined, compact, hard. He has a firm chest dusted with dark hair, a hard abdomen with six-pack and that V that dips below his waist. He removes his shirt and his biceps are exquisitely defined, veined, firm. He moves an arm forward, and that's when I notice the tattoo on his right forearm—a simple infinity symbol inked in black.

I swallow, feeling that desire build again inside of me. I didn't think it could be possible to feel so satisfied and yet so hungry at the same time.

His hand goes to his belt and then it stops. He steps forward and reaches around the back of my dress where I'm still sitting like a vegetable on the table. With one swift motion, it's completely unzipped and he has peeled the bodice away from me, but I'm still watching the sweat sheen on his muscles as he moves. He smells of clean aftershave, sweat and sex. That hunger stirs in the pit of my belly again like a thing alive.

I need him inside me. *Now.*

But I won't be the one to decide that. *He* will.

Chapter 15
Marked

I SLIP OFF THE TABLE, LETTING THE DRESS FALL TO THE floor. Soon, the shredded scrap of lace that were once Sam's new panties join it. I'm completely naked except for the silver strappy heels. I bend to remove them, but he stops me.

"No. Leave them on."

I swallow. He hasn't moved as his eyes rove over every inch of my body, and I suddenly feel self-conscious. His gaze rests first on my beaded nipples, then slides across my belly to rest at the apex of my thighs. Slowly, very deliberately he licks his lips.

"I can't wait to feel that delicious little pussy wrapped around my cock, Madeline, to feel you pulsing with your orgasm, squeezing me." He reaches for his belt, unbuckles it and then unzips his trousers, reaching into the pocket to grab something before letting them slide to the ground. Beneath, he's wearing boxers and those quickly follow and he's naked before me, his large cock swollen and jutting out from his perfect, hard body.

I moan at the sight of him.

"Get back on the table," he grinds in a thick, husky voice. I pause for a moment, confused that he doesn't want to move this to the bed. He senses that, revealing the wrapped condom in his hand. "I'm taking you right here. Right *now*."

With a deep breath, I slide back onto the table. The marble surface is hard and cold underneath me. He approaches me again, like he did before, pressing my knees wide apart.

His hand sweeps up to grasp my hair and pull my head to tilt my face up to his. "My turn now," he grates.

With our gazes locked, I do what I've been craving to do since he first took off his shirt. I touch his chest. It's perfect, hard, smooth, dusted with enough hair to feel manly, rough. He stills for a minute and I wonder if he's holding his breath. He seems to want me to continue touching him, so I do.

I run my hands over his hard pecs, palm his nipples and then pinch them just as he did mine. A low growl emits from the base of his throat but my hands have roamed lower, over his hard six pack abs, tracing the lines between them. And then even lower, to land on the soft skin of his erect cock. My fingers wrap around the base of it. He's both very long and thick around. I have not had a wide amount of experience with this part of the male anatomy, but I know he's a lot bigger than Jason was.

Is it going to hurt? Or will it just feel amazing? I swallow…. Or maybe it will be a little bit of both?

The thought of feeling both pain and pleasure as he thrusts inside of me makes me even wetter. I can feel my moisture pool onto the table. I slip my hand from the base of his cock to the tip, pinching it. With a loud grunt, he takes my shoulders and gently pushes me back against the table so that I'm lying down again, looking up at him. He stands over me, never taking his eyes off of me as he rips the foil wrapper on the condom and slides it onto his swollen cock.

He props each of my sandaled feet onto the back of a chair to each side of him. Then, he grabs my knees, pulling me toward him so that my butt is flush with the edge of the table. With my knees as widely apart as they will go, he then takes hold of himself, nudging the tip of his cock against my entrance. The moment I feel him there, I suck in a sharp breath, tensing with anticipation.

"Breathe, Madeline. Relax."

He slowly guides himself into me, stretching me as he pushes deeper but never stopping. When he's halfway in, he lets out a deep groan. "Christ, you are so goddamn tight. Your pussy feels so good, I can barely control myself."

I swallow. He's been gentle up until now and it hasn't hurt much—there's just a bit of tension from where he stretches me in muscles long dormant from lack of use.

But now, his jaw tenses and his eyes glaze over. I realize I'm witnessing his loss of control. He grabs my hips and plunges the rest of the way into me with a sharp, deep thrust. I grunt in pain as he hits a barrier deep inside me. The sensation is deeply pleasurable and painful at the same time. But another jerk of his hips tells me that there's still more of him and the pinch of pain is making my eyes water.

But he doesn't notice. He's too immersed in his own bliss.

"Oh, God," he breathes, stilling, closing his eyes and appearing to savor the feeling of me wrapped around him. Clamping my hips, he slides slowly out, the friction of his movement pulling the breath out of my lungs. He's almost completely out before he thrusts forward, slamming into me again with such a force that makes me gasp in pain. He's so big it hurts. But...it feels good. *So good.*

I wiggle my hips, but he clasps them, holding me still while he continues to push in and out of me with a quick, relentless rhythm. The air sucks out of my lungs and yet I watch him—his glazed, burning eyes, the tension in his jaw and neck. That magnificent chest rising and falling with his heavy breathing.

He thrusts and thrusts repeatedly, pushing me up on the table and then dragging me back to him at the hips. By now, all pretense of gentleness is gone. His hold is forceful, his movements sharp and urgent. Ferocious. *Wild.*

It all feels rather cold and impersonal, me lying back on the table, staring up at him while he, standing, is only touching me at my hips and where his cock is buried deep inside me. His glazed over eyes stare into mine, posture stiff with tension, his gorgeous features flushed.

I grip the edge of the table with my palms to hold myself in place as he slams into me over and over, knocking my breath away. This cold, distant fuck is turning me on, and I moan, though I can't move my hips to meet his thrusts.

It takes him a while…and that's surprising me, too. I had no idea that sex lasted longer than five or ten minutes.

He's been working me for longer than that. But after some time, I detect that he's approaching his own climax—only because that's when he suddenly slows his relentless thrusting. He breathes in deeply, over and over again in an attempt to regain control while moving his hips in shallow circles. He's fighting his own orgasm, actively prolonging the act. Making this moment of deep, bone-aching pleasure last even longer. I feel every movement where we are connected down to my toes, in every millimeter of my skin.

I'm still staring at his face, but his eyes are fixed on my breasts as they bounce with the motion of his body. Suddenly he stops, and the sheen of his muscles coated in sweat fascinates me.

Breathing hoarsely but without a word, he bends and snaps up one of my nipples into his mouth, sucking fiercely. I gasp, arching to push it deeper into his mouth, and he begins to bite me, that sharp pain matching the pinch inside me where his cock is hitting against my inner wall. His thrusts are short and shallow now and he's coaxing me closer to the edge, moving to the other nipple to bite it while pinching the first between thumb and forefinger.

And that's all I need—it's almost without effort this time that I'm up and over the edge, shattering into a million pieces as gorgeous pleasure washes over me again. But this time, it's different because of that full sensation where his hard cock is inside me, stretching me like an immovable rod of iron. I contract around him, locking my legs around his hips as I let go. His breath is ragged as he stills, eyes closed, savoring the feel of my orgasm as the contractions clasp his cock over and over again.

His heavy breathing is only punctuated by moans in his deep baritone. But instead of resuming his thrusts to finish himself, as I was expecting, he suddenly pulls out of me. He tears off the condom and with his savage eyes burning into mine, he pumps his fist over his cock once, twice. And he's coming.

I watch in fascination as his hot semen spurts across my abdomen. He holds himself still as he continues to come, his spray spreading across my stomach like abstract art. This is such a surreal moment, and yet I find it incredibly hot—surprisingly so. I'm breathing heavily now, looking up at him as his eyes slide over me, from my neck, my breasts, my stomach.

I swallow, as he pulls my high-heel-clad feet widely apart on the table. Then he snatches up my right hand and presses it against my clit. "Touch yourself," he orders.

I take a deep breath, puzzled. I've had two orgasms already. I don't even think I'm capable of more. But that command in his voice—and my promise to obey—are still fresh in my mind. Slowly I move my hand against my clit.

His eyes lower to the movement, watching me. "Don't take your eyes away from me, Madeline. You won't think of anyone else but me when you come again."

I'd almost laugh at that if I wasn't so turned on. *As if I even could.* "No. Of course not."

He's breathing deeply again, clearly feeling new arousal as he watches me, and I'm wondering if I have the energy—or the desire—to come again. Both the orgasms I just enjoyed were head and shoulders above anything I've ever had before. And I've never had three in one night. *Let alone in one hour.*

But he's clearly not concerned. His hands reach out to me, splaying across my belly, still coated with his semen. He begins to spread the sticky liquid across my stomach, breasts, and lower, as if he's massaging me with it. It's warm and under his hands it feels so good. His hands move to my nipples, the contact there sticking as he pinches and rolls them between his fingers. He's completely painted my stomach and chest, up to my neck with his come, all the while ordering me to rub myself.

And I'm close again, closing my eyes, I moan.

His voice grates harshly at my ear. "I've marked you, Madeline. How do you like feeling me all over your skin?"

Everywhere his hands aren't, the liquid is cooling now. I shiver, but with more than with just cold. His possession, his *claiming*, have aroused me to yet another level.

"It feels so good," I moan.

"Yes. Remember that. I've *taken* you. Claimed you. *Marked* you. Now, you're mine. Say my name when you come."

"Evan," I moan.

He pinches my nipples again as if in reward for my obedience. My hand moves faster between my legs, and his hands are all over me again, rubbing himself into me. "Mine," he growls.

"Evan," I breathe. I'm almost there, right at the edge.

"Tell me whose you are."

"I—am—yours," I say between grunts and gasps as my hand moves faster. And the orgasm blooms, this one feeling different, subtle, rolling in waves and lasting longer than the others, but lacking the intensity that he'd evoked. It occurs to me that this is how my self-induced orgasms have always felt before he began to touch me today and ratcheted up the standard to an all-new high.

Like this night is the first incredible hit of a drug. I'm in danger of becoming addicted to his touch. When my orgasm finally fades, I open my eyes, and he's watching me. He leans forward, bends over me to kiss me hard on the mouth. Where his body touches mine, his semen causes our skin to stick together. Impossibly, his cock is erect again. I can feel it against my leg.

"Fucking hell, Madeline. Just the sight of you covered in my come is enough to make me painfully hard all over again." He pulls back, looking into my face, pushing my matted hair away from where it sticks to my forehead. "You might need to rest, though…" His voice dwindles, but there's a strange tone to it. Almost like a challenge.

I smile, lick my dry lips. "And you don't?"

He grins that wicked grin. "Ah, not yet."

I suck in a breath, overwhelmed with the desire to impress him…to *please* him. "Then…neither do I."

His smile widens and he kisses me again. "Ah, that's a good girl. That's the best response you could have given." His sticky thumb caresses my cheek. "We'll be at this for a while, I think. I haven't wanted someone with this intensity for a very long time."

That familiar drunk feeling is stirring in my stomach, my chest. My legs are growing cold with that pleasant numbness of intense arousal. "Neither have I."

"Then it's going to be a long night…but I'm quite sure we're going to enjoy every minute of it." His cock twitches against my leg, and I know he's already raging to go again. I open my legs to signal that I'm ready, but he draws back, shaking his head.

Suddenly I'm rife with disappointment as he straightens and reaches to pull me up to a sitting position and then off the table. Has he changed his mind? Are we done now?

I wait for him to step back so I can follow him, but instead, he stoops to pull another condom out of his pants pocket on the floor. I can now see that his cock is as rigid and swollen as it was before. It's as if the last time never happened.

But the soreness inside me reminds me that it *did*. And suddenly I'm scared. He said it would be a long night. How many more times can he even do this?

He's straightening and looking at me again as I bite my lip and return the favor. "We'll do things rather differently *this* time, though." And that harshness is back in his voice. He hooks a hand around his tie that is dangling on one of the chairs and then grasps my shoulder, spinning me to face away from him. And quickly—as he's clearly experienced at it—he takes the skinny end of the tie and holds it up to fasten it over my eyes as a makeshift blindfold.

It's knotted firmly and I can see nothing. Suddenly my heart is racing with new thrill and even a tinge of fear. His mouth presses against my ear. "Can you see?"

"No…nothing."

"Good. You will trust me for the rest. And you will not struggle or resist." I stiffen at the implication. I sense him grasp the long end of the tie—the fat end. Then he stops, shaking me as if to dissipate that sudden tension. "Is that clear, Madeline?"

"Y-yes. Yes, Evan."

He kisses my ear, running his tongue along the shell. I shudder with the sensation. "Very good." His hands are moving again, winding the tie around again. He wraps the fat end of the tie around my neck and throat, tugging the end and tightening it, but not so much that I can't breathe. Just enough that I'm aware that it's there.

Then he's pressing my back, bending me forward over the table. My front is still sticky with his come and he's laying me against the tabletop—even on the papers that we just signed. With his foot, he nudges my sandaled feet wide apart, pushing my ass into the air. Then his hands leave me as I hear the crinkle of the condom package and the telltale snap of him slipping it on.

In seconds, though, he's back to me, bending around me and pressing himself over my back, pushing me harder against the table. "A little warning. This time will be…rougher."

I take a deep breath and am about to swallow when suddenly the tie around my neck tightens—*a lot.* Enough to prevent me from swallowing. His other hand grabs my wrists and pins them both against the small of my back.

Despite my promise, I begin to struggle as he slides his erection deep inside me in one sudden, smooth stroke. I push back against him but there's nowhere to go. He's already impaling me. And though it feels good, I'm panicking from the tightness around my neck, the fact that I can't see, the fact that he's got my arms pinned at a near impossible angle. I'm helpless underneath him, growing anxious.

He eases up and loosens the tie. "Don't fight me..."

"It's—it's too much."

The tie loosens even more. "Then we'll go slow."

"Please take the blindfold off."

His cock twitches inside me. The sensation evokes an image of a racehorse closed within the gates, sidestepping and rearing to be released and start the race.

"Trust has to start somewhere. Let ours start here. I won't hurt you. But *this* is how I want it. If you say now that you don't, then we won't. But..." He lets his voice drift off. He doesn't have to say the rest. *But I'll be disappointed.*

I'm aware that as he's talking, his cock is moving. Just slightly, but it's pressing against the right spot inside me and my arousal level is shooting through the roof. The tinge of fear I'm feeling only enhances those sensations. In spite of myself, I moan and gasp.

I still haven't responded.

"Well, then?" he prompts.

I grit my teeth together. He's shifted and that enjoyable pressure is even stronger now. His cock feels huge and intensely pleasurable inside me. And, goddamn it, all I want to do right now is give him what he wants. *Please* him. Become the reason he can't stop himself. *All night.*

"Do it this way, then…but…go slow."

That's all it takes. He's suddenly moving again, sliding in and out of me. "Trust me, Madeline. Give yourself to me completely and…I promise you'll feel things you've never before experienced."

He's right…. I've climaxed three times recently, and yet I feel like the hill I'm climbing now is higher, each sensation more intense. Each tiny slight movement of his sends ripples of response in me. My body convulses around him, and I'm not even at my climax yet.

But his soft groans indicate that he's felt my response. And that he enjoys it as well. He's still holding my wrists tightly together in his one hand, not letting up. My head is lolling against the table, and as he continues to pump slowly, gently into me, his other hand once again takes up the end of the tie that is wound around my throat.

He pulls it taut, but no farther, and at the same time, thrusts himself deeper than before. We both groan in unison, as if singing a duet we know very well.

"Goddamn," he hoarsely moans. "You are making me lose my mind."

Suddenly his thrusts are jerky, wild, and he's straining, moaning against me. And before I even realize it, the tie around my throat is tight, so tight that I can't breathe. I'm holding my breath because I have no other choice. His body crashes violently against my ass once, twice, a third time until I feel him stiffen and shudder on my back.

His orgasm lasts and lasts as he convulses against me. But I don't move. Suddenly he's still and loosening the tie around my neck, rubbing the skin underneath. He has not hurt me...only scared me a little. But that fear had acted like an amplifier for my arousal. He hasn't pulled out yet. And even though he just came, he's thrusting into me again.

He's still hard. *Still.*

Fuck. He's like some kind of sex machine.

He releases my hands and presses his now free fingers in between my legs, rubbing harshly against my clit, evoking the orgasm that's been hovering along the edge of my consciousness since he first penetrated me.

And when I come, it's a brain-frying experience. I hold my breath, see stars, and I can't think straight for minutes afterward, just drift down in a buzzing cloud of pure pleasure. I collapse against the table, unable to think. Unable to speak for minutes.

Before I realize exactly what he's doing, he's removing the tie and turning me over, picking me up gently and finally carrying me toward the bedroom. My limp head lolls against his massive shoulder, and I get a glimpse of the clock. It's been a little over an hour since we arrived and signed the papers and yet so much has happened.

He's fucked me. *Twice.* He's made me come. *Three times.* He's marked me, claimed me, commanded and dominated me. *And this is just the beginning.*

CHAPTER 16
WALK OF SHAME

OT WATER SLUICES DOWN MY BACK, SEEPING INTO MY sore muscles. Last night, Kohl fucked me for *hours*, the entire night really...as he'd promised. After our encounters on the dining table, he carried me to the bathroom, slowly and languorously bathed me in steaming, scented water before joining me in the lavish sunken tub. He touched me everywhere until the water grew tepid, then made me come twice more. Once when he ordered me to sit on the ledge of the tub while he buried his head in my thighs, and once when I, again, came on his cock.

Then we finally made our way to the bedroom, but it hadn't stopped there. Though exhausted, we spent silent hours touching each other, getting to know each other's bodies intimately, and kissing before drifting off for a catnap.

When I woke, he was penetrating me from behind while spooning me, swaying slowly, gently against me, taking his time and wringing every ounce of pleasure from my body and his.

Hardly any words were exchanged all night. It was just mindless animal heat. I managed to fall asleep again as the sun came up. But when I woke up this morning, he was gone.

I have to confess to feeling a bit relieved. None of that after-morning awkwardness. None of the meaningless idle chatter.

After that epic night of endless sex, it would have been anticlimactic.

I step out of the shower and towel off. I opt to throw the ruined panties away and only have the dress from last night, as I brought no other clothes with me. And I sure as hell wasn't going to interrupt things last night to call Sam to bring me some. As it is, she's going to have a field day with this.

After combing my hands through my wet hair, I slip on my whore-heels, grab my clutch, and head into the living room, where I give the space a cursory glance.

That's when I spot it—a small, rectangular and trademark blue Tiffany & Co. box tied expertly with a white ribbon sitting on the dining table. The very same elegant marble table we'd been all over the night before.

There's a note tucked under the box.

Wear this for me. All the time.

My assistant will call you this afternoon to coordinate the details of our arrangement.

- E

I groan at the thought of an assistant "coordinating" the most intimate details of my life. I don't even want to know what that means. I wouldn't be surprised if she'd been assigned the task of buying me a whole new wardrobe of lacy underwear and fancy hooker-heels. One pair for each day of the week. And extras, for shredding.

I open the box and there's a small blue satchel with a necklace inside, a silver or platinum chain with a diamond encrusted infinity symbol in the center—the same symbol I saw on his forearm last night—with two shimmering beads on either side.

Shit, are these real diamonds? Bead diamonds?

I blink down at the necklace and run my fingers over the glittery stones. They're beautiful and most definitely real. I've never worn anything this expensive before—even when I was growing up and had plenty of money, I never allowed myself to indulge in things like fancy jewelry. I never wanted my dad's money. After what he put my mom through, I never wanted anything to do with him at all.

And what did this symbol mean to him? Beyond the generic meaning of infinity, which seemed to have the implication of a deep and loving commitment—like marriage. But perhaps it meant something more concrete. It was a link to him. A binding link, like the contract.

And then I take in a breath with a new realization at the memory of his passion-filled declaration the night before. *I've marked you.* It's his mark and he wants me to wear it openly. *All the time.*

I close the box and head out the door, clicking it shut behind me. I plan on taking the bus back to campus. But when I step outside, I see Evan's driver from last night waiting for me. He's leaning against the limo, a book in his hand.

He closes the book, looks up at me and touches the shiny bill of his chauffeur hat. "Miss Swanson," he says.

I smile tightly and tug on the hem of my dress, suddenly embarrassed at the realization that I'm completely bare underneath and somehow this driver knows about every dirty thing that went on in that beach bungalow.

I'd never really understood the phrase "walk of shame," but now I get it. I totally get it.

The driver opens the door for me and smiles. If he's secretly passing judgment on my moral character, he doesn't show it. "I've been instructed to take you anywhere you'd like to go, miss."

"Just back to Harper House, where I live. Thanks," I manage.

Once home, Sam launches off the couch toward me as soon as I open the door. "There you are! Nice mysterious midnight text, *'Don't wait up. I'm fine.'* Soooo, what happened? Tell me everything." Her eyes are aglow, but she lowers her voice. "Did you sign the contract? Did you have sex with him?"

Her questions hit me in a tidal wave of excitement. I toss my clutch down on the couch and gingerly sink down next to it. I'm still sore from him. I wasn't a virgin but I hadn't had sex in years and I'd never ever been fucked like *that*. Four times in one night—and that didn't even count the numerous times he'd fucked me with his fingers and his tongue. Not even in our randiest post-drunken teenage party moments had I approached that with Jason. "I signed." I sigh. Suddenly I'm exhausted. "And the sex was…incredible."

I've marked you.

His words flit through my mind again and the flood of heated arousal washes over me. I swallow, remembering the feel of his teeth on my nipple, his cock moving deep inside me, as he brings me to my umpteenth orgasm that night.

Sam claps her hands together and laughs. "I *knew* it! The guy looks like he knows his way around a clit."

I want to deny it, but I can't. "He definitely knows what he's doing." I sigh. "I need to get out of these clothes and get some studying done. My exam is Friday."

I've got five solid days to study, and I need to stay focused, which is easier said than done with an unbearably sexy billionaire taking possession of my body and my life.

Who knows what else he'll take possession of?

CHAPTER 17
PUNISHMENT

THE CALL COMES AT THREE O'CLOCK IN THE AFTERNOON. I'm stretched across my bed, studiously trying to figure out why supersonic or hypersonic speeds cannot be solved using a steady solution, when my phone lights up.

The other person on the line is Miriam, Evan's assistant. She introduces herself and gets some basic information from me—my schedule, my address, my measurements—before telling me the moving van will be here in the morning to box up my stuff and move me to the new house. It's just a block away, on the other side of campus.

She also informs me that Kohl will see me this Wednesday. I'm on his calendar for six o'clock in the evening. On. *His.* Calendar. She actually says those words to me. I'm not sure what I'm more horrified about—the fact that my sex life is penciled in on some guy's calendar, or the fact that his secretary is on the phone telling me about it.

It all feels so cold and impersonal. But maybe that's a good thing. The fewer emotions that are involved, the better, right?

The next two days pass in a frenzied blur. In between classes and studying, my days are filled with movers, doctor appointments, and a meeting with my new personal shopper. I'm overwhelmed, to say the least, and I start to wonder if maybe this was all a big mistake.

The house he puts me up in is a gorgeous Tudor-style cottage, directly across from the Caltech campus. It's fully furnished and way too much house for a single person. When I ask Miriam why Evan didn't just rent me an apartment—which would be far less conspicuous—she tells me Kohl has owned the house for years, since his collaboration with Caltech first began. She also informs me that he'd specifically insisted on me staying there. It makes sense, I guess, for the sake of privacy, for him to want to be in his own house when he visits instead of a much smaller apartment.

And if I'm being honest with myself, the house is fucking gorgeous. The decor is breathtaking—all whites and medium to light-blue tones, giving the house a soothing, airy feel. Along the walls in the living room are hundreds of books, all covering a wide array of subjects—history, physics, mathematics. It's a scholar's dream, and I don't hesitate to pick out a few to read later, after quals.

I don't hear from Kohl at all until Wednesday—three whole days after our fuck-a-thon at the hotel. I'm sitting outside the cafeteria with Sam and Keith, eating lunch, when a text pops up on my phone. It's Evan.

I have a meeting downtown at four. I'll be at the house by six-thirty. Wear the necklace and the red lace.

The red lace. The personal shopper had loaded my dresser drawers with every color of lace imaginable. Not silk, not cotton—just delicate, expensive lace. That's all I'm permitted to wear. Apparently Kohl has a thing for it.

I put my phone down on the table and return to my pizza. Taking a bite, I savor it. True to his word, Kohl had put money on my student spending account, almost twenty grand. Just days ago, I'd been living off ramen noodles, and now I could afford to eat whatever I want. I'm going to enjoy it while I can.

Sam lifts a brow in question. "Was that who I think it was?"

I slide a glance at Keith, who's trying to look disinterested, but I can tell he's curious. I just nod tightly.

Anticipation swirls in my stomach. I can't help it. It's been days since Kohl has touched me, and my body is aching for it.

Keith clears his throat, drawing me back to the present. "So, um, Sam tells me you quit the coffee shop," he hedges.

"Oh, yeah, it was too much," I lie. "I was having trouble staying focused on my studies."

"Ah," he says, and I can't tell if he believes me or not.

Eager for a change in subject, I search for something to say.

"Oh, hey, do either of you know how to pick a lock?" I ask.

"It depends. What type of lock are you trying to pick?" Keith asks.

"It's a closet, actually. The new place I'm, uh, renting"—I shoot Sam a look—"has a locked closet."

I'd noticed the locked closet door as soon as I moved in. When I asked Miriam for a key a couple days later, she told me that Kohl had the only key—which, of course, piqued my curiosity. Why lock it? What could he possibly be hiding in there? I'm dying to know.

"Ah, those locks are pretty easy. You just need two paper clips." He takes a pen and a scrap of paper out of his cargo bag and draws me a diagram. It looks way more complex than he lets on, but I nod anyway, convinced I can figure it out.

***

It's about four o'clock when my last class finally lets out and I rush over to the house to shower, shave my legs and get ready for Kohl's visit. But my first order of business is trying to break into that damn closet. I find a couple of paperclips at the bottom of my backpack and bend them exactly as Keith instructed. For fifteen minutes, I struggle to turn the tumbler, but it won't budge. No matter how hard I try, the damn thing won't move. Finally I just give up.

I don't really have time to be breaking into closets, anyway. Kohl will be here in a couple hours. I need to finish getting ready for his visit. I take my time in the shower. When I'm done, I step out of the stall and towel off. Music is blaring from the speakers in the bedroom—playing from my super secret boy band playlist. If my friends ever find out I have these songs on my Spotify, there will be no end to the torment they'll inflict on me.

But right now, it's just me, and I let the music carry me away. I slip on a matching bra and pantie set, then brush out my hair as I move my hips to the rhythm of the music and belting out the lyrics at the top of my lungs.

I hop onto the bed and jump to the beat, singing so loud my throat feels raw. By the last chorus, I'm breathless and exhausted. As the song ends, I turn to jump off the bed, but I stop dead when I see Kohl leaning against the door frame, an amused smile tugging at his lips. He reaches over and disconnects the speakers.

All the blood drains from my face, and I'm awash in humiliation. I take a deep breath, feeling the slow burn of a blush wash over me.

"How much did you see?" I ask.

"Enough to admire the very pleasant view of your backside."

I grab my white, fluffy robe off the chair, slipping it over my shoulders. Glancing at the alarm clock next to the bed, I note that it's just after five.

I swallow. "You're early. I thought you had a meeting downtown." I haven't brushed out my hair or done my makeup yet. Self-consciously, I run my fingers through my hair and clear my throat.

I allow my gaze to rake over him. He's wearing a white button-down shirt, open at the collar, and dark jeans that hug his powerful thighs perfectly. And he's as beautiful as ever, those blue eyes never leaving me.

He pushes off the wall and moves to stand in front of me. Opening my robe, he gently pushes the fabric off one shoulder. Apparently I'm not supposed to hide myself from him. The robe falls to the ground at my feet. "Miriam messaged your medical files over to me. You've received a clean bill of health."

"So have you." When I got home, his test results were waiting for me in the mailbox, and I read them over meticulously.

"And birth control?"

"The depo shot," I answer.

"Good girl." His finger traces the line of my jaw, then drops to my collarbone. He frowns. "You're not wearing the necklace."

Oh, right. He did ask me to wear that, didn't he? It totally slipped my mind. "You're early. I was going to put it on before you came." I smile up at him. "Thank you, by the way. It's beautiful."

His eyes narrow as his finger trails along my collarbone. "Where is it?"

"On the dresser."

He grabs the box off the dresser and takes the necklace out of the little blue sachet it came in. He walks back to me and places the necklace at my throat, his fingers brushing against the back of my neck and sending tingles of arousal as he works the clasp until it's secured.

"You are to wear this *all* of the time and never take it off."

As in…*ever*? "Why?"

"So you'll think of me, even when I'm not here."

I touch the pendant and worry my bottom lip. Evan doesn't strike me as the romantic type, so his words surprise me. "You are so sweet," I finally say.

"I'm many things, Madeline, but 'sweet' is not one of them."

I smile, reach out and fiddle with the button at the base of his throat. "It will be our little secret, then."

His eyes drop to the necklace at the base of my neck, and he runs a finger along the chain. "I'm glad you like it. You deserve pretty things. You shouldn't hide yourself under old jeans and faded T-shirts. Or even a borrowed dress."

I frown. How had he guessed that the dress had been borrowed?

"I wasn't hiding myself," I say in a whisper, unable to meet his gaze.

His hand moves to my chin, to lift it up, forcing my eyes upward until they are trapped by his beautiful blue gaze. "There's something that wasn't in the contract but I would like to exist between us at all times—complete, open honesty. Can you do that?"

I nod.

He smiles, bends his head, and his lips are on mine. The kiss is unusually tender, heartfelt. His mouth doesn't claim me or dominate me. This kiss is like an honest conversation, a give and take. He advances, then recedes, and I follow him. Our tongues touch and it is electric. Something I can't name sizzles between us, and I'm afraid to think it's something more than mere desire.

When he pulls back, he's smiling down at me. I return the smile and lick my lips. My heartbeat is racing.

He fingers the necklace again. "A statement of who you belong to."

His smile fades, and I sense something in him shift. Like a blind coming down over his features, closing them off. Then, he brushes his thumb across my lips, pushing the very tip of his thumb between them.

"Such gorgeous lips." His voice is suddenly harsh. "I'm going to come inside this pretty little mouth."

Something stirs inside me. The thought of taking his cock in my mouth makes my heart race and my core ache. He raises a brow at me, as if belatedly asking the question.

"Yes," I breathe.

His lips curl up with satisfaction. He glances at the ground between us. "Get on your knees, then."

That command in his voice compels me to obey, and without hesitation, I sink to the ground. I look straight at his crotch, noting the outline of his swollen cock through his jeans. I draw an unsteady breath.

I want him. Been craving him since the morning he left me sleeping in that Exeter House bungalow. I want him so damn bad it hurts.

Slowly, he unzips and frees his erection from his boxers. As I remember, it's huge, the thick, swollen head already beaded with precome. Leaning forward, I lick my lips and gently press my mouth to the very tip.

He lets out a long breath and pushes my hair back from my face so he can see what I'm doing as I bend over his cock. Very slowly, my mouth slips down over the tip, my tongue rolling up the underside of his length, savoring the salty, earthy taste of him.

He groans and threads his fingers through my hair, cupping the back of my head to begin guiding my movements. He won't even cede control to me here. But I'm quickly losing myself in the moment, closing my eyes in concentration. There is only the feel, the taste of him as he slides in and out of my mouth.

I take him in greedily, my tongue sliding over his velvety softness. He fills me. And then he holds my head firmly, refusing any give as his hips thrust forward and he fucks my mouth, his deep, guttural groans echoing off the walls. I feel powerful with him in my mouth, at my mercy.

"Christ, Madeline," he moans. "Your mouth feels so good."

I pull back a little and run my tongue along the underside of his cock, then swirl it around the swollen tip, before taking it back into my mouth.

His grip tightens on my hair, and my eyes water with the pain. Moisture and arousal gather between my legs and I moan. He pushes deeper into my mouth, his cock hitting against the back of my throat. I can only breathe in between his thrusts. And he seems aware of this, varying the length of his thrust, sometimes pushing all the way in and holding it there on purpose. It reminds me of that second time on the dining room table when he had the tie around my neck, getting off on the fact that he had control over my everything, even my breath. And, strangely, giving him that control has excited me, too.

"I'm going to come," he moans. "Swallow it…"

Holding my head still with one hand and my jaw with the other, he pumps in and out of my mouth, his thrusts clipped and frenzied. Desperate.

His cock swells even thicker, and he stills, letting out a long groan. He comes in a hot, powerful rush. I savor the taste of him, continuing to suck as the contractions of his orgasm fade in intensity. With my mouth, I'm squeezing his cock until he lets out a low, tormented growl of pleasure.

His breathing is hard and ragged as he pulls out of my mouth, recovering. I sit back on my heels, swallowing everything. I wipe my mouth with the back of my hand, already missing the feel of him filling me up.

He reaches down and brushes his thumb across my bottom lip. "Shit…" he breathes, looking down at me. "That mouth of yours was made for sin."

I smile up at him. "Always glad to be of service."

"You're very good at that…" He pauses as if he wants to say more. A cloud passes through his beautiful blue eyes. He draws back, still staring at me, his eyes traveling down my near-naked body. "Made for me to enjoy."

"How much enjoyment will there be tonight? Looks like we're off to a quick start…" I say, overtly noting that he's already semi-hard again. One thing I've learned from our first night at the hotel was that once wasn't close to enough for him. It was just barely a warm-up. Twice might not be, either. Are we in for another sleepless night like the first night we spent together? The thought sends a hot thrill through me. I feel powerful with the knowledge that he can't get enough of me. That his need is as insatiable as my own.

"Oh, there will be plenty. We'll both be quite happy."

Something stretches between us—something I really can't explain. The air is thick, heavy, and I have trouble pulling it into my lungs. I look up into his eyes, trying to decide if I should stand before he tells me to. Crazy, that thought. It would have never occurred to me before this to await his permission.

He bends, taking me by the elbow, pulling me to my feet. Our gazes catch and hold for a long, breathless moment.

His eyes wander over my body. From the necklace, which he touches again, over the red lace demi-cup bra that barely covers me. He lowers his hand from the necklace to slide down along the edge of my bra, his finger slips inside to glance against my nipple, sending shivers through me and causing it to stiffen. He watches my face as he does this, not missing anything.

"You look gorgeous in red…" His head dips even as his finger hooks into my bra, pulling my breast free. He shoves the cup underneath, forcing my bare breast up and out. Before I can catch my breath, his hot, wet mouth is sucking my nipple to a tight point, in seconds doing the same with the other after extricating it similarly from the bra—which he refuses to remove. My head lolls back, enjoying the sensation of his mouth on my tender, hungry nipples.

When he raises his head, I can see hunger in his eyes. It's the same hunger that burns inside me. For days, I've been waiting for this, almost since the moment I'd opened my eyes the morning after our all-night fuckfest at the hotel. I'd been daydreaming about having him here with me. The feel of his cock. That intense look in his eyes…

During the day, at night, that look is all I think about.

Now he's here. I can't wait any longer. I'm struggling for breath.

He flicks his chin. "Turn to the wall."

I hesitate, frowning, unclear about what he's asking. Everything in me wants to refuse, to make him work for my compliance, but I'm desperate for release and he seems to know that. I haven't come in days, and sucking him off has me hungry for his cock inside me.

When I don't move, he firmly grasps my upper arm and walks me to the far wall opposite the bed. "That and the necklace…you have some learning to do. In the future, Madeline, you *will* be quicker to obey me."

I blink, saying nothing. There's something underlying in his voice. Not quite anger. It's more like the tone of a disciplining parent—or someone who trains an animal.

"Put your hands behind your back and your forehead on the wall. And keep it there. Don't move."

I bend forward, complying.

He walks out the door into the hall where the locked closet door is located. I hear the rattle of keys, then the distinct sound of a door being opened, drawers pulled out. I pull my head away when I hear it, straining to pick up any more details—all I hear is the squeak of the door on the hinges. He's opened the secret closet. My heart races in my throat. What is he pulling out of there?

A minute later, he returns, and though I've got my forehead back on the wall, I peer out of the corner of my eyes as best I can. He's holding black leather cuffs chained together in one hand and a riding crop in the other. My sex clenches at the sight. I itch to feel its sting on my skin, the rush of heat surging through my veins. I'm desperate for it.

His gaze hardens as it falls on me. "You're disobedient today. In too many ways. I think someone wants her punishment."

Punishment?

CHAPTER 18
NO BOUNDARIES

KOHL'S EYES TRAVEL OVER ME AGAIN, CHUCKLING AT the obvious flush on my features, as if pleased with himself that he's guessed right—that I'm anticipating punishment. While I'm still against the wall, he tosses the things from the locked closet onto the bed. Then I hear him shuck his clothes. I sneak peeks at him, relishing every graceful movement, every inch of flesh he reveals, gasping at the beauty of him. Finally, he stands beside me naked, his thick cock jutting out, ready to fuck.

Lifting the strip of silky fabric off the bed, he leans over and secures it around my head, blindfolding me.

"Now," he says. "Time for a little fun."

"W-what are you going to do?"

He places his mouth against my ear, the pulses of hot breath sending shivers down my spine. His words rasp in a hoarse, harsh whisper. "I'm going to use you, Madeline. And maybe, if you deserve it, I'll make you come. This time there will be no barrier. I'll ride you hard and come inside you."

He turns me from the wall, guiding me to lie down on the bed, pointedly pulling my ankles apart. And moments later, the tip of the riding crop touches my arm, first lightly and then gradually firmer. Excitement trips through me as he drags the tip of the whip across my stomach, circling my navel, before gently tapping it on my thigh. It's not enough to sting, but the promise of pain is there. He's teasing me.

"Have you been thinking about me, Madeline?"

The way he says my name, slow and deep, with that erotic accent, makes my channel clench. The whip stills as he waits for my answer.

"Yes," I breathe.

"Good." Though I can't see him, I hear the smile in his tone. "And when you're thinking about me, what am I doing?"

I hesitate. I don't know why. Maybe it's because I've never told anyone what I'm about to tell him. My secret fantasies. The twisted things I imagine him doing to me.

"Madeline, tell me what I'm doing."

I swallow. "You're...you're punishing me."

His fingers brush across my collarbone and push my bra strap aside, freeing one breast, then the other. "You crave domination," he murmurs, pulling my bra down. "You crave pain."

"Yes," I whisper.

"That pleases me. *A lot.*"

Suddenly he delivers a sharp blow on my nipple, and a sting zings through me, down to my core, making me feel alive. It takes my breath away. Then his hot mouth is there. His tongue soothes the pain, swirling around the tip before sucking it into his mouth. I moan, arching my back. I can't help it. His mouth feels so good.

When he pulls away again, I have no idea where he is. He makes no move, no touch. The breast where his mouth was now feels cold, tender, raw. I swallow, at once exhilarated and frozen by the fear of another strike.

It comes without warning, this time on my other nipple. I let out a yelp, but more out of shock than of pain. As before, he soothes the sting with his mouth. Now I'm shivering with anticipation.

The tip of the crop strokes up the inside of one of my thighs to rest at the apex. With it he traces the seam of my sex. My heart races, and I hold my breath.

"What do you say, Madeline?"

A deep breath. I tilt my head toward the voice of the man I cannot see. "Thank you."

"Good girl." He taps his approval with the crop on my clit, not nearly enough to cause pain but likely a warning of what he might do. My legs stiffen and my hands move to cover myself. I'm in the dark and completely vulnerable, open to him. And I'm not sure I trust him to give me what I need.

Instead, he removes the crop and pushes my hands aside. Then, his hand strokes down my belly, and I jump at the initial touch. The fingers trail down to my hips, pulling my panties down, his nails scraping my skin as he removes them, then tosses them aside.

"Turn over onto your stomach," he commands.

Without hesitation, I flip over and settle onto my stomach, my legs straight out, arms at my sides. Evan pushes my legs open with a hand while the other pulls my hands over my head. "I want your hands on the headboard. Do not remove them."

I swallow.

"Do you understand?"

"Y-yes, sir," I say.

A light touch trails down my spine, the small of my back. He rests his hand on my ass. "Good," he murmurs.

The whip slices through the air, landing on my ass with a crack. I let out a shriek. Pain slices through me. My legs close, and I tense, anticipating the next strike.

"Legs open, Madeline. Do *not* make me say it again."

Without a word, I open my legs, swallow and tense, waiting for the next strike. He quickly lays another blow across my ass. It feels hot, like fire against my skin.

Then *another.* I'm breathless, panting. I can't seem to catch my breath.

Another strike, another yelp. And when I think I can't take any more, he gets on the bed behind me, reaching a hand between my legs.

"Soaking wet. I knew it."

He hooks an arm under my hips and pulls me up against him. I feel his erection against my tingling ass, and I gasp, pain and pleasure co-mingling with the contact. He enters me from behind. Groaning, he pushes deep, so deep that I gasp—his cock hitting the wall of my cervix. One hand reaches underneath me, and finds my clit and he begins to pump into me, moving in sure, strong strokes.

"This is what you need," he says, his fingers moving over my clit in rhythm with his thrusts. "My cock inside you, filling you."

"Yes," I say, but the pillow muffles my words. I grip the headboard, bracing myself against it as he moves behind me. I'm already so close—ready to shatter.

"You're *mine*, Madeline."

He pulls out, plunges into me again, laying his body across mine as he continues to stroke. His hot breath is scorching my neck, sending tingles clear down to my core. My mind is blank to everything but the feeling of him inside me, his weight pressing me down into the mattress, his movement against me, his hand stroking me, making me moan.

"*Mine,*" he repeats. "Mine to command. And you'll obey me. Do you understand?"

But I'm panting, barely hearing him. I'm. So. Damn. Close. The pressure inside me is building and my body begins to tighten, anticipating another orgasm. He can feel me tightening around him because he slows. His hand leaves my clit, and he stops moving.

"Answer me, Madeline. Do you understand?"

"Yes," I gasp, twisting restlessly beneath him.

But he doesn't relent, grounding out between his teeth. "Tell me you're mine and that you'll obey. *Say it.*"

I gulp, vaguely aware that I should be annoyed by his words, but I just want to come. I need that orgasm as much as I need to breathe right now. God. "Yes, I'm yours. I'll obey you. Evan, please. I'm so close."

Pulling out completely, he grasps my shoulder and flips me over onto my back. He pins my wrists above my head with one hand. Then he slides his cock into me slowly, and begins to move, his hips moving in shallow, even thrusts.

I sigh in frustration. It's fucking torment.

He's in complete control of my body, and he's enjoying every minute of it. Underneath the blindfold, darkness surrounds me. I wish I could see his face, look into his eyes as he fucks me, but I can only feel and hear his moans of pleasure. Every nerve in my body is alive with sensation.

He bends to kiss my neck, fastening his mouth at the base, sucking. My ankles hook around his hips as he pistons into me so hard the headboard slams against the wall over and over, in rhythm with each powerful thrust. Then he sinks his teeth into my skin, biting me hard.

Everything draws tight inside me, and I arch my back. This orgasm slams into me with such force that I can't catch my breath. Hot waves of pleasure overwhelm me, pull me under as I struggle to breathe. His teeth sink deeper into my neck, even as his cock continues to move. The feeling is so intense, too much really. My entire body is electrified, and I climax so hard, I'm sobbing his name.

"*Fuck*, Madeline." He pushes deep, and with one last thrust, he stills, coming hard with a loud groan. His hot seed pours into me, and my legs tighten around him, pulling him tight against me. "Fuck, fuck, *fuck*."

For a long moment, we say nothing, lying completely still. He's buried inside me, my legs clamped around him. We're breathing heavily as we drift back down to earth. Finally, he releases my hands and rolls off of me, collapsing onto the bed beside me.

I'm listless, exhausted and utterly awash in the high of our lovemaking, lying there in the darkness as I try to get a handle on my breathing. A fine sheen of sweat coats my skin, and my heart is still beating wildly against my ribs. Fuck, that was so damn good.

Evan reaches over and pulls the blindfold off, then he tugs me over to lie across his chest. The steady beat of his heart is soothing, and I sink into him. Our sweat is causing our skin to stick together and my mind is reeling.

Part of me had thought the night at the hotel was a fluke—that it had been so amazing because it had been such a long time for me. But if possible, this was even better than the previous times we'd been together. I swallow, wondering what this means. None of this is what I expected. *Kohl* isn't what I expected. He's brilliant, gorgeous. And the sex is just…beyond words. Is he just that good?

As if answering my unspoken question, he sighs deeply, clearing his throat. "I knew it would be like this between us," he says, stroking along my spine. "From almost the first moment you walked into that interview, I knew."

But how could he know? And did this imply that it wasn't like this for his previous lovers? Before I can voice the question, he brushes a strand of hair off my shoulder, and I catch sight of the infinity tattoo. I reach out and brush my finger across the black ink on his forearm, wondering at the special meaning. Why has he marked himself—and now me—with that same symbol?

"What does this tattoo mean? And why does my necklace have the same symbol?"

I can feel him stiffen beneath me, the way he does whenever I ask him anything personal. There's a long pause as he continues to stroke my back, and I feel like he's forcing himself to relax against his own instinct.

Eventually he clears his throat. "The infinity symbol represents limitless possibilities, which has always served me as a philosophy in life and in business."

I turn my head to look into his face, but his eyes are fixed on my necklace. He fingers it, twisting it idly. "Between us…it means no boundaries."

No boundaries. Uh, what the hell does that mean? There are clearly boundaries between us. Maybe not physically, but emotionally he's practically Fort Knox.

I sit up, and his hand falls away. "Of course there are boundaries," I counter. "Isn't that what this is? The contract, the whole *mistress* arrangement? You even said it yourself when we were at dinner. The contract establishes boundaries that are essential to you."

"Madeline…" His tone is gentle, pleading.

"I'm right, though. I don't know anything about you. All I know is what it says on your Wikipedia page." How fucking pathetic is that?

He releases a heavy breath and rubs both hands down his face. "This arrangement is meant to protect you. *You*, Madeline. It's better if we don't get too close."

"Why?"

Crickets.

I let out a long sigh of frustration. There's no response from him, because that would require revealing something *personal*. His guard is up and at full attention at all times. Even when he's fucking *inside* me. He can ask me all about my life—or find it out in other ways, but I can't know anything about him. One thing is clear, whatever this twisted arrangement is, it doesn't exist to protect *me*.

CHAPTER 19
GRACE PERIOD

I SIT UP FROM THE BED, SHAKING MY HEAD. "THIS WAS A BAD idea." What the fuck was I thinking? This never could have worked long term. The fucking w amazing while it lasted. Thank God we'd negotiated a grace period.

"Christ, Madeline." He sits up next to me. "Why does this need to be more than it is?"

"Yeah. You're right," I say, standing up. I fix my bra and snatch my panties off the floor. "We're just fucking. That's all this is."

I head into the bathroom and lock the door, sinking against it. This is too much. Kohl is too much.

I quickly wash up and slip on the jeans and baby tee that I'd left in the bathroom after my shower. When I open the door and walk out, Kohl is dressed and sitting on the edge of the bed, tying his shoes. He looks up at me. "Are you hungry? I have about an hour before I need to be downtown."

"No, thanks," I say, grabbing my backpack off the floor. "My exam is Friday, and I really need to study."

He nods, but I can see the disappointment on his face. "Would you like help studying?"

If I didn't know better, I would say he was looking for a reason to stay a little longer. A reason that doesn't involve sex. A complete contradiction to the way he'd just been acting.

Time to give him a taste of his own medicine. I shake my head. "Thank you, but Keith is coming over to help me study."

His eyes narrow. "The guy who works at the coffee shop?"

"Yes, he's been helping me out with my studies. He's very good."

Something dark crosses his features—jealousy? "He's coming here? Will you be alone?"

"Yeah, you don't mind, do you?" I set my backpack down on my desk.

He stands. "Yes, I bloody well mind. Christ, Madeline, I saw the way he looks at you. Stay the fuck away from him."

My eyebrows shoot up. "So, what, you own me now, because you're paying for this house? Because of a fucking contract?"

He rakes his hands through his hair. "That's not what I said."

I fold my arms across my chest and look down. "Well, it's how you're acting. Keith is a *friend*. Not all men just want just one thing from me."

A muscle ticks in his jaw. "I saw the way he looks at you," he repeats, as if that proves anything.

"It doesn't matter how he looks at me, does it? I signed a contract, and I stick to my agreements."

He looks skeptical. "That isn't enough."

Whaaaaat?

"Well… you're going to have to trust me, then, aren't you? Are you capable of that?"

He continues to scowl, his jaw working but he says nothing.

With a sigh, I throw my hands up in frustration. "Well, if you can't, then this whole thing is fucked up. *Already.* And it's been, what, three days?" *At least I still have that grace period.*

"What's fucked up?"

"This." I gesture between us. "Me, you. This crazy arrangement. What was I thinking?"

His features soften, and he steps toward me. When he speaks, his voice is quiet but tension underlies it. "Madeline, don't do this. Don't give up on us."

I almost scoff at that. Is there an *us* to give up on?

I glance down at my bare feet. "I don't think this was such a good idea."

I'd signed that damn thing in the heat of the moment, singularly overwhelmed by the desire to sleep with him. I hadn't thought all this through like I should have...

He takes me by the shoulders, and I look up at him. For the first time, I see vulnerability in those blue eyes. He places his hands on my cheeks. I refuse to meet his gaze. He can't break me down again. He does it too easily.

I open my mouth to continue, but he cuts me off.

"I won't let you walk away, Madeline. I can't."

"I have a grace period," I remind him. "It's in writing."

"Hold on just a moment, please? You're just feeling stressed. About this, and about sitting your exam." His thumb brushes across the line of my jaw. "I'll be at XVerse on Friday. Why don't I have Henry pick you up after your exam to celebrate? I'll give you a tour."

I finally meet his gaze, blinking at him. A personal tour of XVerse from the company's CEO? Holy crap! Ever since I enrolled as an aero student, I'd been dying to get my foot into that place.

That offer is just too irresistible to pass up. "Um, okay. My exam is at three, and it'll probably only take an hour." Unless I fuck up. Then it will be over much sooner than that.

He flashes me a quick smile. "I'll send Henry over to pick you up at four-thirty. Be ready."

I nod. "And about Keith..." My words trail off. I'm not exactly sure what to say, except that Evan's an ass for not letting me study with a friend who just happens to have a dick.

"I'd rather you not bring him here," he says, his eyes almost unconsciously wander back toward the bed.

I push out a breath at the implication. "*Fine.* We can study at the library."

His face is somber as he places a kiss on my forehead, but he pushes the subject no further. "I'll see you on Friday."

***

"I'm going to puke." I clutch my midsection and breathe deeply, trying to stave off the nausea that has suddenly overtaken me. "I can't do this."

"Well, if you want to be in the PhD program, then you don't have a choice," Sam says. "You've got this, Maddy. You've been studying for weeks."

I press my lips together and nod tightly. "Yeah, okay, you're right. I've totally got this."

With a squeeze of my hand, Sam shoves me in the direction of the conference room where my exam is taking place. When I walk in, the three professors on my committee are already sitting around the conference table, waiting for me.

Over the next hour, countless questions are thrown at me. By the end, I'm exhausted and ready to go home and fall into bed. Between studying for the exam and Kohl, I haven't been sleeping well.

Professor Naveri closes his notebook and smiles. "Thank you, Miss Swanson, you will receive an answer by the end of next week."

I thank the committee members and get the hell out of there, my heart still pounding. Thank God that's over with. Waiting for their answer will be hell, but I feel good about how the exam went.

I glance at my phone. It's just after four—Henry will be at the house soon to pick me up and take me to XVerse. I should call Evan and cancel. If I go, it will only prolong the inevitable. This can't last. I was crazy to think I could do this and not develop feelings for him.

But the opportunity to visit XVerse is too tempting to resist. And it's too late to cancel now, anyway. Henry is probably already on his way.

With a deep breath, I formulate a plan. Go to XVerse, have a nice afternoon, and tomorrow when I see Kohl, I'll tell him I want out. Or maybe I'll just tell Miriam. She seems to talk to him more often than I do anyway.

Rushing home, I change into a white graphic baby tee and the black flower skater skirt I bought at the mall last week. His prescribed infinity necklace at my throat and lacy underwear underneath, just like he likes. Not that he'll see it today, of course. This is my field trip day!

Just as I'm slipping on my black ballet flats, the doorbell rings. It's Henry. I grab my purse and hop into the back of the town car. My phone lights up immediately. It's a text from Kohl.

Are you on your way? I need to see you.

I smile at his words. He misses me. It's unlike him to be effusive, but I think I like it.

XVerse is in La Cañada, only about a twenty-minute drive from Caltech. I close my eyes for the short drive, trying to catch up on a little shut eye. But as we pull off the freeway, I open my eyes and I reply to Kohl's text.

Just got off the freeway. Be there in a few min.

When we enter the parking lot and pull around to the front of the building, Kohl is standing at the curb. My heart skips when I see him. Wearing a blue short-sleeved shirt that hugs his biceps and gray slacks, he looks so fucking delicious, I moan to myself.

Damnit. Walking away from this man might be harder than I thought.

Before Henry can come around the front of the car, Evan steps forward and opens the door for me. I step out of the car, and he immediately pulls me into his arms.

"Christ, I've missed this."

I've missed it too. I didn't realize how much, until I felt his arms around me. Inexplicably, I feel safe. Wanted. Desired.

I pull back and smile. "It's only been two days."

"A lifetime," he says, planting a quick kiss on my lips. He threads his fingers through mine and tugs me toward the large building. "How was the exam? Do you feel you passed?"

I shrug. "I think I did all right. But I won't have any idea until next week."

He smooths his thumb over my cheek. "I'm certain you did. Shall I show you around?"

He leads me through the stark white-marble lobby, and everything from the receptionist desk to the sitting area is sleek and modern. Likewise, the office space is wide open, each cubicle separated by white frosted glass—including Evan's. Despite being the Founder and CEO, he has a cubicle like everyone else.

"Shouldn't you have your own office?" I ask.

"I have an office for conference calls and confidential meetings, but otherwise, I prefer the cubicle. The open floor plan fosters free communication."

Over the next hour, he takes me through the server room, the avionic test facility, the shaker room, the electromagnetic interference testing chamber, but it's when we approach the warehouse filled with rocket engine components that my interest is truly piqued.

"Are these the engine parts for the Pegasus?"

Pegasus I will be the most efficient reusable launch vehicle in history, as soon as it's up and running. It's groundbreaking, and for the first time, it will make commercial space travel more affordable.

"Yes, they'll be assembled and then sent out to our testing facility in Texas."

I crouch down to inspect the individual parts. "Have you ever thought about eliminating the fuel-oxidizer turbine interseal? That's typically where a chemical rocket engine fails."

"Yes, actually," he says, but when he hesitates, I glance up at him. He looks stunned. "That's the direction we are taking with the next generation of engines."

I stand up and brush my hands down my skirt. "Excellent."

The look in his eyes is something I've never seen before—it's tenderness, desire and surprise, all rolled up into one smoldering gaze.

"I'm impressed, Madeline." He reaches out to brush a strand of hair behind my ear. "You never fail to surprise me."

My mouth feels suddenly dry. "Um, thank you."

Leaning forward, his lips brush against mine. Startled, I take a hasty step backward, out of his embrace. My gaze darts around the large warehouse. Several employees are working in plain view of us.

"What are you doing?" I ask. "Someone will see us."

He folds his arms across his chest and gazes down at me, looking powerful and in control. "And if they do?"

I blow out a breath. "I would be mortified."

He almost seems affronted by my statement. "Mortified to be seen with me?"

"Yes!" I whisper harshly. "I mean, no. I mean...I don't want to be seen kissing you in the middle of XVerse." Geez, I bungled that.

His eyes narrow. "Why not?"

"I just...don't typically go around kissing men in public, that's all."

Not the entire truth, but he doesn't need to know that. If I ever secure a job here, I don't want people thinking I fucked my way in. Especially since I'm thinking about backing out of this whole sordid arrangement. The less people know, the better.

"Madeline, you're mine. And everyone will know it, sooner or later."

"Yeah, about that," I hedge. This isn't exactly the time or place, but I can see he's going to press the issue. Doesn't look like it can wait until tomorrow. "Since we're still within the grace period, I think it'd be best if we…reevaluate this whole thing."

He visibly stiffens, his entire body turning hard as granite. He shoves his hands into his pockets and bows his head, as though trying to rein in his reaction. Suddenly I can't breath and my heart is racing as I witness his fight for control. I'm almost afraid of the result. After endless moments, he finally looks back up at me, his eyes meeting mine. There's an intensity in his gaze that's utterly captivating, and despite all my thoughts of backing out, it turns me on.

When he speaks, his voice is even and controlled. "We aren't reevaluating anything, Madeline. If you want to speak further about this, we'll do so in private."

I lift my chin. "Fine. I can do that."

With a hand at my back, he guides me across the warehouse through a double door and down a long hallway. To the left is another door. He quickly keys in a code on the security lock, opens it, and ushers me inside.

The room is completely dark. There are no windows, no lights. But before I can ask where we are, he pulls out his phone and presses an app open. The room instantly comes to life—blue lights glint from beneath the clear tile floor, giving the room a surreal otherworldly look. Two massive screens, now blank, are mounted on the far wall, and several rows of desks and computers fill the room. He moved down the slope of the room toward a large table as I gawk at the displays.

Then I spin around to face him. "Is this a Mission Control room?"

He nods once, his expression solemn. It's clear the tour is over. I have a feeling he has something much more lascivious in mind. "Come here," he commands.

With hesitant, shaky steps, I obey.

Once I'm within his reach, he places a finger beneath my chin and lifts my face up, forcing my eyes to meet his. A shiver moves through me. That cold, hard look in his eyes tells me he hasn't forgotten what we are about to discuss.

Might as well get it out in the open. "Evan, this isn't working…. I think it's best if we don't continue with it." Then I reach up and unhook the necklace, holding it out to him. "Here, I can't keep this."

Nausea gathers in my stomach when I imagine his next mistress wearing it.

He ignores the proffered necklace, his eyes still fastened on mine. "You said you'd obey me," he says quietly. But there's something in his eyes, a spark of flame that makes cold fear clamp around my throat.

"In the heat of the moment, I did. But we also signed a contract that gave me a grace period."

He takes the necklace from my hand and places it back around my neck, hooking the clasp. Though it's only been off of me for less than a minute, it feels cold. I frown, unable to process this. He's absolutely refusing to take no for an answer.

"We're not through until I say we are."

CHAPTER 20
BEAUTIFUL AGONY

We're not through until I say we are.

His crisp words settle in my stomach, and I swallow. "That's not what the contract says," I counter.

"Fuck the contract." His tone is hard, clipped, verging on angry. "Only I can give you what you need."

Before I can answer, he pulls me into a rough, passionate kiss. His tongue pushes into my mouth and takes control. Like before, it overwhelms me, sweeps me under. His tongue and lips dominate mine, and I'm pierced to the core with want. His hand slides up to the back of my head, holding me in place even as my hands move up to press against his chest.

"Evan—" I murmur against his mouth but he smothers the protest. I can feel his body hardening against mine and my own responding, fire in my belly, hollow, aching desire in my core. I don't just want him. I *need* him.

Catching my wrists with one hand, he pushes me, stomach first, against the table. I'm breathless, still reeling from his kiss, when he lifts my skirt with his free hand and finds my core.

A growl escapes his throat. "You are so fucking wet." His finger circles my entrance, before pushing inside. "You say you don't want me, but this is how I know you're lying."

I let go a long breath but don't deny it. It's no use anyway. He already knows my body far better than Jason ever did. He seems to know exactly what I want, what I need.

"I never said I didn't want you, Evan," I pant. "I said—" I moan as his fingers slide over my clit. "I said this wasn't working."

He leans down and kisses my neck. "What isn't working?" he murmurs against my skin. "Surely you aren't talking about the sex."

My mind spins. I'm hardly able to tear it away from the sensation of his mouth on my neck. "I'm talking about emotions." He kisses his way up my neck and nibbles my earlobe. "I'm not sure I can keep this strictly physical."

He slides one finger into my slick channel, than another. "We've started something good here. Something strictly physical that works. This is all it can be. I'm not the man for you for anything beyond that, Madeline. And you know it."

"Do I? I don't even know enough about you to determine that."

His fingers pump into me, delving deep, then pulling out again, driving me to distraction. I can't have a conversation like this. I wonder if he's planning it this way.

"If you are enjoying this and it's beneficial to you in more ways than one, then you're smart enough to keep your feelings detached, especially from a man like me."

"And if I'm not?"

"You *are*," he says. "It's why I chose you."

"Evan—" My voice cuts off when he slides his fingers across my clit again. I grind against his hand. In spite of my desire to keep this a calm, business-like discussion, like always, he's quickly taken control and manipulated everything to favor him, like always.

His free hand grips my chin, tilting my face back and up toward his. And he captures my lips in a fierce, possessive kiss. His next words are murmured against my mouth without pulling away. "I can't let you go, Madeline. I won't."

"Evan, *please*." Am I begging to be free of him, or begging for sexual release? I'm not sure, and right now, I don't care. The feel of his fingers inside me is intoxicating, like a drug I can't get enough of. "Please."

"Promise me you won't end this." I shake my head. His fingers slow. "Madeline. Promise me."

"Stop it," I say, I twist my hands free of his grip and push my body back against his chest. "You are overwhelming me."

In one fluid motion, he removes his fingers and steps away from me. Cold air sweeps into the space where he was, and I almost whimper at the loss of him. I face off with him, and his expression is grim, determined.

"Do you want to end this?" His tone is calm and controlled, but I sense anger just beneath the surface. And more than a little fear. "Is that what you want? If so, then end it. *Say it*." He grinds between his teeth.

My body is still humming from his touch, but I struggle to ignore it. Do I want to end it? He's giving me an out, and part of me wants to take it. But another, stronger part of me has been ensnared by this man. I can't imagine walking away. I guess the real question is, can I do this without involving my emotions? Can I turn that part of myself off? I swallow a huge lump in my throat. *I don't know.*

The answer is...I don't know. I hoped that I could, but don't trust that I can.

"I don't know what I want," comes my miserable reply, finally.

"Then you need to decide." His voice is flat, lifeless. His beautiful features are shuttering from me. I can't even read his desire except for the bulge at the front of his pants. "I'm not the man for you in any other way but this. I can't be. I'm not capable of anything but—" He cuts himself off, running a frustrated hand through his hair and shaking his head, as if afraid he'll reveal too much. "I can only give you this," he finally concludes. "This is all I have..."

The vulnerability in his eyes guts me. What has done this to him? When I Googled him weeks ago, there was very little information about his love life. Just pictures of him with beautiful models hanging off his arm. Nothing about an ex or a breakup or anything. As far as I know, he's a serial dater, never allowing himself to get close to a woman. Maybe some of them were contracted mistresses, like me? Though I can't help but think this is the first time he's attempted something like this.

And he's attempting this contractual relationship in response to something that's happened in his past. Because the way he's done things before hasn't worked.

I remember his words at the restaurant not long before I signed the contract. *There will be no talk of love at all.*

"Will you tell me why?" I ask in a small voice.

His jaw tenses, and he looks away before shaking his head.

I release a heavy breath, my decision made for me. "Then I can't do this."

As I move to push past him and walk out the door, he catches my wrist again and spins me around to face him. His eyes are dark, hooded. He looks like a man tormented, and I can't help it, I lift up on to my tiptoes and place a gentle kiss on his lips.

"Don't walk away from this," he says against my mouth.

I nibble at his bottom lip, savoring the taste of him. "I won't. Under one condition…"

I feel him smile, certain he's already won. "What's that?"

"Tell me what happened to you. Why is sex all you can offer?"

He pulls away from me, physically recoiling from my question. "Does it matter?"

"Yes," I say. "It does. We agreed to open honesty, didn't we? Can you be honest with me?"

His Adam's apple bobs visibly as he swallows. As if I've just asked him to walk through a pit of poisonous cobras for me. As if I've asked him to face his darkest fear. But if he wants this badly enough, then he'll have to comply, because I've already determined that I can't back down. It's too late for that.

He steps away from me and moves deeper into the room, leaving me. A hand comes up to rub the back of his neck. "There are things in my past…. It's not easy to talk about."

I fold my arms against my chest and lean against the table, as if to remind him that I can't back down and won't let him off the hook. "We all have skeletons in our closet," I say quietly, thinking of my own heartbreak in the past, that same heartbreak that has prevented me from seeking out a relationship all the years since. And maybe even tempted me into this contractual deal. Maybe he has a story like mine? Maybe we can find a way to console each other in that?

He doesn't turn to see if I've bolted out the door yet. His hands slip into his pockets again—a posture I'm now associating with his being uncomfortable. Clearing his throat, he begins in a quiet voice. "My father was not a good man. And there are days when I fear that I am just like him, despite the fact that I loathed every breath that he took."

I blink, suddenly confused. I was expecting a tale of heartbreak. Of his one true love cheating on him or something. But he's talking about his father? I'm completely lost and confused at his direction. But I dare not say anything, dare not even ask lest he back off and let me go. Because with each passing minute that I am here, my desire to leave fades.

He turns and glances at me and then starts to pace the entire length of the long room. My eyes follow him as he begins to talk. The story comes out of him quickly, as if a dam has broken inside of him and letting out the words in a rush. "I never discuss this. With anyone. It's not easy."

He takes a breath and then lets it go as if to underline the painfulness of it. I shift where I'm leaning but don't say a word. "He abused her. I can never remember a day when he didn't lay a hand on her—or threaten to do it."

My breath catches. He must be talking about his mother. "I begged her to leave him. I was only ten years old, but even then I knew we could have a better life without him. He was wealthy and powerful, but I knew, I knew if I could just convince her..." He shakes his head.

I lick my lips, silently urging him to continue without threatening to break the spell.

"She wouldn't listen to me. Said we needed him. *We.* I never needed that bastard." He shakes his head again. "She didn't have the courage. Didn't have the faith, and I had to watch her wither away and die—all because of what he was doing to her. She wouldn't eat, wouldn't take care of herself—" He sucks in a breath.

I push off the wall and intercept the path he is pacing. He halts a foot away from me, blue eyes burning with remembered hurt, relived pain.

"You can't believe that you are just like him," I say quietly.

"The apple doesn't fall far from the tree, Madeline."

"Bullshit."

He takes a breath and stares at me, his eyes bearing that same intensity. "I have never and will never lay a hand on a woman in anger. But there is more than one way to destroy a person."

I take a tentative step toward him and then another. "You're wrong," I say.

Something passes through his eyes, something that reveals he clearly does not believe me. I stop when I'm standing so close to him that I can feel his body warmth. I place my hands on his cheeks.

"Evan, look at me." And he does. "You're not like him. You're nothing like him."

He doesn't move. Even when I stand on my tiptoes, bring my mouth up to touch his. This time he lets me control the kiss as I pull his head down to meet mine. I'm the one applying pressure, pressing him for more. I close my eyes and let loose a small sigh, and suddenly his arms are hooking around my waist, pulling me fast to him.

I can feel his erection straining against his zipper, pressing into my stomach. I realize with a sudden rush, that I would never have walked away. Not really. I might tell myself I would have, but the truth is, I'm just as addicted to him as he is to me.

I rub against him shamelessly, moaning as he grips the globes of my ass, then lifts me onto the table, his lips never leaving mine.

He pulls something out of his pocket—four metallic balls, the size of large marbles, connected by a string.

I lick my lips. "What's that?"

He doesn't answer. Instead, his hand slides upward, under my skirt, until his fingers find the edges of my black lace panties. Pulling them down my thighs, slides them off and tucks them into his pocket. "I've been craving this sweet pussy for days."

Instinctively, I arch into his hand as his fingers push inside me. Already, it's almost too much. Just his hands on me—*inside* me—is enough to send me over the edge. Clenching my teeth, I throw my head back and try to stem the orgasm that's already building.

"Open for me."

I do as I'm told, bracing my heels against the edge of the desk, spreading my thighs wider. That's when I feel his fingers leave me, replaced by something cold and metallic. The balls he'd taken out of his pocket, I realize. I gasp as he pushes one ball into me, then the other, until all four balls fill my channel. They feel hard, ungiving and heavy. They start out cold but are soon warmed by my body's heat.

Then he dips his head and buries his face between my thighs. I gasp at the feel of his hot tongue gliding up the length of my slick folds, swirling over my clit. The onslaught of sensation is so intense, I moan and twist beneath his mouth. His strong hands grip me, his fingertips digging into my hips, holding me steady.

"Oh, God, Evan. I'm going to come."

"You taste so fucking sweet," he says hoarsely. "I can't get enough of you."

"Less talking. More licking," I mutter breathlessly.

I'm near the precipice, so close to the abyss that I could weep. His tongue feels so good. He knows how to work my clit just right, adding just enough pressure to drive me frantic with need. Still writhing, I thread my hands through his dark, wavy hair and tug, desperate to pull him closer.

Every muscle in my body tenses as a violent orgasm slams into me. My channel clenches tightly around the balls, convulsing, sending ripples of heat radiating through my body. I fight for breath through my gasping moans. His hands grip me tightly, hold me still against his mouth as he works on me through every last convulsion.

Just as the ripples slowly begin to ebb, he removes the balls from my sex and tosses them aside. I'm staring up at the white square ceiling tiles, trying to catch my breath, when I hear the distinct sound of a zipper.

He places his palms on my knees and spreads me wider. I'm completely open to him, more vulnerable than I've ever felt in my life.

"I'm going to fuck you. Do you understand?"

I lick my dry lips. "Yes."

"Don't make a sound." He places a finger against my mouth. "I'm going to take you fast and hard, the way you like it. But I don't want to hear a sound from you."

I nod eagerly, desperate to feel his hard length inside of me. It's all I've thought about for days.

The swollen head of his cock slides over my clit and nudges the slick folds of my entrance. In one swift motion, he slams into me, his cock stretching me impossibly wide. I almost gasp, but somehow I manage to catch the sound before it escapes my throat.

Holy fuck.

He feels so damn good I could weep.

Then he moves inside me, each thrust quick, clipped, focused. His heavy balls slap against my ass as he drives into me, over and over, each thrust taking me closer to the edge of oblivion.

Leaning over me, he dips his head, and bites my nipple through the fabric of my shirt and bra. The sharp sting is electrifying. It feels damn good, and I check myself before I let out a moan—then decide to test him. What will he do if I don't obey his command? I let out a long, loud moan.

His hips immediately stop in their jerking motion against me. He pulls out of me and, taking me by the wrist, tugs me up and flips me over so my stomach is pressed against the edge of the desk, my ass completely bared to him.

"I believe I told you not to make a sound."

Braced on my elbows, I nod, not daring to speak.

"You disobeyed me." His voice sounds ominous. "And you will always obey me, as you said you would or there will be consequences." Lifting my skirt, he gently strokes my ass with the palm of his hand. "And when you do not obey, you will be punished."

His words excite me, and my body tightens, anticipating the first blow. Seconds later, his hand comes down on my ass with a thunderous *smack*—then another and another. Tears sting my eyes. This is harder than he's ever hit me. But even as the pain jolts through my body, I crave more.

Biting my bottom lip, I swallow the cries I'm desperate to let out. Pain is entwined with pleasure, and each hard slap sings through my body, humming through my veins. Tears stream down my cheeks.

Several blows later, I've lost count of how many times he's hit me, but I'm not sure how much more I can take. The pain is almost unbearable now. Exquisite torment. Beautiful agony.

Then suddenly, it's over.

His lips brush across my hot skin, kissing the places where he has just hit me. The sensation soothes my sore backside, cooling my hot skin. My nipples tighten and my channel clenches with need.

"Good girl," he murmurs, stroking my sex. "If you stay a good girl, I'll let you come before I do."

Oh, God, yes.

CHAPTER 21
DEFIANCE

AND WHEN YOU DO NOT OBEY, YOU WILL BE PUNISHED. IF YOU *stay a good girl, I'll let you come before I do.*

I must have made a small sound of approval, because less than a second later, he rams himself inside me, reaching around to stroke my clit as he thrusts against me with quick, sharp strokes. The onslaught of sensation is overwhelming. All I can do is feel. Everything is centered on where we are joined, the glowing soreness in my backside as he rubs against me there. Nothing else in the world exists but each steady thrust and the wild beating of my own heart.

"You're so tight," he groans. "Your pussy is squeezing me like a fist. Feels so fucking good."

I would moan, just for spite, but I know he'll punish me if I do, and right now I just want to come again, so I clench my jaw to keep from making a sound. But it's hard.

Threading his fingers through my hair, he tugs my head back, still pounding into me forcefully. The desk sways beneath us. "Do you like that, baby?"

When I don't say anything, he growls in my ear. "You can respond. Tell me."

"Yes," I cry out. "I like it."

"Do you want to come again?"

I grip the edges of the desk to give him better resistance. "Yes...."

He slows his pace. "Say 'please, sir'..."

Seriously? I'm about to shatter. "*Please, sir,*" I breathe.

His pace picks up again, and I'm so close. Tension builds in my core, every muscle tensing in anticipation. Then he adds more pressure to my clit, and I fall apart, coming hard until I'm writhing beneath him, gasping for air.

My channel squeezes him, and he stills, pushing deep inside me. I feel his cock swell even bigger as he finds his own release. He lets out a long, satisfied groan before collapsing on top of me, his arms supporting his weight.

Minutes later, he pulls out of me and smooths my skirt back down over my backside. His touch is gentle, almost reverent. I straighten and turn around to face him just as he's tucking himself back into his tailored gray slacks.

We share an awkward moment of silence before he leans over and kisses me. His lips capture mine in a slow, gentle kiss that completely engulfs me. His scent, the warmth of his body, the velvety softness of his tongue sliding against mine...

At that moment, the door to the mission control room opens. Evan jerks back and places himself in front of me, shielding me from whoever has just walked into the room—which happens to be a group of unsuspecting XVerse employees.

I blanch when I see the shock on their faces. It's obvious what we were doing. Even without the smell of sex that lingers in the air, our startled reaction to their sudden intrusion is enough to give it away.

"I'm sorry, Mr. Kohl. I didn't know anyone was in here."

"Just…give us a minute." Again, he's the cool, confident CEO, and not the man who just wildly fucked me against the desk.

"Sure," the man says, then ushers the group out of the room, shutting the door behind him.

Evan expels a breath and rakes a hand through his hair, shaking his head. Nearly being caught has rattled him, and I'm not sure why. Evan seems like the reckless type. The type of man who does what he wants, takes what he wants, and be damned the consequences.

"Thank goodness they didn't walk in five minutes ago," I laugh, trying to ease the tension. "Then they would have really gotten an eyeful."

He explodes, slamming his palm against the wall. "*Fuck!*"

His sudden outburst takes me by surprise, and I flinch. He catches my reaction and turns toward me. The look on his face is pure anguish, and all I want to do is reach out and soothe him. But something stops me.

"I'm sorry, Madeline." He shakes his head and slips his hands into his pockets. "I should have been more careful."

"It's okay," I say.

"No, it's not." He releases a heavy breath and reaches up to stroke my cheek with the pad of his thumb. "Someone could have seen us. It was careless of me. Come," he says, taking my hand in his. "I'll walk you out to the car."

He's sending me home? "Wait, why? I haven't seen the rest of the building."

"I…have work to do."

My jaw drops. "Then can someone else show me around?"

"No," he says in a dead voice. He leads me out of the mission control room and down a long hallway. "Everyone here has work to do. We have a big launch in a few months."

I open my mouth to protest again and then shut it, studying his body language. His shoulders are stiff, hunched. Henry is waiting outside at the curb, right where we left him. He'd been there the whole time, and I suddenly feel guilty for making him wait so long while Evan and I fooled around.

Before Henry can step out of the car, Evan opens the door for me. I can't help but feel like he's upset at me for something. Since that moment in the mission control room when we were interrupted, he's been acting cold and distant.

Leaning forward, he places a quick kiss on my forehead. "I'll call you this weekend."

I nod, get into the car, and watch as he disappears back into the building.

****

It's been six days. Six long days since I've heard from Evan, and I can't seem to focus on anything *but* the fact that he's *not* calling me. I'm lying on the couch, clutching my phone, watching old *Friends* reruns when Sam walks through the front door.

"Maddy-bear!" She walks through the house until she finds me in the living room. "Oh, God, Maddy. This is ridiculous."

"I'm watching *Friends*. What's wrong with that?"

"Aside from the fact that you *never* watch TV except when you're sick or depressed? And did you even shower today?" She plops down next to me on the couch and releases a heavy sigh. "Still no call from Kohl, I gather. Have you tried texting him?"

I glare at her. "I have no idea what you're talking about. And *yes*, I did shower." She flashes me a side-glance, and I know she sees right through me. "Fine." I push out a breath. "I've texted him twice. No reply."

God, saying it aloud is so much worse than thinking loser thoughts to myself. I should have a tub of ice cream between my knees and a spoon in my hand to complete the full picture.

"I checked your cubby at school and I found something that might cheer you up." She hands me a plain white envelope, an excited grin on her face. "I rushed right over, and if it's what I think it is, some celebrating is in order!"

I sit up and snatch the envelope from her hand. *Holy shit.* The results of my exam. Fear knots in my stomach and my hands shake as I open the envelope and read the letter. "Oh, my God." I jump up and turn to Sam. "I passed!"

"I knew it—I'm so happy for you." She throws her arms around my neck. "We are *so* going out tomorrow night! Let's do some drinks and dancing. We'll ask some other people to come with us. It'll cheer you up."

I'm so damn relieved, I could cry. I didn't realize just how much the exam had been weighing on my mind. Letting loose is exactly what I need. "Awesome," I say.

"Can we go to The Playroom? It's a new club on Colorado Boulevard, and I've been dying to go."

I nod. "Yeah, whatever. As long as they are serving alcohol and lots of it."

At that moment, my cell phone rings. Glancing down at the caller ID, I see that it's Miriam, and my heart leaps into my throat.

"Hello?"

"Hello, Madeline. Mr. Kohl would like to see you tomorrow night for dinner. Henry will pick you up at seven o'clock."

"Wait, tomorrow night? What happened to the forty-eight hours notice?"

He's been ignoring me for a week and now he just expects me to be at his beck and call? No way.

"Mr. Kohl would like to see you," is all the answer I get from Miriam, as though that is reason enough for me to drop everything.

"Well, you can tell him that I have plans. My friends and I are hitting The Playroom tomorrow night."

"Mr. Kohl won't be happy. He had meetings rearranged so he could schedule with you. He was quite insistent."

"Then he should have given me more notice," I say unapologetically.

When I get off the phone with Miriam, Sam is staring at me like I've grown two heads. "Did you just blow off Evan Kohl?"

"I didn't 'blow him off.' He knows damn well what the rules are."

"You've been moping around here for days because he hasn't called you, and when he finally does, you refuse to see him."

"First of all, *he* didn't call. Miriam did. And second, he can't just snap his fingers and expect me to come running. I'm not his slave." I smile at Sam. "Besides, I already made plans to go out with you."

Sam's brows lift. "Oh...okay. So tomorrow then. Seven o'clock?"

"Sounds good. I can't wait."

She leaves not long after, and with new exhilaration, I go about the rest of my evening. I get a few more texts from friends congratulating me on my good news once I post it on Instagram. I invite Keith and some of his friends along on our bender. It's shaping up to be a fun night out—one that will be well-earned. I've got a lot of steam to blow off, much of which is due to the maddening behavior of Mr. Kohl.

I had to admit, if only to myself, that I was curious how he'd react to my pushback. Just the thought of it brought a little thrill.

But I tucked that aside and went about my day. I didn't have time to obsess over him. And this good news was enough to remind me that I was a strong and intelligent woman. And if he didn't appreciate that, well too bad for him.

Chapter 22
Playing with Fire

THE NEXT DAY, I'M RUNNING ERRANDS, SUCH AS BUYING my books for the next term, doing my laundry and getting the place straightened up for the cleaning lady when my phone chirps with a text from Kohl.

I heard you are busy tonight.

His annoyance is unmistakable, which is exactly what I was counting on. Kohl is a man who gets what he wants when he wants it. Most people don't have the balls to tell him no. I'm a little surprised that I do, actually. But if I don't make a stand now, then he'll walk all over me later.

I wait a half hour—while I fold my whites—formulating a reply that should sufficiently express my level of irritation with him. Part of me wants to not reply at all—like he'd done with me. But my snarky self gets over that pretty quickly.

Oh, I see that you do actually remember how to use the texting app on your phone. I'd thought you may have forgotten.

His reply comes less than a minute later:

I had a v. busy week. I want to see you tonight. Pick you up at 7.

Much as I would like to wait another half an hour, I can't let that stand.

Sorry. I made plans & your scheduler called me too late. It's 48 hrs notice, as agreed upon in the contract.

Not two seconds later, his reply lights up my phone.

Touché, Miss Swanson. You've made your point, now stop being insolent or I may have to punish you.

I smile at his text, but I'm still annoyed. Maybe a little bit turned on, if I'd care to admit that to myself.

Guess I'll just have to take my chances.

As soon as I hit "reply" I turn my phone off and toss it into the laundry basket. Already, I'm tempted to turn it back on and see if he's replied, but I resist. He needs to know he's not the only one calling the shots. He can't just trample all over that contract. He signed it, too.

***

"Another lemon drop, please!" I wave my hand at the bartender, and he acknowledges me with a nod. It's my third drink of the night, and I'm feeling a nice, warm buzz.

"Maddy, come on. You haven't had anything to eat," Sam scolds.

"Hey, if I want to get shift-aced…I mean shit-faced then I'm allowed! We are celebrating."

Keith, on the other side of me, grins. "We sure are. Welcome to the program, Maddy. It's going to be an awesome year." As the bartender sets the pretty yellow martini down in front of me, Keith holds out a bill. "This one's on me."

"Awww. Thank you," I say, tilting my head to rest it on his shoulder. "You're so sweet." Greedily, I snatch up my drink and sip at it.

One of my favorite songs comes on, and people start flocking to the tiny dance floor.

I feel a tug on my arm. "C'mon," says Keith in my ear.

I turn to him, eyes widening. "What?"

"Let's dance. Come on!"

"Hmm. Just a sec." I tilt my head back and polish off the martini in one gulp.

Sam's eyes goggle so that they almost fall out of her head. "Slow it down, Mads. Don't do anything stupid."

I scoff at her. "Stupid? What stupid? I've got my man Keith here. He'll take care of me, won't you?"

His arm slides around my waist, and he smiles. "Of course I will."

Sam glares a warning at me, but I ignore her and let Keith guide me to the dance floor where we rock it out for the rest of the song. For geeky aero students, our moves aren't bad—or maybe my perception of our dancing is dimmed by the fog of the alcohol. That last martini really pushed me over the edge of buzzed into mildly impaired but it feels good. Being out with my besties is helping me forget my irritation and the mild hurt I've been nursing from Kohl's insensitive behavior all week.

As soon as the song ends, I head back toward the bar to order my fourth drink when Keith's hand hooks around my arm. Another song begins, the beat pulsing in rhythm with the blue, purple and pink lights. He's got a hopeful smile on his face, and a gleam in his eyes.

"C'mon, Maddy. Let's dance again…"

He's cute and *so* sweet. And so much more attentive than certain *other* males of my acquaintance. How could I say no to that?

I laugh as he pulls me back onto the dance floor and begins moving against me. He's got a hand on each hip, and we're feeling the beat. Every so often he starts grinding on me, and I'm so buzzed I think it's the most hilarious thing in the world. Soon I'm turning around and twerking at him in response just to crack him up.

"What the fuck are you doing?"

The familiar English-accented voice carries over the din of music, and I instantly freeze, too afraid to turn around. I see Keith's face go white as a sheet and I know exactly who is standing behind me.

Yesterday, I'd mentioned in passing to Miriam where I was going. She must have passed that little tidbit of info along to him. Taking a deep breath I turn around to face Kohl, who's got his fists clenched at his sides.

"What are you doing here? I didn't think these kind of places were your thing."

His face is hard, unreadable, but I can tell he's fighting to control his anger. "I'm taking you home."

"Uh. No, actually, I'm just getting started here. I was going to get another drink right after this song."

He reaches out to grab my wrist, when Keith intervenes. Bravely, he steps up to stand between me and Kohl. He slides a protective arm around my shoulders.

"Keith—" I try to stop him.

"Hands off," Kohl snarls, his voice low and commanding.

He tugs on my wrist and pulls me toward him, dragging me off the dance floor, through the club and out into the cool night air. Keith has followed us, and I see Sam heading up the rear, her eyes wide with concern.

"Keith, it's okay. Just go back inside," I say, but I'm so taken off guard and foggy from the alcohol that my voice sounds shaky, fearful.

"I'm not leaving you out here alone with him," Keith bites back, his hard gaze fixed on Evan.

"What the fuck is going on?" Sam asks.

"Nothing," I say. "It's okay, guys. Really. He's not going to hurt me. We just need to talk."

"Then why do you sound like you're scared of him?" Keith asks, darting an unspoken challenge at Evan. Oh shit, no. No. *No. No.*

Evan steps forward, getting right in Keith's face, his hand still circled possessively around my wrist. His grip tightens as he speaks to Keith between clenched teeth. "Stay the fuck away from Madeline. Do you understand? She's off limits."

Keith takes a step back, his eyes darting to me. "Is he imposing himself on you, Maddy? Do you agree to this?"

I wrench my wrist out of Evan's powerful grip. "It's fine. I'm okay, Keith. Really."

Keith seems to relax a bit at my words, but I can still see the fight in his eyes. Thankfully, Sam comes to my rescue. She steps up and grabs Keith by the elbow. "Come on, let's give them a second alone."

It takes a minute, but finally he gives in. "We'll be right inside," he says.

As Sam and Keith walk back into the club, I hear Keith mutter to Sam under his breath. "Is that really Evan Kohl?"

Evan doesn't hear or pretends not to—or maybe he doesn't care. He seems far less motivated to keep our relationship discreet than I am. I close my eyes and take a deep breath. Evan and I are finally alone. Tension arcs like electricity in the air between us.

He is visibly angry—jaw clenched, beautiful features flushed, and there's this look in his deep-blue eyes. It actually scares me a little. Makes me think of that story he told me, of how he feared himself prone to violence and destruction because of his father's history.

He seems at a loss for words, his hand working at his sides. His gaze fixes on mine. "Why aren't you wearing the necklace?" His voice is as hard as granite.

I swallow, suddenly a little afraid. My hand flies to my collarbone, to the necklace I know isn't there.

"It didn't go with my outfit," I say with a toss of my head to bring an air of flippancy that I most certainly do not feel. The alcohol has definitely lent me lots of false bravado.

Fury flashes in those eyes and he bends, his face very close to mine, and I'm suddenly given a taste of what Keith must have been feeling with Evan right in my face. I jerk away from him, but his hand comes out, clamping around the back of my neck, holding me still.

"You seem to find it funny to continually defy me. It's obvious that you need to be taught a lesson on how you are to behave while we are under contract together."

With a huff and a swallow and not a little bit of a thrill, I wonder what this lesson will entail.

Because I had a lesson to teach him as well—*ignore me at your own peril.*

As I took a breath and tried to calm the beating of my heart, I couldn't help but anticipate the imminent clash of our wills, with an almost inevitable sense of who would win.

Chapter 23
Promises & Ultimatums

For the first time since meeting Kohl, I feel something like real fear. My bravado falters, and I struggle to find something witty to say, but my mind is frozen and the words are caught in my throat.

He's standing in front of me—looking both furious and fucking hot—waiting for my reply.

Finally, I manage to regain my voice. "I told you—and Miriam—I already had plans."

It's all I can muster, and already I can see it isn't what he wanted to hear. His eyes narrow and a muscle starts pulsing in his jaw. Shit. I can see the anger he's struggling hard to control, and suddenly my heart feels like it's going to beat right out of my chest.

Maybe it's stupidity or just a test, but I turn on my heel and head back toward the bar. If I'm being honest with myself, I want Evan to follow me. I want him to take control and insist I stay with him.

Halfway to the door, he grabs my elbow from behind, pulling me to a stop. "*No*, you are coming with me."

I whip around to face him, almost tripping over my own heels, but his powerful body is there to catch me. I struggle against him, but the alcohol has taken away my fight. I glance up at him through my lashes, his grip still tight around my elbow.

"What do you want, Kohl?"

His gaze is hard and unforgiving. "I want what's mine."

He pulls me to his car—a brand new black Tesla—which is parked haphazardly in a red zone on the street, and opens the passenger door, ushering me inside. I sink into the soft leather, clutching my purse in my lap as he shuts my door and gets into the driver's seat.

Excitement rushes through me as we zip through the streets of Pasadena before hitting the freeway headed west, the opposite direction of the house on Hill that he rented for me.

"Where are you taking me?"

He doesn't answer, he just keeps his gaze fixed on the road.

It's not until we reach the 10 freeway that I suspect we're headed toward the beach. It's a balmy night, and he has the windows rolled down. The wind whips through my hair, ruining my hour-long fight with the flat iron, but I welcome it. The fresh air feels good on my skin and it sobers me up.

After thirty tense minutes of silence, we make our way down a long, dark driveway that leads to an underground parking garage. Evan presses a button on his visor, and the gate slides open.

That's when the realization hits. *Holy everliving fuck.* He's taking me back to Exeter House.

He parks the car and gets out, coming around to my door and yanking it open. I step out, my heels clicking on the smooth cement as he shuts the door behind me, grabs me by the wrist and pulls me to a bank of five elevators. We take the first one, and with his key, he hits the button for the top floor. We stand in awkward silence as the elevator climbs several floors, before spilling us out directly into a huge, contemporary-style penthouse. It's all smooth white planes, steel, and glass.

It's absolutely stunning.

He doesn't bother showing me around. Instead, he leads me up the massive staircase—it's a spiral, all white, with curved glass windows overlooking the ocean.

Without pausing, he pulls me down a long hallway. His strides are long and urgent, and I struggle to keep up with him. At the end of the hallway is a pair of double doors. He throws them open and strides inside, tugging me along with him.

I take in my surroundings. We are in an en suite bedroom, which is decorated in white on white. There's a huge bed, a fireplace and a couple of upholstered chairs—all in a slightly off-color of white against a snowy carpet. Everything is simple yet elegantly so. So that it's clear that he paid a fortune to have it decorated, everything designed to give the impression of incomprehensible wealth.

My fists knot at my sides and I fidget while he removes his jacket and tosses it across the back of one of the chairs, then unbuttons his sleeves and rolls them halfway up his powerful forearms. "So…why am I *here*? I thought you didn't bring women up here." I could guess at the reasons, but I want to hear what he says.

He doesn't answer. Instead, he whips around to face me and says, "What the *fuck* was that tonight?"

I startle at the white-hot anger burning in his pristine blue eyes. Have I crossed the line? I'm oddly excited at the thought of pushing the always-in-control squillionare too far.

"I was just out blowing off some steam with my friends. If you'd bothered to check in with me this week, you'd know that I have something worth celebrating."

"I know damn well about what you have to celebrate," he grits out between clenched teeth. "And I intended to take you out for a celebration of my own. But you refused to see me. Have you forgotten so soon?"

I open my mouth to reply hotly but stop when he begins pacing the length of the room, his fists knotting and then relaxing at his sides. He won't look at me. I can tell he's getting more frantic, more unhinged, with every stride. "That guy had his hands all over you, for Christ's sake."

"Keith is just a friend. *Seriously*. Evan—"

He snatches a vase off the mantle, and he smashes it violently against the wall. It explodes into a million little pieces, scattering across the plush carpet like confetti, and I jump about six feet out of my skin when he does it. *Fuck*. "No one touches you, Madeline. *No one*." He turns to me, breathing hard, and I swallow, thankful for the respectable distance between us. "Only *me*."

I'm frozen, my eyes glued to the tiny bits of glass strewn along the carpet, glistening under the recessed lighting. Fear knots tightly in my chest. What the fuck have I gotten myself into?

I take a deep breath and release it, thankful for his silence. "Evan—"

But he rides over me, holding up his hand to stay my words. "I'm giving you one chance—one out. You leave now and walk out that door. The contract will be dismissed. You'll stay in the house until you can find another place to live and with my support, as agreed upon in the contract. But you will never see me again." He takes a deep breath and appears calmer, his fists relaxing. "*Or* you can choose to stay. But if you do, you agree to obey me in all things. You will be mine, no questions asked. Mine to do with as I please. And you will not question or refuse me again."

I blink, stunned by his offer, my mind swirling with the possibilities. He's offering me my absolute freedom—including freedom from financial difficulties. I can go out when I please, spend time with whom I please. But...I'll never see him again. That thought brings an ache right down to my toes, and it shocks me to realize how much I need him. How much I crave him. I squeeze my eyes shut. *Mine to do with as I please.* I have no idea what that means, but I have to admit that the thought of it excites me. His domination excites me, and it has from the very beginning. I sigh, realizing that I'm already in far too deep.

I search his face but say nothing, trying to puzzle out his unreadable expression. "*Well?*" he barks. "What's it going to be?"

I swallow, trying to force away the unmistakable feeling that I'm stepping over a precipice. "I'll stay, then."

His eyes narrow, and a faint, knowing smile teases the edge of his lips. It's suddenly clear. This was all a bluff or maybe a test. Perhaps he never would have let me go. "Then you agree to obey, unequivocally. And *not* defy me."

I nod.

"Speak it, Madeline. Say the words."

Heat rises up my neck, and my fists knot tightly. My brain is screaming in protest, but my mouth forms the words. "I will obey."

"And not defy me," he repeats.

"And I won't defy you."

That smile increases, like a pleased pet owner rewarding a dog for performing a trick. "Your body is my property. To use as I please."

A long, charged silence while he stares at me expectantly. "My body is yours to use...as you please." Much as I hate to admit it, his claim over me is fucking hot. I'm already wet and aching.

Now he's smiling such that his even, white teeth are showing. He reaches for his belt and unbuckles it. "Good girl."

I lick my lips and hesitate.

"Remove your clothes."

With shaky hands, I unbutton my shirt and slip it off my shoulders, then unzip my skirt. They both fall into a pile on the ground beside me. His eyes devour me hungrily, and I note that he slips off his shoes. Then I reach around and unhook my bra, letting it fall too. His breath catches as he takes in my bare breasts, and I feel desirable, powerful, that I have this effect on him.

Lastly, the panties go. Neither one of these undergarments are the lace that he stipulates that I wear. It doesn't seem to curb his heated reaction to my naked body. His erection is an easily noticeable bulge in his pants.

"On your knees. *Now*," he orders.

I only hesitate a second before lowering myself onto the plush white carpet. My heart is thundering like a riot in my chest.

"Eyes closed. Hands clasped behind your back."

I do as instructed, and wait. As several breathless seconds pass, I hear him removing his belt. Then he moves to his dresser and opens a drawer, closes it and opens another. Soon, the carpet is registering his footsteps as he comes closer to me. He's right in front of me now and my eyes are squeezed shut. I don't even dare peek at him. The unmistakable sound of a zipper splits the silence. I know exactly what's coming and I start to tremble.

"Open your mouth."

Again I comply immediately and the head of his cock touches my bottom lip. Then he stops. "Suck me, Madeline. Take it deep."

I lean forward greedily, taking his salty, musky length into my mouth. He's huge and he stretches me wide as I suck him. He groans, shifting his hips, forcing me to take more of him until he hits the back of my throat, and I can no longer breathe. He stops for a long minute as if to prove that he has control even over my basic need for breath. Panic starts to rise inside, but I will myself to calm. As if to reaffirm this control, he's got his hand cupped around the back of my head, holding me there to keep his cock deep in my mouth.

I fight the instinct to unclasp my hands and push him away, hoping he'll move soon. I'm in no danger of passing out—yet. Nevertheless, his pleasure is mine to give him. Every shudder of his body is *mine*. In this moment, I have power over him and that knowledge makes my channel ache.

His hand threads through my hair, tugging me closer, holding my head in place as my tongue swirls around the underside of his cock. He slides slowly back, lets me catch my breath quickly before shoving forward again, even deeper. I can feel him in my throat and I'm willing myself not to gag as he stills there again.

Suddenly, his hand leaves my head and something cold encloses around my neck with a distinctive *click*. I jerk back, startled but his hands are still on whatever is around my neck, closing a clasp? My hands fly to my throat and I feel a thick metal band hugging my neck like a choker and from it hangs a pendant—no, not a pendant. A *padlock.* He's locked it around my neck.

The bastard *collared* me. Like a damn puppy.

I look up to see him watching my reaction closely before he puts his hand in my hair again, ready to pick up where we left off. But I turn my head away, my anger growing more palpable by the second. "What the *fuck* is this?"

With one hand still in my hair, he tugs on a chain held by the other—that I quickly discover is attached to the collar like a leash. "My assurance of your obedience. Will you protest now? So soon after promising that I could do as I please?"

I blink, speechless. My hand flies to my throat again. A collar, an *assurance of obedience* to him. In shock I realize that this is only the very beginning of the *lesson* he seems so eager to *teach* me.

CHAPTER 24
CUFFED & COLLARED

M Y LIPS TREMBLE, AND I THINK ABOUT WHAT I'VE JUST promised him—that I'd obey him unquestioningly, that my body is his to use as he pleases. But before I can reply, he's nudging his cock toward my mouth again. Without another word, I accept it, letting him thrust into me. Letting him fuck my mouth.

My eyes close, and though I'm still burning with rage, I'm also burning with desire, feeling his powerful will coil around me and take me to places I couldn't have even imagined in my darkest fantasies.

My tongue is caressing him as he thrusts into my mouth, pushing against my throat, and as it's been a while since he last fucked me, it doesn't take him long to come. His cock swells in my mouth as he lets out a ferocious growl, pushing impossibly deep so that I actually do begin gagging. He ignores me for several seconds as his hot semen pumps into my throat and I have no choice but to swallow and fight the gag reflex.

He pulls away from me with a long sigh and then steps back. "Don't move," he commands as he steps away, into the en suite bathroom, which I can see only a fraction of from this angle. The minute he's out of sight, I begin pulling at the collar, the padlock, trying to determine just how immutable this thing is. The chain is permanently attached to it, too, not clipped like a leash that can be removed. And it's thick—tugging on it is not going to break it.

Soon he's back in the room standing in front of me again. He reaches down and lifts my chin to look up at him. "Well done," he breathes as if I should be crying with joy that I've pleased him. "You have a very fuckable mouth—that I intend to have more of soon. Along with the rest of you."

I grind my teeth but don't reply, letting my eyes drift away from his. He reaches down and grabs the chain attached to the collar and gives it a firm tug, pulling me up to my feet wordlessly. He could have just told me to stand up but chose to do this instead, as if to emphasize the existence of this damn collar and leash.

Shit. I can't wait until this night is over and he takes the damn thing off. I'll go home and curl up in my bed and pretend he wasn't ordering me around like his slave tonight.

"Now for the rules..." he says, his blue eyes glittering, and my heart hammers with fear. This isn't over yet.

"First, while you are in this apartment, you will always be naked and collared." He tugs the chain again and smiles at the flare of fury in my eyes as I bite my lip. He's enjoying my anger too much, pushing it on purpose. "Second, when I am fucking you, you will not be permitted to climax without my express permission, which you must beg for beforehand. And you may not bring yourself to orgasm unless I command it."

My mouth drops. Is he fucking *serious*? He brings his face down close to mine, then turns so that his mouth is centimeters from my ear. And he speaks in a low, seductive voice. "And lastly, you will always, *always* surrender to my will. In. All. Things." We are both still as he lets that sink in and then he turns to look at me from this close angle, studying my suddenly calm, blank features as my fury fades and I accept these terms.

"Is this clear, Madeline? No nods. You must speak it clearly."

I swallow. "Yes," I say. He lifts a brow, and I belatedly add, "—*sir.*"

He smiles, raising a hand to my hair and petting it like the aforementioned puppy. But I'm no longer burning with fury for him. Instead, I'm burning for release. "That's a good girl."

I can't help it…a rush of satisfaction swells in my chest. As fucked up as it is, I crave his praise and approval. It's like a drug coursing through my veins, and already I want more.

"On the bed," he snaps. "Now. Facedown, legs apart."

With a hop of fear, I turn and comply, just as he's asked, pressing my cheek against the smooth, satin finish of his white comforter.

"Hands behind your back." And when I do, he grabs another item off the dresser and settles the cold metal around my wrists. *Handcuffs.*

I suck in a breath, my cold fear returning—but also a thrill, a question of what will happen next.

The weight on the bed shifts, and he settles beside me. He lets out a long breath, which scurries over the skin of my naked back. "This is the test of the depth of your obedience to me, Madeline. You will not remove that collar. Nor will you leave until I say you may." My mind freezes in shock, trying to process his words as he cups a large hand around my shoulder and pulls me so that I'm now face up. His hand travels to caress my face. "You promised to obey? Well, this is your chance to prove it." He smooths my cheek, gazing over my features adoringly. "And in your complete submission, you'll find a pleasure you never thought possible. I assure you."

So much for going home to crawl into bed and forget about this miserable collar around my neck. I should have known this had all been too easy. It isn't like Kohl to let something go without first exerting his control.

He touches the collar. "It's locked in place and I know that you hate it now. But when this is done…you'll love it. You'll crave for me to put it on you."

I turn my face away and bite back my reply. *Like fucking hell I will.*

Instead, when I speak, my voice comes out shaky, weak. "My roommates will worry about me. Especially after that scene at the club."

"You'll be allowed to call them. But you are not permitted to speak to *him* again. I won't allow it. Not to study, not even in passing on the street." My mouth drops open, but again, I don't find the voice to protest. "You may make *one* phone call. But that is the extent of my generosity." He grabs my cell phone off the dresser and plugs it into a headset. "Your security code?"

I clench my jaw, reluctant to give it to him. So even in this move of "generosity," he is using this as an excuse to get even more control over me, via my phone.

"The choice is yours, Madeline. You can call them or not."

With a heavy sigh, I tell him the code and he keys it in, opening up my contacts. "Let's see, the girl I met the other night, the one from the club. Her name was Sam, right? Here she is. Let her know that you will be staying here for the week."

I gape at him. "A *week?* Evan, I'm a full-time grad student. There's no way I can skip out on a week's worth of classes."

He glares at me. "I will handle your professors." He slips the headset on my head and dials the number. Then he leaves the room after having gathered my clothes from the floor.

Sam doesn't answer her phone and I'm actually relieved that she won't pepper me with questions that way. I leave a message telling her that Kohl surprised me with a last-minute trip to Mexico. It seems the easier explanation than the almost insane reality of me collared and handcuffed and naked on Evan's bed.

Evan returns a few minutes later with a tray of food—cheese and fruit and some sort of thinly sliced meat, a tall glass of ice water and some ibuprofen. He sets them down on the nightstand, then bends to scoop up my phone and remove the headset from my head.

"You need to sober up. Eat and hydrate so you won't be sick." And then he continues darkly. "You'll also need plenty of energy for what comes next."

With that, he rolls me over again, unlocks one side of the cuffs and attaches it instead to the wrought-iron headboard. He points to a service button by the lamp. "When you need to use the bathroom, you'll press on this button and I'll free you for that."

"How kind of you," I bite in reply.

Instead of the angry reaction I'm half expecting, he actually grins, amused. "Now, now, Madeline. I know you intend to strike back with your angry words, but it only excites me more. I look forward to taming my little wildcat."

And then he walks out the door, leaving me naked, chained up and alone.

My mind races, playing quickly over everything that's happened between me and Kohl since the moment I stumbled into that penthouse suite for an "interview."

Jesus. How the hell did I get into this?

Chapter 25
Master

Through the haze of sleep, I feel a pair of strong hands travel up from my waist to my ribs, tugging on me, pulling me out of my dream. Then I feel a hand on my knee, spreading me open, exposing me to the cold air.

I hardly have time to contemplate what's happening before I feel a tongue pressed to my center, licking the length of my entrance. My back arches off the bed as I come awake immediately, pure pleasure infusing me from the base of my spine up to the beaded points of my breasts.

Oh, Jesus.

Instantly, I'm assailed by sensations. Pleasure courses through my veins like liquid fire, spreading through my entire body. I let loose a breathless moan. But when I reach down to run my fingers through his hair where his head is pressed against my center, I realize I can't.

Both of my hands are cuffed to the headboard. Evan has wrapped the chain from my collar's leash all the way around my chest so that it's tight across my nipples. He tugs on it lightly as he continues to work his mouth against my clit. With each dragging breath, he pulls that chain tighter, making my nipples raw with pleasure and pain. His hands press against my thighs, pushing them impossibly wide. I'm spread out before him on the bed like a starfish.

His hands tighten on my thighs as he forces my knees even wider apart. His mouth never leaves me, continuing his relentless assault. His tongue connecting with my clit and then thrusting into me by alternate turns until I'm out of my mind with pleasure, every nerve ending set aflame.

And I'm crying out with animal grunts and calling his name, willing him to bring me to release. After earlier this evening and his abandonment, I'd fallen asleep, still unfulfilled. Now, hours later, I'm *this close* to coming.

But it doesn't take long for me to figure out that he's toying with me. Just when the sensations start to build and intensify, he pulls his mouth away to lick the outsides of my labia, or my thighs, or even up to my navel. As soon as he pulls his mouth away from my center, the build peters out.

Over and over again, he does this so that it becomes a game—how close will he get me before he pulls away again?

"Please—" I finally gasp.

He pulls his head away and looks up at me. "You're on the right track, Madeline. If you beg me nicely enough, I may just let you come."

I twist beneath him, suddenly enraged. Fuck if I'm going to beg him. Making me come brings him pleasure, too. He wouldn't deny me. I can feel his hard cock against my leg. He wants it again—*needs* it again—and if he fucks me, there's no way he can prevent me from coming.

So instead I very visibly bite my lip. He watches me, a smile on his lips. His finger slips down to lightly stroke me, and I almost leap off the bed, panting.

"*Beg*, Madeline. Beg me."

"Evan—*fuck!*" I say as he shoves two fingers into my pussy, his lips twist in a wicked grin as he curls his fingers, touching me at that spot deep inside. *I will not beg.*

"You will beg, and you'll call me *sir.*"

I ignore him, mindless with ecstasy and agony thrumming with every beat of my heart. "Evan—"

Abruptly, he pulls away from me, removing his fingers from my channel. I wait for a second, panting. He can't possibly be serious. His hard-on looks painful, straining.

So I taunt him. "You think you're punishing me? You're also punishing yourself. I can see how much you want to fuck me."

His smile widens, and my heart races. I'm starting to learn to fear that smile. Evan sits up and then swings a leg over me, straddling me over my belly but not resting his full weight on me.

"I'll fuck you soon enough. *How* and *when* I want. Don't you worry about me."

He grasps his cock and starts to stroke it. I rest my head back on the pillow, closing my eyes.

Seconds later, he jerks the chain on my collar and my eyes snap open. "Eyes open. I want you to watch me."

"I don't want to watch you," I snap waspishly.

"I don't care what you want. You will obey. You swore to. And that collar around your neck is that promise. Watch me, Madeline. Watch me come on you."

And I take a deep breath and focus my eyes on the erotic motion of his hand over his cock as he slowly, lovingly strokes himself. The other hand comes down to finger my nipple under the chain and it beads to a point, but that's not nearly enough stimulation to help me along in my quest for an orgasm.

He lets out a low moan as my nipple responds under his firm attention. "Fuck, you feel so good. I want you writhing underneath me, Madeline. I want my cock deep inside you. I want you calling me *master* and begging me to let you come."

I bite my lip and watch as his erection stiffens so that it's pointing straight up. And I'm almost forgetting about my own throbbing sex as I watch him—this smoking hot man—bring himself to orgasm as he fantasizes about me. I admire his cock. It's a thing of beauty, long and girthy, veined and powerful.

Then his grip tightens and his pace quickens and his breath is hissing between clenched teeth. He leans forward and presses his thumb in my mouth, pulling it wide open as he stops, arching, his hot semen spraying on my stomach and breasts. He sits, frozen for a few moments as he continues to pump himself, taking a long time to come. My own sex is throbbing so much it's painful.

"Evan, *please.*"

But he ignores me, reaching down draw a finger through the pool of semen on my belly. He then starts to "mark" me with the sticky liquid, much as he did that first night, massaging his come into my skin—everywhere. He seems absorbed in the task for several long, silent minutes, oblivious to my labored breaths, my throbbing, pleading body.

Soon, he lifts a leg and gets up to go to the bathroom, returning with a hot, wet towel minutes later. He spreads it across my belly and breasts, carefully cleaning me up.

"Please, Evan. Finish me..."

He wipes me dry with another towel and then goes back to the bathroom to deposit them. When he returns, he doesn't come anywhere near the bed. "Do you need to use the bathroom?"

"I need you to finish what you started!" I hiss.

He holds a finger up and wags it at me. "It's too late, Madeline. Consider that for next time."

"Fuck you!" I kick my leg at him, nowhere near close enough to connect. "There isn't going to be a next time!"

That goddamned grin again. "We'll see about that. Sleep well."

And then he's gone. And I lay back, aching, exhausted from pulling against my restraints. Like I'm going to sleep like this?

My body is still thrumming, so flushed with such intense desire that I'm not sure it can ever be satisfied. I'm in real danger of flipping the fuck out. I want to punch him in the balls. He's goddamn lucky that my hands are chained up. Perhaps that's why he did it.

It's hours later when I finally drift off, probably around three in the morning or so and very dark. I manage to make myself comfortable, rolling on my right side to let up on the pressure of my arms. Then, I sleep.

Chapter 26
Hot Desire

THE NEXT MORNING, I'M LYING IN BED, BARELY conscious when he quietly enters the room and stands at the foot of my bed without a word. He watches me from beyond the footboard as I'm stretched out in quite possibly the same position he left me hours before.

I turn my head to look at him and—in contrast to last night—neither his mouth nor his eyes smile.

"Good morning," he says.

"What's good about it?" I reply, stretching my legs out as far as I can as I shift position. His eyes travel down my form, taking in my legs, my hips, my nakedness. The desire there is clearly evident, but I'm not about to let that sidetrack me.

"You hungry?" he asks.

I don't answer, trying to sit up. Both of my hands are still cuffed to the headboard where he'd left me last night.

He comes around the side of the bed to stand about a foot from my knees, his eyes more closely inspecting my naked body. There are marks from his confident possession the night before, across my belly, my thighs. I wonder silently when he'll replace those with bruises. I swallow, trying to ignore how much that thought arouses me.

Actually *everything* is arousing me, him standing so near that I can smell him. The memory of his head between my legs early this morning as I was sleeping. The feel of his mouth and tongue pressing against my center, licking, sucking.

Hot desire streaks through me even in my tired, achy state, and he watches hungrily as my erect nipples betray my arousal, giving him a full report. I curse my traitorous body for giving him the intel.

And I'm aching again—like I never stopped. The unreleased tension is so strong it's almost painful. He quickly bends over me and unlocks the handcuffs around my wrists, and I rub the marks they've pressed into my skin.

"Time for the bathroom, I think. And a shower," he says quietly.

I swallow, my throat dry. I throw a glance at the glass of water he'd left at the side of my bed, and he dutifully takes it up and hands it to me. I drink greedily until there are only a few swallows left, and then, I can't help it, I feel the need to express my rage.

I flick my wrist, dumping the last bits of water into his face. He blinks and straightens, but his expression changes in no other way, and I'm wiggling off the bed, free of him.

I really have to pee, but I have to get out of this goddamn bedroom even more. I'm looking around for something to cover me—a sheet or a towel—but there's nothing. So I head straight for the door when he strides up behind me and grabs that fucking leash and yanks it back.

Not so hard as to break my neck, but definitely hard enough to express his own anger. He wraps the chain around his fist and buries his other fist in my hair, pulling it tight and pulling me back against his heaving chest.

"What was that?"

When I speak, my voice is raspy, tinged with fear. "What did it look like? An expression of my displeasure."

A dry laugh sounds in my ear. He presses his mouth to the side of my head, his hand tightening in my hair so that tears form in my eyes. He pulls me up to my tiptoes, tugging my head backward, and I gasp.

"Your pleasure or displeasure is completely irrelevant."

I swallow, fear streaking down my spine, but I say nothing.

"Do you want to leave?" he repeats his offer from last night. "Or will you submit completely? Those are your only two choices."

"But—"

"Those are your only two choices, Madeline. Go and be gone forever or stay and submit to me *completely*."

"I don't want to leave," I finally say in a shaky whisper.

"That wasn't one of your choices."

Another pause. Neither of us moves. "Fine. I'll stay and submit."

"I won't ask you again. You stay and submit now, you're here for the entire week."

I must be insane. But my body is already responding to him, and as he's pressed up against me, I feel his hard cock against my ass. He's unbelievably turned on as well.

I lean my head back to relieve the pressure of his hand in my hair, but also to relax against him, send him a sign that he can trust me. "I'm sorry."

"Apology not accepted."

He releases me, and I turn to face him. We hold each other's gaze for a long moment and then he glances pointedly at the floor without saying a word or making a gesture. I sink to my knees, face still pointed toward him. "I'm sorry, Evan," I repeat.

He says nothing, moving his gaze away from mine, refusing to look at me. His hands open and close at his sides.

I'm confused. I have no idea what to do, what he wants from me. And apparently I'm supposed to figure it out without him prompting me. On instinct, I fall forward on my hands so that I'm now on all fours. It's humiliating as hell, but it has to be what he wants.

"I'm sorry, sir."

"Lower," he growls from above.

Slowly, I lower myself so that I'm now lying on the carpet at his feet, my face in the floor. "Please forgive me…" I trail off, and then, for good measure, I add, "Master."

His quick intake of breath tells me that I did something right. I don't dare move or look up but I feel him move, step around me. Then things shift and he's kneeling beside me. He runs a hand from the back of my neck, down my spine to my tailbone. His touch burns, igniting my every nerve ending.

"Good girl," he murmurs like he's stroking a dog. "Your submission pleases me. It pleases me a lot."

I'm shocked to note that his admission makes *me* pleased. Almost overpoweringly so. I don't move. I'll wait for his permission to rise. But he doesn't give it. Not yet.

Instead he reaches up and fingers the collar around my neck. "How does this please you, Madeline?"

I swallow, biting back my first instinct, which is to give him an angry, sarcastic retort about taking his fucking collar and sticking it where the sun don't shine.

"My pleasure or displeasure is irrelevant, sir," I reply. His hands stills for just an instant, and I'm suddenly holding my breath, intensely curious.

"Your pleasure will come from pleasing me," he echoes my exact thoughts from a few minutes ago when he was clearly happy with my apology.

"Yes, sir," I reply.

"You've given me your body, Madeline. To do with as I please. Your words should reflect that submission."

I hesitate. "As you command...Master."

Without another word, he bends and scoops me up from the floor, turning me over and pressing me against his broad chest. He turns and heads into the bathroom. I keep my head down, my heart racing in my throat, but I sneak a peek at his beautiful face under my lashes.

He's flushed and slightly sweaty, clearly as turned on as I'm feeling. Except that *he* has had two orgasms in the last twelve hours—one in my mouth, and one when he'd pleasured himself while straddling me, the bastard. I'm still sore and suffering from lack of release. Everything between my legs feels heavy, uncomfortable.

If I'm good, maybe during that shower....

He deposits me near the toilet and says he's going to get some towels. He hasn't given me any instructions, so once I'm done relieving myself and washing my hands, I stand in the spot where he left me. I'm unable or unwilling to move until he returns to tell me what he wants me to do.

When he returns, I see he's removed his T-shirt and jeans and is only in his underwear. He deposits the stack of towels on the counter. "You only use those to dry off. *Never* to cover up. While you are here and collared, you will always be naked."

I bow my head, look at the floor. "Yes, Master."

"In the shower," he says, and I turn to comply.

I enter the shower, which is plenty big for both of us, but he stands outside, instructing me to turn it on and warm the water, which I do. He's standing and carefully watching me through the clear glass. Handing me a new bar of soap that smells wonderful, he orders me to wash myself. And as I comply, he watches me with heated eyes that devour me. I shampoo my hair and soap up every inch of my body.

But before I can step back into the stream to rinse myself, he stops me. Then he turns and pulls a taper candle from a fancy gold candlestick near the sunken bathtub and enters the shower still in his underwear.

He turns me toward the tiled wall and massages my back slowly, his hands gliding over my soapy skin. Every firm stroke of his hands pulls me tighter and tighter, like the string on a bow.

"Touch yourself, Madeline," he says in a voice that brooks no argument nor hesitation.

Flooded with relief that he's going to reward me with an orgasm at last, my hand slips down between my legs. "Slowly, Madeline. You may not come yet."

"But—"

"You do not have permission to speak," he interrupts when I'm about to ask him if he'll let me come today or if this is just still more torture. Stiffly, I comply and say nothing, my hand moving slowly between my legs.

"This is me showing you trust, Madeline. I know how badly you want to come. I know how much you *need* it. And soon, I will give you what you need. *Everything* you need. Even the things you don't yet realize you need. Is that clear? But *you must obey*."

I swallow and continue to rub myself between my legs, each stroke bringing me closer to that elusive release. His hands are moving in circles over my skin, lower and lower until....

His fingers slide into the cleft in my ass, to wash me there. I immediately tense up.

"Relax," he commands, and with a deep breath, I force myself to comply.

"Good," he purrs and that one word rips a hole right through me. I'm suddenly *very* close to coming so I pull my hand away. He notices. "That's a *very* good girl, Madeline..." And his fingers slip lower along the crack of my ass until...his fingertips brush the edge of my anus. I gasp in shock. His other arm, wrapped around my front, tenses, as if he's preparing for my resistance. So I force myself to accept what he's doing to me, realizing that this is the test.

And strangely, as weird as this sensation is—all of it, him washing me, him putting his hand and fingers in my ass, all of it is his way of staking a claim, proving to himself and me that he *does* in fact have complete control of my body, just as he wanted.

"Hands on the wall, Madeline." I brace myself there by doing just as he asks. I shift against him and feel his engorged cock throbbing against me. He groans low and deep, letting out a long breath and an expletive. "I'm going to fucking explode right here and now and it will be your fault. Your submission is driving me insane with lust. I've *never* desired a woman like I want you right now."

His fingers push inside me and there's sharp pain. I let out a yelp and push back.

"Hold still. Remain silent. Your body is mine to do with as I please. And you *will* please me, Madeline."

I feel something cold and hard between my legs and realize that it's the taper candle that he'd grabbed. He's running it along the slit of my sex, as if gleaning my natural lubricant. He rubs it against me over and over again, but not hard enough to allow me to come. My head tips forward to press against the cold tiled wall, and I force myself to relax.

Suddenly he's pressing the blunt end of the candle up to my rear entrance and I jump, balking.

"Take a deep breath and unclench your muscles."

But I don't want to. I don't want him to invade me like this.

His mouth consumes my ear. "Do you want to come, Madeline? Do you want your orgasm? Then you do as you're told and you do not hesitate. Resist again, and I'll chain you to the bed for another day."

I slowly nod and force myself to relax. The minute I do, he's pressing that candle into me, pushing it slowly inside me, applying intense pressure to the closed opening until my muscles give way and it gains entrance.

And he keeps pushing it until it's halfway in.

At first it hurts. He slides it a few times, once pulling at it and pushing again, a few times twitching it to the side. Soon it feels like it's softening, as if absorbing my body's heat.

He's breathing grows more labored and hoarse the more he manipulates the candle inside me. I can tell it's intensely exciting him. But he says nothing, just moans into my ear, telling me how sexy my complete submission is.

With a quick pull that evokes a gasp from me, he yanks out the candle and drops it on the floor of the shower. He grabs me, pressing his mouth to my neck and biting *hard*. I jump, and his erection is hard and huge against me. Then he pulls back abruptly. He's completely sopping wet, his underwear clinging to his straining erection. I can barely take my eyes off his massive cock—the wet material leaves little to the imagination.

"Rinse and then get out and dry off. Wait for me in the bedroom." He pauses. "Kneeling."

I only hesitate a moment. "Yes, Master," I breathe before following his commands.

Ten minutes later, he enters the room. I'm kneeling at the foot of the bed, my eyes on the floor, my hands clasped behind my back. I'm shaking with the cold and also with hunger, but I refuse to say anything. He has a towel wrapped around his waist. And that's all I can see from my angle.

Suddenly, he bends and drapes a bathrobe around my shoulders. "Put it on," he orders me. "I'll be back. But you aren't to leave this room unless I allow it. You aren't even to *ask* to leave. Is that clear?"

"Yes, Master," I say without trying to sound like a robot, though I'm starting, strangely, to feel like one.

My heart can only race with anticipation and even a little fear, unable to wrap my mind around what he might have in store for me next.

Chapter 27
Complete Submission

Once Evan leaves the room, I pull my arms into the robe he's given me and belt it up. The thick, velvety inside warms my cold skin and the shivering stops. I'm still aching from unfulfillment, hoping I get my orgasm soon. Since the night before when I was chained to the bed and later in the shower, he's done nothing but tease me, bring me to the brink and then leave me hanging. It's infuriating, and it's all I can do not to touch myself now for a little relief.

I ponder my next move. Should I get off my knees? But he didn't give me permission. They are starting to hurt from all this time kneeling on the carpet. I could get up and sit on the bed, but he hasn't explicitly allowed that either.

On the other hand, he hadn't actually said not to move. He did say I couldn't leave the room without his permission. I make to get up, grabbing onto the footboard to pull myself up, when I stop, remembering his instructions in the shower. *Wait for me in the bedroom...on your knees.*

Wouldn't it please him more to see that I had taken his commands literally? If I stay as I am...I'll be uncomfortable for a few minutes longer, but the payoff may be a lot greater. It might even be worth it.

I have no further time to dither before Evan steps back into the room with a large tray. He sets it down on the table beside the fireplace, then he takes the chair and sits. He watches me for a moment as I keep my eyes on the floor.

"Come here, my darling."

My heart lurches with joy. He's never called me that before. He's never used any term of endearment. And that one, the way it rolls off his tongue with his British accent—it's delicious and intoxicating. I hobble to my feet, and then, eyes still fixed before me, I stand in front of him, forcing myself to ignore the food. I want to bury my face in that fucking food tray, I'm so famished. I want to strap it onto my face like a food bag. But I resist even looking at it.

"Kneel here, in front of me, and I'll feed you."

One second of hesitation. My fists tighten at my sides. He's *feeding* me now? My one last shred of resistance is rearing its ugly head. He waits, watching. He's tense, poised, almost as if hoping I'll fight him on this.

"Must I repeat myself?" he snaps tersely when I make no move.

I blink, jolting to my knees. "I'm sorry, Master."

"You'll be making up for it later, Madeline. For every indiscretion." He shakes his head in disdain. "You were doing so well there that I'd forgotten you are just a beginner."

Just a beginner.

Suddenly I'm awash with curiosity. Has he done this before? Has he been a dominant to other submissives? He certainly knows what he wants. He seems to know how to "train" me and get me to perform for him, too. A sick, dark feeling roils in my belly. I'm ill with jealousy at the thought of some other woman kneeling before him, accepting his cock into her mouth, swallowing his come, receiving his praise. My face flushes, and he raises a hand to my cheek, smoothing it.

"And you'll learn to hide the anger, too. But we have time. Lots of time for you to improve." His thumb traces my trembling lips and my eyes flutter closed. "And the thought of teaching it all to you makes my cock throb. So let's feed you, shall we? Your lessons await."

And he proceeds to do just that—feed me as I kneel before him. He places small pieces of fruit before my mouth, pushing them in slowly, erotically, forcing me to lick his fingers as he does. He feeds me yogurt that way, too, with his fingers instead of a spoon, indicating that I should suck them clean. There are pieces of cheese, cold sausage. The few times I reach to take the food with my hand, he pulls it away, then finally tells me to clasp my hands behind my back until he's finished feeding me.

When I close my eyes to try to forget this humiliation, he orders them open. He orders me to lock gazes with him. And without a second's hesitation, I do it. For each bite, after I swallow it, I'm to thank him and call him master.

And with each passing second, I'm becoming more and more his.

But still there's this feeling, like the other shoe is about to drop. Those lessons he spoke of...I wonder about them with not a little fear and trepidation and, I'll admit, a spark of excitement.

After he's pushed a ripe berry into my mouth—placing it deep near my throat and slowly withdrawing his finger as my lips close around it—he says, "There you are. You've had enough. We can't have you too full..."

I gulp and swallow the berry whole instead of chewing it. Cold fear streaks through me, and I'm suddenly so wet that the moisture is dripping down the insides of my thighs. He smiles and bends to pull open my robe, pushing it apart and exposing my breasts to him.

"Mmm, now for *my* breakfast." He watches my face closely as he uses both hands to fondle my breasts and teases them to ripe, aching points. Then he's feasting on my neck. He tugs me into his lap so that I'm straddling him. My heated pussy is pressed flush against his hard, straining cock and only the layer of his sweats between us. He strokes my clit and murmurs about how ripe I am. He also tells me that he's going to make me scream so much I won't have a voice left.

I can't wait until he delivers on that promise, too. I'm almost positive that if he breathes on me in a certain way that I'll come at this point. What he's doing to my nipples alone is getting me close. *Again.*

Close but no cigar.

Speaking of cigars. His cock is impossibly hard and straining against me. He can't possibly wait much longer.

"Does it feel good, Madeline?" he asks in a dark, hoarse voice.

I'm about to answer when I realize I may be walking into a trap. "I only want to please my Master," I say.

With a growl, he stands up and pulls my legs so that I clasp them around him. He walks over to the bed but deposits me by the footboard instead. He doesn't tell me to move so I stand and watch as he moves to the headboard and removes the dangling handcuffs there. I swallow a thick lump in my throat. He also grabs two pillows and lays them down across the top of the footboard.

He attaches one set of handcuffs to each of my wrists. Then, bending me over the footboard, cushioned by the pillows, he pulls the other end of each set of the cuffs to lock against the bottom frame of the bed. I'm now on my tiptoes, splayed over the footboard with my ass high in the air. He grabs yet another pillow for my head and front of my chest. I'm now poised in a super awkward—but not uncomfortable, thanks to the pillows—position.

He stands back to admire his handiwork, running an almost reverential hand over my ass. Then, I pick up in my peripheral vision that he's discarding his clothes and going over to the dresser to pull something out of the drawer.

My heart races. Another riding crop? A paddle?

I'm in the perfect spanking position. Perhaps this was what he meant by payment and complete submission?

I could do spanking. I'd actually *enjoy* it.

Maybe if he hit me hard enough, I'd come just from that. I'm almost excited as I adjust myself. The footboard is so high that I'm on my tiptoes and it's hard to readjust. Evan returns to stand behind me and he starts touching my ass again.

"Unless you want your ankles tied down, too, you'll keep your legs open and not move them. Am I clear?

"Yes, Master." My reply is muffled against the pillow.

He continues to rub me. "Such a pretty little ass…"

And he's about to make it *allllll red*. I hold my breath in anticipation. He hesitates, doing something…maybe grabbing for his toy of choice—when suddenly, something very cold touches me right in the asshole.

I yelp and jump, and he places a hand across the base of my spine, holding me still. "Shhh, relax."

"But—"

"You will not speak."

My mouth hangs open as he enters my ass with first one finger, then another. The feeling is strange…not painful, but not comfortable either. I'm tight back there, and I think I know where this is going.

I tense again, fighting with myself on whether or not to protest this. I was a fool to think that he wouldn't test me in this way. I remember that night at the restaurant when I'd told him that anal was a hard limit. His reply is still branded in my brain. *I will own every inch of you. I will dominate you in every way imaginable. There can be no boundaries between us.*

He's been working up to this moment for weeks, but he planned this all along. Because letting him take me this way—in this way I'd told him felt like a degradation—will prove his total domination over me.

Soon he's pumping three fingers slowly in and out of me, and I'm trying hard not to make any noise. I'm still foolishly hoping against hope that his test stops here. That he's going to finish with this and then take me in the pussy, the way we both enjoy it.

But a few more minutes of him murmuring about how much he *needs* to fuck my ass, and he pulls his fingers out, I feel something *much* bigger than fingers at the entrance point.

I jerk up, the cuffs restraining my movements. He might not even listen to me. I'm in no position to fight him. He can take what he wants when I'm like this and he knows it. Slowly, he exerts pressure against my anus, pushing to enter me.

I gasp and tense, clenching.

He pulls back, thank God. I breathe a sigh of relief.

"So you don't want to show me your complete submission? After all this?"

I'm breathing so hard that I'm gasping. "What?"

"This is your chance to show me beyond mere words that you submit to me completely. That I am your *Master*. I intend to take you in the ass, Madeline. Will you stop me?"

My mind races, and I'm so dizzy I'm almost nauseous. "Please."

"Please, what? Take you or don't take you? You make the decision. But remember that there are consequences if you deny me. And remember that you vowed to please me. You *know* what will please me right now. So choose well."

"I don't like how it feels."

"Does that matter? Should I remind you of what you just said to me five minutes ago? That you only wish you please your Master." He pauses, and he shifts how he's standing so that he's pressing up against me again. I squeeze my eyes shut. But somehow I know he won't initiate until I tell him to. "Who is your Master, Madeline?"

"You." My voice comes out small, tiny.

"*What?*"

"You are my Master. *Sir.*"

"And what will please me right now, Madeline?"

"If I let you take me in the ass," I practically sob.

"And will you do that? Will you please me?"

I'm so frustrated right now that I want to bang my head against the wall. Everything is turning, and inside I'm screaming in protest even as my mouth says, "Yes."

"Yes, what?"

I suck in air, fighting my frustration as every muscle in my body tenses. He's pressing the tip of his cock against my ass just enough to remind me that he's there and he's ready.

"Yes, I want to please you. Please take me in the ass." Another deep breath. "*Master.*"

Without hesitation he presses himself into me. There is a sharp burst of pain, and he pushes harder as my body tightens against him. He murmurs to relax again, and I try, but the pain is preventing it.

Soon his hands are on my ass cheeks, spreading me wider. He's ignoring my gasps and grunts and penetrating deeper with each movement of his hips. Only when he's completely buried in my ass does he stop with a growl.

"Do you like that, baby?" I can hear the strain in his voice, the pent-up aggression that I know he's holding back.

The sensation of him buried deep inside my ass is overwhelming, and it's all I can do to breathe, let alone speak. When I hesitate too long, he slaps my ass cheek—hard. I flinch at the sharp sting and squeeze my eyes shut.

"Answer me," he commands.

"Yes, Master."

"Good girl. You *need* my cock in your ass. You'll understand soon."

His hips start moving again in a slow, steady rhythm that stirs something inside me. The pain begins to ebb, and pleasure takes hold. Heat rushes through my body as his fingertips dig into my hips, pulling me toward him.

Just when I think I can't take any more, he reaches around and strokes my clit. I jump at the contact. It's too much, and I try to twist away, but I'm pinned beneath him. Helpless. His touch intensifies, as does his hoarse breathing.

Steadily, with each thrust and stroke, he fucks me harder, deeper. His fingers never leave my clit—swirling, pinching, stroking—as his cock pounds harder into my ass. I'm close. I'm so damn close, and I bite the inside of my cheek to keep from crying out.

With his free hand, he grabs my hair and pulls my head up. The pleasure and pain of it is more than I can take. "I want to hear your moans while I'm fucking you," he growls roughly into my ear.

My climax comes hard and fast, dragging me over the edge and into the abyss. I scream out as pleasure pulses through me, over and over. His cock is still buried deep, his fingers still caressing me, wringing every moan from my body.

This orgasm is incredible, tensing and pulsing all over my body. Wow. Just wow. I don't know whether it was the prolonged buildup to release, the anal, or both that led to *that,* but I can't remember an orgasm this good in a long, long time.

My brain is so fried I can hardly speak and am only peripherally aware of what's going on around me.

With one forceful thrust, he stills inside of me. "Oh, fuck, baby. *Fuck.*" His cock hardens and swells inside my ass, and I feel his orgasm pulse into me, over and over as he gives a hoarse roar.

Minutes later, when he finally pulls out of me, my head falls back onto the pillows. I'm completely exhausted. Unlocking my handcuffs, Evan frees my wrists and pulls me up so that I'm standing toe to toe with him on wobbly legs.

He brushes the hair back from my face and looks me in the eyes adoringly. "Darling Madeline. You've pleased me. *Very much.*"

Those words shouldn't have any power over me, but they do. Tears well up in my eyes, and I can't stop them. He's broken me. He's forced me to look at a part of myself that I never knew existed.

Silently, I weep before him as he kisses my tears away and gently holds me against his warm body. My last shred of resistance has been obliterated.

I am his. Unequivocally.

CHAPTER 28
MASTER'S ORDERS

TEARS STREAM DOWN MY CHEEKS AS I STARE UP AT EVAN. He quietly pulls me against his chest and holds me there and just allows me to cry, rubbing my back and my arm with soothing strokes. His strength wraps around me, holds me up.

A few minutes later, he pulls back and brushes my tears away with his thumb. I see a softness in his gaze that I've never seen before. "Come on, let's get cleaned up."

Threading his fingers through mine, he pulls me toward the bathroom and guides me into the shower again. He steps in after me and turns the water on, adjusting the temperature. I stand there, half dazed, as he lathers me up, his strong hands smoothing gently over my wet skin.

It's over quickly, and I'm a little confused. I half-hoped, half-feared he would bend me over and fuck me again during the shower. Instead, he turns the water off, steps out of the shower, dries himself off.

And then he reaches for me. "Come."

I go to him without hesitation, stepping onto the bathmat and into the dry towel he's holding up for me. With quick, efficient movements, he dries me, and then tosses the towels aside.

And then he does something completely unexpected—he sweeps me up into his arms and carries me out of the bathroom, past the bedroom where I spent the night, then into the hallway. I crane my neck to look around. Where is he taking me?

"I can walk, you know," I say quietly.

I watch him out of the corner of my eyes and notice how the right side of his mouth slants up into a half-mile. Nevertheless, he doesn't respond to my comment. He carries me down to an open door at the end of the hall, walks through and places me on the large bed.

Sitting up, I take in my surroundings. The room is huge, minimalist, decorated in black, white, and shades of gray. Fine art hangs on the walls, and there's a sitting room to the right with a floor-to-ceiling window that looks out over the beach and the relentlessly crashing ocean. It's insanely beautiful.

Then it hits me. This is *his* bedroom.

"Why did you bring me here? I thought I wasn't supposed to leave that other room?"

I get a nice view of his firm ass as he walks to the bed to pick up a remote. "Because..." he says as he presses a button to lower the shades on the windows, "I want you here with me. I know neither of us slept much last night."

Pulling back the thick down comforter, he slides beneath, holding it open for me. I narrow my eyes, wondering what he has planned. Evan is twisted enough to lure me into his bed with the promise of sleep and then fuck me again for hours.

But when I join him under the covers, he turns me onto my side and tugs me against his warm body.

We're spooning. I'm *spooning* with Evan Kohl.

Before I can even contemplate that crazy fact, he nestles his head in the crook of my neck, and we fall asleep.

We sleep for hours, it's late afternoon once we finish napping. I awake to the feel of his skin pressed to mine, the feel of his fingers idly tracing patterns on my bare flesh. When my eyes flutter open, I see that he's staring off into space, propped on his side with me pulled in as close as I can fit, flush against him.

"Mmm," I say, snuggling in tighter to him. "*This* is nice."

His vivid blue eyes snap back to the present, and he smiles down at me, bending to press a kiss to my forehead. "Yes, it is. Are you hungry?"

I smile. "Yeah…I could eat."

"You would be eating regardless," he said. "Master's orders."

Much to my surprise he instructs me to dress in my clothes from last night, handing them to me in a folded, laundered stack. "We'll be going downstairs for a bit. I need to show you around, since you'll be here for the week."

I have to admit to some small relief that I won't have to just sit inside the room the entire time I'm here as his house guest— or pet, or sex slave, or whatever it is that I am.

I hurriedly slip on my clothes from last night while he's inside his giant walk-in closet. But my underwear is missing and I suspect that was no mistake. Instead of complaining to him, however, I end up going commando under the miniskirt. Oh well, at least the rest of me will be covered while out in public.

Though I had heard rumors of certain sections inside Exeter House where clothing was optional or even banned, sex dungeons, orgy clubs and what-have-you. Probably all salacious rumors only. *Too bad.*

Once dressed, I wait for Evan, standing with my hands clasped behind my back and my gaze on the ground. It's stunning how naturally this comes to me now that I know what he expects. I don't even have to think about it. He appears, dressed in jeans, flip-flops and a polo shirt, gorgeous as ever.

Then he takes a hairbrush from the bathroom counter and starts to brush my hair for me. I tilt my chin up, and he seems focused on getting every strand of my hair, arranging it around my shoulders. "There, all ready to go?"

I blink. "Uh…you forgot…" I reach up and tug at the collar.

He tilts his head and stares into my face, eyes intense. "I didn't forget anything. But *you* just forgot to address me properly. I won't tolerate that a second time."

My eyes flick down to the carpet between us. "Forgive me, Master."

He smooths my cheek. "Much better. As for your collar. That will stay on."

"But…"

"As a matter of fact…that gives me an idea, now that you've reminded me how much you're *enjoying* your collar. Giving you still another reason to appreciate it can't hurt." I blink and he turns away from me, steps back into his closet. I suck in a quick breath, cold with fear.

I squeeze my eyes closed, chastising myself for daring to protest. It was probably going to get worse now. Before another second goes by, he's back standing in front of me, holding a small metallic object and two large black marbles in his hand. I peer at them, brow furrowing but don't dare open my mouth again, for fear of making things worse.

He unscrews the handle from my leash and attaches the round object, then demonstrates for me to see. It's a magnet and the two marbles are attracted to it.

"Heavily magnetized hematite," he says.

My heart races with dread and excitement at once. Where will those go?

He pulls one of them off the magnet with some difficulty and tells me to open my mouth and he places it inside. "Get that nice and wet for me, Madeline. There's a girl."

I roll it inside my mouth while staring at him with wide eyes. The ball is very heavy on my tongue and about the size of those jawbreaker candies I used to love as a kid. When he tells me to open my mouth, he pulls it out and replaces it with the other one.

"Open your legs," he breathes. Then he puts both of the balls on the end of the magnet, which is now attached to the end of my leash. He threads the leash down the front of my skirt and pushes the balls firmly inside me.

They feel cold, heavy. Somehow I'm supposed to walk with these inside me? And the leash hangs down the front of my shirt before tucking into my waistband. I'm supposed to go out there looking like a puppy dog with a visible collar and leash? My face flushes with heat—though whether from humiliation or anger, I couldn't say.

Evan is watching me closely.

"Do you have something you'd like to say to me, Madeline?"

Fuck. Damn it. This is bullshit. Couldn't he just make it easier by *not* asking my opinion?

I look up at him, and I'm sure the internal war is evident on my face. His mouth turns up in an expectant smile, a flame of desire licking the back of his blue, blue eyes.

"Well?"

"I—uh." I swallow and look back to the floor. "Thank you, Master," I finally whisper.

"You are most welcome. I think you'll enjoy how they make you feel. More importantly, I'll enjoy knowing that they are inside you, making you feel good. And as for the collar..." He fingers the infinity symbol that dangles from my throat. "Well let's just say there are some definite benefits to wearing this downstairs, too. You'll see."

With puzzlement, I wonder at that, following him out of the bedroom. The first few steps I take, I walk with a weird, wobbling gait, all too aware of the heavy balls inserted in me, pulling everything down. Every step makes me more and more aware of them and my sex starts to throb with arousal. These balls readily remind me that I am a sexual being. *And* they remind me that while I'm here, I live to receive and give pleasure to Evan Kohl.

My master.

Chapter 29
Something Dangerous

ONCE INSIDE THE ELEVATOR, EVAN PULLS ME TO HIM and kisses me deeply. I return the thrusts of his tongue with my own, and his breath hitches, holding me flush against his rock-hard erection. "Fuck," he whispers against my mouth. "You are intoxicating."

His hand slips under my skirt and he tugs against the chain a couple times before rubbing it, cold and rough, against my wet clit. I jump, like I've been jolted by an electric shock. He breaks the kiss and presses his mouth against my temple, breathing deeply. "I can't stop thinking about all the things I'm going to do to you this week."

I swallow and let out a small whimper instead of speaking. The thought and anticipation of what this week will bring are undoing me, too. But first, I'm dying to see the rest of Exeter House.

We ride the elevator down to the fourth floor, which, Evan explains to me, is the main floor for members. The first three floors of the building are part of the public-facing part of the establishment. Rooms can be taken there by hopeful members of the house or even non-members who pay high premiums. There are restaurants, bars, various designer boutiques, a coffee shop, and even a nightclub on those levels, as well.

I glance around. "How will they know I belong here?" This place is so swanky, *I'm* not even sure I belong here.

He taps on the infinity symbol that dangles from my collar. "This will identify you as *mine*." That last word rolls off his tongue like a caress and sends a hot ember of desire skipping down my spine.

My thoughts are cast back to earlier, when he entered me from behind, sending a wave of sharp pleasure rocking through me. He was right. It turns out, I like being fucked in the ass, and I already want more.

During his "dime tour," Evan demonstrates that the place has everything the decadently wealthy could want—and even some special locked doors he doesn't explain, but which instantly stir my curiosity.

He checks his phone after it's chimed insistently several times. Then he sighs, pulling me close and kissing me deeply. "It looks like I have to run to the office for a little while. I want you to grab something to eat and have some fun exploring. And you can always do some shopping. Get anything you want. They know to charge it to me. Don't leave the premises and back upstairs before four."

"Do you have to go?" I hate the petulance in my tone, but the thought of him leaving me here, alone, is a little intimidating. Only the elite and their "associates" wander these halls. I'm just a broke grad student, and I can't help but feel inferior.

He must sense the direction of my thoughts because he smiles and kisses me again, this time quickly on the lips. "You belong here with me, Madeline, so you'd better get used to all of this. You'll do just fine."

I nod and force a smile. "Yeah, you're right. I'll be fine," I echo.

As much as I enjoy submitting to Evan Kohl in the bedroom, I'm still an independent woman, and this is a perfect opportunity to prove that to both him *and* myself. I've got this. *Totally.*

With one more swift kiss, Even trots off to get his work done, and I'm left in what amounts to America's Kensington Palace, sans the history. The lobby area where I'm standing is huge, circular, with gorgeous frescoes covering the ceiling. The mosaic tiles beneath my feet are equally ornate and colorful and, together with the white, decorative pillars all around, give me a Greco-Roman vibe. The forest of fresh flowers arranged in huge vases all about just scream insane wealth. This place is unreal.

It doesn't take me long to figure out that the members are almost all men and their "close associates" are all women, many very elegantly dressed. Nearly every one of them is wearing a collar similar to mine.

"Can I be of assistance to you, Miss Swanson?"

I spin around to see a pleasant young guy in a gray vest with red hair, green eyes and a wide smile on his face. His name badge says Andrew.

"Oh, you know my name." My hand flies to my collar and I touch the infinity emblem. I don't know why, maybe it's my anchor to Evan.

Andrew's smile grows larger somehow. "Mr. Kohl was kind enough to inform us of your stay, and I'm happy to assist you with anything you may require while you're with us here at Exeter House."

"Oh. Cool, thanks. I was just exploring, wondering what I should do first."

Andrew steps to the side and indicates a door to the far right. "May I recommend the spa? Our massage therapists are world-class, and many associates enjoy the exquisite treatments we offer before starting their day."

There's that word, again. *Associates.* Well, at least it isn't *mistress.*

"Great," I say.

He indicates the front desk. "I'll be here if you need anything. My shift ends at seven, then Chloe will be on duty."

"Thanks, Andrew."

I make my way over to the spa, and I'm immediately whisked inside, stripped and swathed in the softest terry cloth I've ever felt in my life. A lovely woman leads me into a private room, where a massage therapist is waiting.

The next hour is pure, unadulterated heaven. I've never had a deep tissue massage, but by the end, my limbs are jelly and I feel so relaxed, I have trouble retaining the balls Evan inserted inside me. Honestly, he'd never know if I chose to remove them and slip them back in later, but I *want* to do as he has told me. To please him. And if I cheat, I'll feel like I failed him.

After my massage, I'm offered a light meal of spa food— sandwiches, fruit and cucumber-infused water. Then I'm led to a room full of reclining beds, where I'm given a twenty-four-carat gold face mask. The mask is cool, and soothing, and after that massage, I'm practically falling asleep on the bed.

"You must be Evan Kohl's new girl."

I open my eyes to see a woman lying on the bed next to me. She's about ten years older than I am, but with her long brown hair and full, curvaceous figure, she's beautiful. Perfect. And she's wearing a collar much like mine, except the medallion on hers is a stylized lion head. She studies me with a set of wide brown eyes. Even without makeup, she's stunning. More power to her.

But what I would give to know what she's thinking... I'm not Evan's usual type. I'm not *any* billionaire's usual type, as a matter of fact. I'm just a broke graduate student with daddy issues, so it must be a shock for her to see me here, wearing Evan's symbol at my throat.

"Yes, I'm Maddy." I shake my head. "I mean, Madeline."

She nods, smiling before laying her head back down on the pillow. "I'm Grace. Welcome to Exeter House."

"Evan Kohl is so fucking hot," another woman says. She's lying on the bed across from us, swathed in terrycloth, wearing a mud face mask. "It's too bad what happened last year."

That piques my interest. "What do you mean?"

Grace clicks her tongue. "Jess, don't scare her." She glances at me briefly before placing her head back on the pillow so her mask doesn't slide off. "Don't listen to her. Nothing happened. She's right, though, Kohl is hot as fuck. You're lucky you landed him, as long as you don't get too attached."

I mentally scoff at that. It's more like *he* landed *me*. I didn't want any of this, initially. And as for getting attached, Evan wouldn't allow that, even if I wanted to. He was quite explicit about that when we started down this sordid path.

"He's a bit of an enigma," I say cryptically. I don't know these women, so I don't want to confide too much. But I'm so new to this world, and it'd be nice to talk to someone about it.

Jess laughs. "Enigma is putting it lightly. He has a reputation at Exeter House for being dangerous. *No one* is going to fuck with you here, that's for sure."

Dangerous?

Evan can be intense, but I've never been fearful. Though, I remember the brief flash—him throwing a vase across the room, shattering it to bits. When I went to that bar with Sam and Keith, he was upset, almost violent. It just reminds me how little I actually know about Evan.

"What do you mean by *dangerous?*" I ask.

I'm still lying down with my mask on, so I can't see Jess, but I hear her sharp intake of breath. "You don't know?"

"Jess!" Grace snaps. "Honestly, Madeline, don't listen to all the gossip. One thing you'll learn about Exeter House is that there's *always* drama. Most of it is harmless."

After that, there was no touching the topic again. Grace was determined to talk about nothing but the weather and which shoes were appropriate to wear to afternoon tea.

After the spa, I'm loose and languid, relaxed, and most of the soreness from all the sex with Evan has been worked from my body. I emerge feeling rejuvenated and ready for another night of passion with the man I now call *Master.* A heady thrill shivers down every nerve as I pass down another elegant marble hallway. I'm so lost in my thoughts that I don't realize that I'm *actually* lost until I've forgotten how I got where I'm currently standing.

Retracing my steps, I turn down another hallway that dead-ends in one of those mysteriously locked black doors that Evan didn't explain to me during his quick tour. There are several visible mechanical locks and a keypad as well. There's little chance of someone wandering in by chance, though I try the knob anyway, unsurprisingly unable to open it.

The surface is black enameled paint, shiny and glossy, the fixtures brass and almost old-fashioned and decorative. Before I have any time to turn back and try another route, the door opens abruptly and I jump about a foot, eyes and mouth so wide I'm sure I look like a cartoon character who's been caught committing some heinous crime.

The man on the other side of the door is gorgeous beyond belief. Tall, elegantly dressed in a designer suit with no tie, dark hair. I blink. Is this some kind of gorgeous-only billionaires club? Beautiful people are everywhere.

"Oh, well hello there, darling. Aren't you lovely?" His deep voice complements a disarming British accent, only a little different from Evan's. His face splits in a grin, and he winks at me affably.

My face heats immediately. "I, uh, I'm sorry. I wasn't trying to—"

His eyes flick to my collar, and a dark brow ticks up. "I'd invite you inside, lovely, but I'm certain your man would not approve. In fact, he'd have my hide if he knew I was the one inviting."

I blink and swallow. "I was just…I'm lost. Looking for the elevator."

He nods. "Allow me." And holds out a hand in the direction I came. I precede him back down the hallway after he's carefully shut the mystery door.

"It can be rather confusing when you're new. You're, ah, quite new, aren't you?"

I toss him a quick glance over my shoulder. "Yeah, new to here, anyway."

"Well, you'll have it down in no time. I'm Ash, by the way. Ash Grayson. Evan is my mate."

At that moment, the hallway widens, and he directs me to turn left. "I'm, ah, Madeline. Madeline Swanson."

His head turns to me, and now that we are walking side by side in the wider hallway, I feel his appraising stare sweep me from head to toe. "Yes, I seem to recall him mentioning you once or twice. Good to finally meet you. You'll be sure to let him know I said hello? Turn right, here."

We round the corner and are now standing at a bank of burnished gold-mirrored elevators. Without a word, Ash swipes a black card, enters a code and the doors open. "This one will go straight to his penthouse."

"Thank you," I breathe in relief. "You've been so kind. I'll definitely tell Evan you said hi and were very helpful."

His features sober for a moment, and he looks up, meeting my gaze. "Yes, definitely tell him I never touched you, right? Never even laid a finger on you."

I bark out a laugh but quickly realize he's not laughing with me. Then, I sober. However, just before the door shuts, he sends me another charming wink.

I swallow, frowning. What is all that about?

When Evan gets home that evening, I have my textbooks spread out across his giant bed. I'm on my stomach, earphones in, reading about solid mechanics, so I don't even hear him come in. I feel his warm hand on the back of my thigh before it moves upward, slipping beneath the mini skirt I'm still wearing.

I flip over with a squeal, slapping him on the arm. "Hey!"

He's already on top of me, capturing my laugh with a deep, hungry kiss. My mini skirt is now up around my waist, exposing my lower half. His fingers find my entrance, tugging on the chain between my thighs. Somehow, I managed to keep the balls in all day. "You've been a good girl," he says, and my heart soars at his approval.

"It wasn't easy," I say.

He pulls back and looks down at me. "I couldn't stop thinking about you today."

I smile up at him. "Oh, really? What exactly were you thinking about?"

"That pretty little mouth wrapped around my cock."

"Mmmm, that could be arranged," I tease. I've been thinking about it all day, too. That, and something else... "Hey, um, can I ask you something?" I say, abruptly switching topics.

He shifts his hips, so his rock-hard cock is pressed against my wet pussy, the only barrier is the fabric of his suit pants. "Yes?"

"A couple of girls at the spa mentioned you and said something happened last year. What were they talking about?"

His brows twitch together only momentarily before he shakes his head. "Just gossip. It's nothing to worry about." He threads his fingers through mine, kissing my knuckles and looking down at me with those dazzling blue eyes.

"Now, what was the rule, Madeline, do you remember? While you are here..." he prompts.

I sit up, stiffening, putting a self-conscious hand on my clothed chest. "I'm sorry. I forgot to take my clothes off, Master."

The corner of his mouth quirks up. "Do it now, then. And if you please me well enough, I'll let it pass—*this* time."

Immediately, I jump from the bed and comply, pulling my clothes off, almost frantic to obey him. When I start to kneel, he stops me.

"Right now, I'm going to feed you some dinner." He presses his thumb to my bottom lip. "And *then* you're going to suck my cock dry with that pretty mouth."

I smile and nod, and try to push the uncertainty away. Maybe he's right. Didn't Grace say there's always drama at Exeter

House? I desperately want to believe that's all it is. Idle gossip. But I can't shake the feeling that Evan is hiding something from me. Something dangerous.

CHAPTER 30
CHAMPAGNE AND SECRETS

THROUGHOUT THE COURSE OF OUR PRESCRIBED WEEK together, Kohl's agenda seems intent on emphasizing the fact that I am a sexual being and that, during this week, I exist in this context to serve him.

So our somewhat regular routine starts the very next day. Instead of waking up and getting ready for my Monday morning classes, I am awakened and commanded to suck him off.

Every morning starts with a blowjob. After waking me in the early hours before he goes off to work, he either directs me to get on my knees or I go down on him while lying on the bed.

Then, as is his new habit, he feeds me my breakfast by hand. At first I'm annoyed by the insistence, but the routine starts to feel somewhat...comforting.

As he'd promised, my schoolwork is sent to me daily by my professors, and I spend much of the morning studying before being permitted to dress and explore the lower levels of Exeter House. Sometimes to go shopping, sometimes to visit the spa. One day, I surprise him with a Brazilian wax.

His response to that surprise could not have been more amazing. He spends hours giving me oral, exploring me in all my depilated glory, bringing me to orgasm after orgasm until my voice is hoarse from moaning and screaming his name.

Nights give me the hot thrill of anticipation. He texts me when he leaves his office, and I'm freshly showered, naked and ready for him, kneeling in the front room when he arrives.

Dinner comes soon after, and he feeds me that by hand as well, while I sit in his lap. Then, the entire night stretches before us. Sometimes, he has an entire scene in mind. I'm cuffed to the bed and whipped or tied up while he fucks me into oblivion. Other times, he denies me his cock, teasing me, drawing out my desire until I'm practically screaming for release.

But it's late at night, when we're both spent and every last drop of pleasure is wrung from our bodies that I really feel connected to him. We feast on snacks, cuddling beneath his five-million-thread-count sheets, and watch something completely inane, like pottery-making on YouTube, or a documentary on bees. It doesn't really matter what it is. We're together. And then we fall asleep that way, all tangled up in each other, with the TV still on.

The week flies by as if we're immersed in some alternate reality, and I'm wondering how the transition back to my normal real world will go when I wake up late on Saturday morning and realize I'm alone.

The tempting aroma of coffee hits my nostrils, and I roll over onto my side, opening my eyes. The bed stretches for miles, but except for me, it's empty. Kohl is gone.

On the bed next to me there's a large, flat box with a smaller box on top of it, an envelope taped to the top. An insulated cup of Starbucks sits on the nightstand.

I reach for the coffee and turn my attention to the boxes. Taking a sip of my latte, I tear the envelope off and open the short, handwritten note inside.

Madeline,

Gala tonight. I will be home at 8 p.m. to pick you up.

E

Typical of Kohl. No explanation about where he is or what he's doing. I stare at the note and will it to be charming and flirtatious, or at the very least, informative. It's neither. Charming and flirtatious just isn't Kohl's style. Neither is informative, for that matter.

Setting the note and my coffee down, I pull open the large box. I dig through the tissue paper until my hands find soft, buttery satin. It's a dress.

Standing, I pull out the miles and miles of deep-blue fabric. There's a full-length mirror on the other side of the room, and I stand in front of it, pulling the gown up to my naked body. It's beautiful. Gorgeous, actually. Strapless, form fitting, with a strip of satin gathered at the left hip—flowing down beautifully into a slender, elegant skirt.

And it looks like it will fit me perfectly.

The smaller box is a pair of silver strappy heels that complement the dress. And they're exactly my size. Of course.

For a second, I wonder if this is Miriam's work, or if Kohl managed to pick these out himself? I'm going with Miriam. No straight man should be able to pick out a gown and shoes this beautiful.

A cell phone rings somewhere in the room, and I jump. Placing the dress on the bed, I search for the source of the ringing. I find it on the coffee table, hooked to a charging cord, in the adjoining sitting room. It's *my* cellphone.

Swiping the screen, I answer. "Hello?"

"Good morning, Miss Swanson. It's Miriam. Mr. Kohl asked me to inform you that the stylists will be there in a few hours."

"Uh, stylists?"

"Mr. Kohl will be there to pick you up at eight."

"Okay. Thanks."

The stylists arrive a few hours later. They sweep inside the penthouse like a small army—one guy and three women—a hairstylist, manicurist, stylist, and seamstress, respectively. For the next several hours, I'm waxed and painted, my hair is cut, given highlights and a blowout, then curled into tight ringlets and sprayed with twenty metric tons of hairspray. My eyebrows are arched, full manicure and pedicure. The works. By the end of it all, I feel like Anne Hathaway in *The Princess Diaries*. Completely transformed.

Smoothing my hands down the satin skirt, I appreciate my reflection in the mirror when the door to the bedroom opens.

Kohl strides in, kisses me on the lips, and heads straight into the closet. When he emerges minutes later, he is dressed in a sharp black suit, starched white shirt and black bow tie.

He is so fucking hot. And he's mine.

He walks up to me confidently, sliding his arm around my waist. "You look so gorgeous in this dress." He tugs me against his hard chest and leans in to nibble on my neck. "And I can't wait to fucking rip it off your luscious body."

Heat twists through my body, and I bite my bottom lip. "Don't you dare," I tease. "This took six plus hours and a team of people to accomplish. Plus, you've seen enough of me naked."

"I don't think so." He shoots me a grin.

I kiss him on the lips. "Thank you for arranging all that, by the way."

He smiles down at me—a genuine smile that makes my insides liquefy. He taps the collar I'm still wearing and shows me a slim key he's holding in his hand. Then he turns me around to unlock it, moves to the nearby dresser and places it inside, pulling out a jewelry box in its stead. He turns to me with a chain dangling from his fingertips. It's the infinity necklace he'd given me weeks ago—the bead diamonds glinting in the evening light.

"You'll wear this instead of the collar tonight. It pleases me to see you bearing my symbol. Everyone will know you're mine. And while the collar is entirely appropriate for Exeter House, out in the world, this necklace will do."

He turns me around and fastens the elegant necklace, his knuckles brushing against my skin, sending a hot shiver down my spine. I've discovered the pleasure in obeying him. And I've discovered the power in giving him pleasure.

"Yes, Master."

He kisses my neck behind my ear, watching my face in the mirror on the far side of the room. "How does it feel to have the collar off?"

I touch my throat, then the beautiful diamonds on the necklace. "I feel a little...well...naked."

He smiles. "Told you that you'd miss it."

While I wouldn't go *that* far, it does feel different. But I say nothing and he studies me in the mirror from behind before reaching up to run a finger under my bottom lip.

"I'm going to fuck this pretty little mouth tonight. In fact, I think I'd rather like fucking you in every opening." He smiles wickedly, probably imagining it, and my heartbeat races. "In the meantime, however, we have a gala to attend and people to wow. Let's get this over with, shall we? So I can get back to enjoying you in every way."

The town car is waiting for us at the grand front entrance of Exeter House. As we settle in, Kohl pours us each a glass of champagne from the ice bucket and waiting flutes in the back. I down mine in one swallow, desperate to calm my rioting nerves. I've been to several upscale events in my life—mostly benefit dinners and garden parties with my parents. But I've never been to a gala, and on the arm of one the world's most brilliant minds, it's more than a little nerve-wracking.

The event is only twenty minutes away, and by the time the car stops, I've had two glasses of champagne. My head is swimming and my lips are pleasantly numb as the door opens and the driver helps me out of the car. Kohl is right behind me, one strong hand clutching my elbow, the other pressed against the small of my back.

"Just stay close to me and you'll do fine."

I look up into his eyes and blink. Can he sense my anxiety? I shouldn't be surprised. In the last week, we'd connected—body and mind—in ways I never knew possible. We shared intimacy I've never experienced with anyone else.

We make our way up a red carpet—an *actual* red carpet— that's been rolled out over the museum steps. We're quickly swallowed by a crowd of famous actors and wealthy entrepreneurs as photographers call out Kohl's name, imploring him to stop for a photo.

We don't stop. Thank God. Instead, he guides me through the museum's Art Deco-style entrance and through to the ballroom. My heart leaps up into my throat as my gaze takes in the elegant room. Round tables, draped in white and topped with golden centerpieces stuffed with fluffy white fresh hydrangeas. Thousands of twinkling lights dangle in beautiful chaos from the high ceiling, drenching the room in a soft golden glow. It's beautiful.

But more than the decor catches my attention. There are several beautiful women in the room, and they all seem to be looking Kohl's way. Of course they are. *He's* fucking beautiful.

And he's *mine*.

With all the confidence of a woman who'd just been fucked by this man almost continuously for six days straight, I thread my arm through his and walk beside him, head high, as we find our table. To my surprise, we're sitting with Jim Carrey, his date, and a few other people I only vaguely recognize.

At some point during dinner, my bladder decides it's had enough. Maybe it's the tight dress, or the three layers of underwear I'm wearing, or the copious amounts of champagne I consumed during the pregame. Whatever the cause, the issue suddenly becomes urgent. I take the napkin off my lap and place it on the table.

"You okay?" Kohl asks.

I smile at him. "Too much champagne. I'll be right back."

Rising to my feet, I make a restrained beeline for the first doorway and find the ladies' room pretty easily. My heels click on the polished tile as I head to one of the empty stalls and fight oodles of satin to be able to use the toilet. When I'm done, there's a woman standing at the long vanity, reapplying her mascara. As I approach the sink, she catches my gaze in the mirror. Her eyes then linger on the infinity symbol hanging around my neck.

Turning, she faces me. "Hey, you're here with Evan Kohl, aren't you?"

Mention of Kohl sets me off balance a little. I take in the woman with new eyes—slender, beautiful with long brown hair, high cheekbones and blue eyes. She looks vaguely familiar, but I can't place her.

"I am," I say with a smile. I pump soap into my palm, rub my hands together and place them under the faucet. "Why do you ask?"

The woman places her tube of mascara into a red sequined clutch she's carrying and focuses her full attention on me. "I dated him once. A couple years ago. He really fucked me up."

I blink at her, stunned that she would just delve into such a heavy topic in the middle of a public bathroom. And with a complete stranger.

"I'm sorry." What else can I say?

She shrugs her slender shoulders. "It's fine. I got over it." She smiles shakily. "*Eventually*. Though it did take several grand in therapy and a shit-ton of vodka."

My mind is buzzing with a thousand questions—who is this woman? Who was she to Kohl? And what did he do to fuck her up so badly? Does this have anything do with what Grace and Jess were talking about at the spa? I could just duck out of the room if she wasn't standing between me and the only exit. This is beyond awkward.

I take a step to the side, a clear signal that I want to leave. "I'm glad you're doing better," I say.

She steps directly in front of me, deliberately blocking me again, and I feel a moment of panic. Suddenly, I'm suspicious that she saw me get up from the table and followed me in here. Who retouches mascara unless they've been crying?

She smiles, clearly trying to set me at ease. "I only mean to warn you—like I wish someone had done for me. Evan is not a good man. He's sexy as hell, but he'll rip your heart to shreds without remorse."

I frown. "What do you mean?" I can't help it. She's baited me.

"Two of his exes were shipped off to rehab for addiction, one is now in a mental hospital. I think she's got paranoia or depression or something."

"Addiction and depression are common enough," I respond. "Especially if they're in the entertainment business. It seems a little unfair to blame Evan for all that."

"His fiancée killed herself last fall."

The words are said so abruptly, I'm convinced she's actively trying to throw me off balance. And she succeeds. *Fuck.* I don't know what shocks me more—the fact that he was engaged and didn't tell me, or the fact that the woman killed herself less than a year ago. Both have me reeling.

"I Googled him months ago. There was nothing about a fiancée killing herself." The gossip sites would have reported that, guaranteed. Sex and death sell, and there's no way they'd pass that up—even if it were only half true.

When I lift a disbelieving brow, she says, "Don't believe me? Just ask him. He told me the first week we were dating." With a smug smile, she opens the door and steps out, leaving me in the bathroom alone with that little bomb.

He'd confided in her the first fucking *week* they'd dated, and months later, he's still said nothing to me? I'm such an idiot. I'd naively believed we'd shared something special—something neither of us had experienced with anyone else.

I glance up at myself in the mirror. My cheeks are flushed and my eyes are watery. I look like I'm about to cry. Maybe I am. The truth is, I don't know how I'm feeling. I just feel numb.

I close my eyes and take a few deep breaths, then walk out of the bathroom and back to my table. When I sit down, Kohl's hand finds my thigh and he squeezes. It's an intimate gesture, one that speaks of the familiarity we've shared over the last few weeks. But after that run-in with his ex, I wonder just how deep that familiarity goes. Is this all just physical? Had I imagined the deeper connection?

When I don't respond to him, he turns to look at me. I can see him from the corner of my eye, daring me to continue ignoring him. I just keep my gaze trained on the stage, listening to some old guy drone on about how thankful the museum is for everyone's patronage. I don't hear any of it. All I can think about are that woman's words to me, her brutal warning: *He'll rip your heart to shreds.*

CHAPTER 31
TERMINATION NOTICE

I'M RELIEVED WHEN THE END OF THE NIGHT ARRIVES AND Kohl ushers me into the town car. As soon as the car door shuts behind us, he turns his focus on me.

"What's the matter?"

I don't want to get into this with him right now—not when I'm feeling so fragile. But I know he won't allow me to shrug him off.

"I ran into one of your exes in the bathroom," I say. "She told me about your fiancée and all the other women."

"*Fuck.*" He tilts his head back and rubs his right temple with the tips of his fingers. "I saw Whitney there with some D-list actor. I should have known she would hunt you down."

"Tell me she was lying. Tell me none of it is true."

Raising his head, his eyes narrow at me, and a muscle ticks in his jaw. I shift in my seat, suddenly aware of his change in mood. He's angry now. It's a subtle shift, but I can practically *feel* the waves of anger rolling off him.

"My past is none of your business," he says stiffly, looking away.

None of my *business*? Is he fucking serious?

I clench my hands into fists, and my cheeks flush with anger. How dare he shut me down and refuse to answer. After everything we've shared, I deserve the truth. He owes me that much.

Then it occurs to me—the women. That's what this is all about. The contract, his need for control. It's all connected.

"Oh, I get it. Okay," I say, nodding. "The contract, everything, is all an effort to control something that no one has any power over."

He turns those beautiful eyes on me. "And what might that be?"

"Human emotion."

He looks away again, and I can see his jaw clench. He's not going to confirm or deny my statement. He's not giving me a fucking inch.

"You can control my body, my orgasms, but you can't control my heart, Evan." I look straight into those intense blue eyes. "You can't control how I feel about you."

He straightens his shoulders and looks away, shutting me out again. So I do the only thing I can—I tell him how I feel. No games, no politeness. Just the raw, honest truth. "I'm in love with you, Evan."

He turns to face me, his face drawn in anger. Reaching over, he grabs my chin and holds it between his thumb and forefinger. "Don't fool yourself into thinking you're special, Madeline. This, what we have, is sex. Two people fucking. Nothing more."

His words cut me deeper than anything else could have. Pain slices through me, and I pull my chin out of his grasp. "You're telling me you felt *nothing* for me in the last few weeks?"

I don't want to believe that. I want to believe he's only pushing me away because he's afraid. That nothing he's saying is true. But when I look into his eyes, all I see is cold indifference staring back at me. No hint of the passion and tenderness I saw in him last night.

"This is an arrangement. Your body for my money. There's no room for emotion."

It feels as though all the air has left my lungs, like I've been punched in the gut.

Your body for my money.

He's making me sound like a prostitute. And that's exactly why it hurts so much, because he's right. My feelings for him don't change the hard facts. I've been fucking him for money.

I sit back, suddenly ill. My stomach is churning. I've become the thing I hate most. The mistress. The *whore.*

When the car finally pulls into the Exeter House driveway, I don't move. I can't. I just stare out of the window blankly. The pain in my chest is intense, too much.

When I don't move, Kohl gets out and comes around to open the car door for me. My legs shaking, I stand, gripping the top edge of the door for support. We're face-to-face now, so close I can feel the heat of his breath on my cheek.

Had it been any other night, I know he would have kissed me. He would have pulled me out of the car, taken me upstairs and fucked me until we were both too exhausted to move.

But something has shifted between us. I can *feel* him pulling away, hiding behind the walls he's put up to keep the world at arm's length.

You know what? Fuck him. Kohl has ripped me wide open, made me feel things he had no right to make me feel—and then has the nerve to pretend our connection means nothing.

"Stay in the penthouse tonight. Tomorrow morning, I'll ask Jefferson to take you home, and I'll have Miriam send over the termination documents."

I blink, confused. "Termination documents?"

The what-the-fuck look on my face must make my confusion apparent because he says, "This is over, Madeline."

He sounds so cold and detached. But that's what this is right? An arrangement. A contracted relationship. Nothing we had was genuine. Nothing between us is real.

Then why do I feel so…heartbroken? God, I sound like a fucking Hallmark movie. But it's true. He's torn my heart to shreds and now he's just going to walk away.

"Yeah," I say, fighting back the tears. "Whatever."

And then I turn and walk toward the Exeter House entrance. As I approach the large double doors, I hear the car door slam shut and the town car take off down the street.

Inside, the penthouse is dark, and a feeling of emptiness washes over me. Tossing my clutch into a chair, I kick my heels off and leave them in the living room, then head into one of the guest bedrooms.

I turn on the light and slither out of my gown, removing the metric ton of underwear, before falling into bed—stark naked and exhausted. And then I do something I swore to myself I'd never do. I curl up and cry.

CHAPTER 32
OFF BALANCE

THE FOLLOWING DAYS PASS IN A TEAR-INDUCED BLUR. My chest hurts, my head hurts. Everything hurts, and all I can think about is Kohl. I fluctuate between hating him and loving him. Between wanting to bite his dick off with my teeth, to praying he'll show up at my door on bended knee to apologize and profess his love for me.

I'm a fucking mess.

The day after the gala, I moved out of Hill House, leaving everything he'd ever given me behind—the necklace, the gown, the underwear, *everything*. If I'd had more energy, I might have burned it all. Maybe it would have given me some semblance of closure. Instead, I begin to throw myself into my graduate work. I have experiments running in the lab and papers that need to be written—plenty of things to keep my mind busy. And yet...every other thought is of Kohl. Enigmatic, fucked-up Kohl.

Nearly a month after he dropped me at Exeter House with his cold declaration that we were terminated, I'm staring at a full bowl of milk and Cheerios when Sam walks into the kitchen. It's nice to be back in a house full of women again. At Hill House, unless Kohl was there with me, I was completely alone.

"Hey, Mads. Ready to head over to the lab?"

I push the bowl of cereal away. "Um, yeah. Let me just grab my bag."

"Aren't you going to eat your cereal?"

"I'm not hungry, actually."

I haven't eaten in days, really. I poured the bowl of cereal with the intention of forcing it down, but I just can't. I'll grab something at the cafeteria later. Maybe.

As we head out the door, Sam turns to me, stopping me on the sidewalk. "Mads, uh, there's something I need to tell you."

It's the way her eyes dart away from me that makes my stomach lurch. "What?" I choke.

"It's, um, about Kohl."

I shake my head. Whatever it is, I don't want to hear it. "Sam, no—"

"He's interviewing for a new mistress," she blurts out. "My cousin told me last night. I know it must come as a shock, but I felt like you had a right to know."

Shock doesn't even come close to what I'm feeling. Anger, betrayal, sadness, it all swirls inside me like a violent storm. In my mind's eye, I can see that line from months ago—models and hopeful actresses waiting outside his hotel room, all competing for the position of his mistress. My stomach wrenches into a twist.

Fuck him.

Fuck the damn models.

It's not my problem anymore, right?

Kohl and I were doomed from the beginning, from the moment I stumbled into his hotel room and saw his beautiful face. From the moment he first kissed me in the garden. If only

I'd known how hard I would fall for him. If only I'd had the strength to stay away…

Maybe that's what his fiancée thought too, before she killed herself.

"Mads, are you okay?"

I swallow and nod. "Yeah, I'm just…thrown a little off balance, that's all. I'm fine." I force a smile. "Really."

"He's a fucking asshole."

"Yeah," I say dispassionately.

"Hey, you know, Keith has been asking about you. And you know what they say about falling off the horse… Or about the best way of getting over one man is to get under another one."

I shake my head. My heart aches at the thought of being intimate with anyone other than Kohl. For a time, he had possessed me completely. My body, my mind, my heart. Maybe in some ways he still has that hold. He'd wrapped his will around me like a thick blanket, and it will take time to find my way out again.

Our connection had run deep. Or, at least, *I* thought so.

I glance at Sam, uneasy with the way this conversation is heading, so my gaze drops to the sidewalk. In the past three days, Sam has tried to set me up with five different men. I think she's feeling guilty and a little too eager to throw me at the feet of any semi-attractive guy who might lure my thoughts—my obsession—away from Kohl.

I clear my throat. "I forgot—I need to stop by the bursar's office. I'll see you over at the lab."

Sam turns to me, reaching out a hand. "Mads, I'm sorry, I didn't mean to—"

"Sam," I say firmly. "I'm fine. Really. I'll see you in a bit."

She squints at me, not at all convinced. "Okay."

I turn on my heel and head into the bursar's office to talk to someone about my account. In just a couple of days, my tuition payment will be delinquent. Weeks ago, I had quit the coffee shop at Kohl's insistence in order to to be "available" for him. Naturally, they have since found a replacement. The money from my graduate work was barely enough to cover my rent and food before. There's still the matter of tuition, books, and living expenses. At a place like Caltech, none of that comes cheap.

The woman at the front desk of the bursar's office looks up at me from behind her computer in that impatient way that makes me feel like a nuisance.

I smile despite my nervousness. "Um, hi, can I speak to someone about my account?" I manage to get out. "It looks like I'll be a bit short this month and need to talk to someone about a payment schedule." I'm not even sure if that's an option, but I'm desperate.

"Name? Student ID?"

I give her the necessary information, and her nails click feverishly on the keyboard before coming to an abrupt stop. She squints at the screen, clicking a couple times before looking up at me through her glasses. "You're all set."

I blink, a little confused. "I'm sorry? What do you mean I'm all set?"

"Your tuition has been paid in full. There's two hundred and fifty thousand dollars in your account."

My jaw drops. Wait, *what?*

"I'm sorry, I don't understand—two hundred and fifty *thousand* dollars? From whom?"

It couldn't have been Kohl, could it? Our contract was voided, all connections severed, as with all agreements. *Your body for my money.* And since were were no longer...

After a couple more clicks of her mouse and some squinting, she replies, "We received payment from Mr. Kohl last week."

Last week. After our split.

"Oh." I reel a bit, shocked. "Okay, thanks."

As I walk out of the bursar's office, my mind is spinning. Why would he pay my tuition? He had no obligation to pay for anything after the termination of our relationship—the contract made that clear. So why, then? Could he still have feelings for me? Was this his way of reaching out and apologizing?

Maybe I should text him...

My phone is out of my pocket and in my hand before I realize what I'm about to do. Sam's news, *he's interviewing for another mistress,* rings through my mind, and I angrily shove my phone back in my pocket.

Knowing Kohl, he'd probably paid me off out of guilt. Because despite what people may say about him, I know he has a heart. Even if he does his level best to keep it locked up tight...

***

As the weeks slowly crawl by, I settle into a new normal without Kohl. I pour myself into my classes and my projects, but Kohl is never far from my thoughts.

There are some nights, I swear, I can still taste him on my lips. I can still hear his voice, deep and commanding, coaxing me to climax. I can feel his hands gliding across my skin...

And as much as I want to forget, he's branded in my memory. He's a part of me, a part of who I've become.

I'm in the lab when Keith walks in looking as confident and handsome as ever. He smiles at me and leans against the worktable that I'm currently hunched over.

"Hey. Let's grab some lunch after this."

I look up from the telescope I'm working on, frustrated that my calculations aren't quite right. "Yeah, okay. I could use a break."

I grab my bag, and we head out of the building toward the cafeteria. Keith has his arm around my waist, and he says something about going to see the new Marvel movie when I catch a glimpse of something—no, some*one*—in my peripheral vision.

I turn my head to get a better look.

Kohl.

My eyes instantly collide with his. He's walking with the President of the Institute and a cluster of several other men and women, all dressed in sharp business suits. They're walking toward us, obviously on their way to an important meeting.

And he looks…*beautiful*, so fucking hot my knees threaten to buckle. He's wearing a gray suit, tailored to fit his large frame, and his dark hair is combed back away from his face. The look in his eyes is level, powerful and commanding. His stoic features reveal nothing.

Keith is talking, but all I can hear is the frantic beating of my own heart. Even as we continue to walk, the world around me falls away, and all I can see is Kohl. He's here. *Why is he here?*

"Hey, earth to Maddy. What do you think?" When I don't answer, Keith glances at my face and follows the direction of my gaze. "Oh, shit. It's Evan Kohl."

Thank you, Captain Obvious.

Kohl's gaze shifts to Keith, and the stoicism melts away. His eyes narrow dangerously, his beautiful face twists into a scowl. Ah, so he doesn't like seeing me with someone else. That knowledge gives me a little thrill. It shouldn't, but it does. And just to rub it in a little more, I lean into Keith and whisper something about the movie in his ear. Keith responds with a smile. Kohl's expression darkens.

Using Keith like this is so wrong. I know it is. But I can't help myself. I want Kohl to hurt like I hurt. I want him to feel the same pain he's inflicted on me. I want him to know I'm moving on.

Happiness is the best revenge. Isn't that what they say?

Seconds melt into what feels like minutes, hours, before Kohl and his group turn a corner ahead of us and disappear. Instantly, I release the breath I'd been holding and the muscles in my shoulders unclench.

"Wow, that was fucking awkward." Keith stops and turns to me. "You okay?"

I push out a breath. "You know, I'm really tired of people asking me that. I'm *fine*. I'm not going to fall apart."

He looks concerned. "It's just not every day that you run into your ex."

"I didn't run into him," I clarify with a shaky smile. "I saw him at a distance. Either way, I'm totally fine."

But even as the words leave my mouth, I wonder how true they are. If I'm being honest with myself, *totally fine* might be pushing it. But I'm nowhere near as delicate as everyone fears. I'm already half over him. *Almost.*

"He must be here for the press conference." Keith says, his head turning to stare after the direction the group had turned as we pass by.

"Wait, what press conference?" I stop.

"Didn't you hear? XVerse is getting ready to launch their new solar-powered rocket."

I shake my head. "I've been putting in extra hours at the lab. I guess I've been out of the loop." And deliberately not reading any aerospace news.

In addition, I've been staying away from the internet and social media. The last thing I need is to come across a picture of Kohl with his new mistress. Yeah, *no thanks.*

"XVerse and a couple of the professors here have been collaborating on the Asteria 3."

"Oh, right. Yeah." I remembered that. I just didn't think he'd be coming *here* to do press interviews. "Whatever. Fuck Kohl. I'm starving." I step forward again, quickening my pace on the way to the cafeteria.

Keith's brows rise sharply, but he sends me a knowing smile. "Let's get a move on."

CHAPTER 33
A CONFESSION

A WHILE LATER, I'M BACK IN THE LAB, WORKING ON THE telescope, when my phone vibrates in my back pocket. It's probably Sam, asking what I want for dinner. She's been on a casserole craze lately, but I really can't complain. It's better than takeout, which is what I usually grab after the cafeteria closes.

I grab the phone out of my back pocket and glance at the screen. I gasp—literally *gasp*—when I see Kohl's name.

I've been thinking about you.

A second later, another text comes through. The ordering tone plain in the words:

Meet me for coffee.

Another one pops up immediately after.

Today. 3 p.m.

I stare at the words. How many times in the last few weeks have I prayed for a text—*any* text—from him? He's ignored me for weeks. But he catches me with another guy, and now he's suddenly blowing up my phone?

Oh, hells to the no. I'm not his little puppet, just sitting around waiting for him to text me.

My fingers hover over the screen. I'm tempted to reply *fuck you*, but in the end, after a ton of mental anguish, I decide no response at all would be more of a *fuck you* than anything I could ever type out. I do get a little satisfaction from flipping off my phone, however, as if he can somehow see it.

Once that decision is made, I scroll through my contacts, block him, and then delete his name and number from my phone. I don't know the number by heart, so now there's *zero* chance I'll be tempted to text him back in a moment of weakness.

Shoving the phone into my back pocket, my heart feels heavy. The finality of deleting his name, of not being able to reach out to him, makes me feel…adrift. Lost. So horribly *alone*.

Pushing those thoughts away, I do the only thing I know how to do. I throw myself back into my work. Again.

The rest of the day passes in a blur, and I spend most of it trying *not* to think about Kohl. In every case, I fail miserably. Every other thought is of him. I can't get the image of his face out of my mind. In that brief glimpse I got of him, he'd looked…tired. Unhappy.

I shake my head. Why should I fucking care? If he's unhappy, that's his own damn fault. But despite my better judgment, there's still something inside me that cares about him.

I'm so fucked up.

Hours later, I'm still in the lab when Keith walks in, his laptop open and resting on his forearm. "Hey, Maddy, take a look at this."

He sets the laptop in front of me on the worktable, and hits the play button. Instantly, an image of Kohl comes onto the screen, and I suck in air quickly in surprise. He's sitting across from an interviewer in a small library. I recognize the locale immediately as the library here, at Caltech's faculty club. I've been inside it many times for lunches and events. Now, Kohl is there, talking about the launch of the Asteria 3, his life, and his hopes for the future. One particular comment catches my attention.

"I know all the single ladies will flay me alive if I don't ask—are you currently seeing anyone?"

There's a long, uncomfortable pause, and I can see the myriad emotions playing across Kohl's beautiful face. Finally, he looks up at the camera and says, "There is someone…" My heart drops, and I suddenly feel nauseous. "There *was* someone," he corrects. "She is…beautiful, extraordinary. I'm in love with her. But I've been an arse and I'm afraid I've pushed her away forever."

The interviewer blinks at Kohl, clearly not expecting such an honest answer. He laughs nervously. "Care to tell us who she is?"

"Her name is Madeline Swanson."

Holy shit. I stumble back a little, shocked. So many things hit me at once. He admitted to being an ass. He called me out on national television. He just said he *loved* me.

"Can you fucking believe him?" Keith laughs, pausing the video. "He seriously thinks he can just declare his love or whatever and you'll come running. What a douche."

"When was that posted?" I ask, biting my bottom lip.

"Today. That's why he was here. For the interview," Keith says.

I nod absorbing that, then I blink up at Keith. Curiosity is eating at me. "Did he say anything else about me?"

He narrows his eyes at me, suspicious. "No, that's it. The rest of the interview is about the Asteria 3. Why?"

I blink, shaking my head. I don't know what to think or feel. "It doesn't matter."

"Oh God, Maddy. You're not actually falling for his douche move, are you?"

"No. Yes." I squint at him. "I don't know. Am I an idiot?"

"Yes!" he says, throwing his arms up in frustration.

Keith does have a point. Kohl knows damn well where to find me. I've been here the entire month since we broke up. If he wanted to contact me before today, he could have. But he didn't. He let me go, and he broke my heart. I can't go back to that, because honestly, the same issue remains: I want more. More than he can give. And a two-second interview confession isn't going to change that.

"No, you're right. He's an ass." I glance at my telescope and push out a breath. My focus is completely shot now. "I just need to get out of here. It's been a long day."

Keith nods and pushes out a relieved breath. "Can I walk you home?"

I just want to be alone, but I don't want to hurt his feelings, so I smile. "Sure. Thanks."

I carefully and meticulously store all my instruments before grabbing my bag so we can head out. The house is on the other side of the small campus, so it will be a short walk, thankfully. One thing I like about Keith, though, is that he doesn't push. He's happy to walk in silence, which is something I appreciate right now.

"Oh, my GOD!" One of my classmates, Becca, comes rushing up to me. "Did you see that interview Evan Kohl did today? He called you out, Maddy. Said he *loves* you! Fuck, if only I could get a guy like that."

I just smile, because I'm not really sure what to say. Do I just deny it, or laugh and pretend it's a joke? Fuck. I didn't think anyone would confront me about it. Especially this quickly.

As I'm considering how to respond, more people spot me and start crowding around, offering congratulations, and asking me questions. Then, of course, the gathering crowd draws even *more* attention, and before long, I'm being suffocated by people—*strangers*—wanting all the details about my love life. There are even several people from the press there, shouting their questions.

I gasp for air, tears welling up in my eyes and my vision spinning. It's just too much to deal with. I don't even know how I feel about the situation yet, and people are pressing me to answer emotionally intimate questions.

"Hey, hey, guys! Back off. Give her some room to breathe," Keith says, grabbing my hand. He tugs me through the crowd until we're free of the tight, suffocating ball of people. His gaze flicks over my face. "Let's get the fuck out of here."

"Yeah," I choke out. "Good idea."

After shaking off even the most persistent stragglers, we head home. Still holding hands, Keith tows me across campus to the house I share with half-a-dozen other female students. On the front porch, he finally lets go of my hand.

"Hey, um, Maddy," he says, stepping close to me. "I know you're going through a lot right now. I just want you to know...I'm here for you." And then he leans in and kisses me.

I'm stunned for a second, and I don't move. His scent, and the feel of his warm lips on mine, just feels weird, and so wrong. In that split second that our lips are locked, it feels like I'm cheating on Evan. I know I'm not, but I just can't shake the feeling that this isn't right.

Pushing on Keith's chest, I break the kiss and take a step back. "Keith," I say. "Thank you for being such a good friend, but…I just can't right now. It's too soon."

Maybe after my heart heals, it won't feel like I'm kissing an eel. A very handsome, kind, and understanding…eel.

Keith glances down, and places his hands in his pockets. "Yeah, I get it. I'm sorry, that was—"

"Don't worry about it," I interrupt. The less we actually talk about what just happened, the better. This entire thing is awkward as fuck. "I know it's cliche, but it really is just me. I'm in a weird place."

"Yeah, of course," he says, taking a step back, then another. "No worries. I'll, uh, see you in the lab tomorrow."

I nod. "Thank you for your help with all that. I'll see you tomorrow."

I slip around the back of the house after saying goodbye, then unlock the door and duck into the house through the kitchen, up the stairs unseen by my housemates and straight to my room. Do not pass go, do not collect two hundred dollars. I sink onto my bed, deflated. I just need some time to figure things out, and get my shit together. I can't go on like this. Being emotionally jerked around by everything Evan does and says.

I need to get over him.

Somehow, I need to forget Evan Kohl.

CHAPTER 34
BROKENHEARTED

THE QUIET SOLITUDE IN MY BEDROOM DOESN'T LAST long, despite my having snuck up here unseen. In minutes, I'm inundated by my roommates, Lexi, Cassie, and Avery, their eyes wide and frantic.

"Oh, thank God, you made it back safely," Avery says, handing me the Hill House landline. "The phone has been ringing off the hook for the last couple hours. Mostly media outlets. They want a statement."

I immediately raise my fingers to my temples and rub instead of taking the receiver from her. *Oh, hell no.* There's no possible way I can deal with this right now.

Shaking my head, I wave the phone away. "I, uh, need to be alone for a while. Just…I don't know, tell them 'no comment' or whatever. Please?"

Avery frowns, clearly confused. "Uh, okay…"

Lexi's brows furrow in obvious concern. "Are you okay, Mads?"

The tears are threatening to spill down my cheeks. I fear that saying *anything* will open the floodgates. And if that happens, there's no way my roomies will give me any peace. With the best of intentions, they'll *insist* we pick the issue apart, analyzing every angle, *ad nauseam*. And there's just no way I'm up for that.

I honestly just want to sleep for three hundred years and then forget Evan Kohl ever existed.

"I'm okay. Please, just let me be alone for a while?" There's a tremble in my voice with the plea.

Lexi presses her lips together and nods tightly. "Sure, yeah. We"ll make sure you're not disturbed."

"Thanks," I say and smile faintly as they file out of the room, each one throwing me a look of concern or pity—or both—over their shoulders.

As soon as I'm alone, I fall facefirst onto my bed. I'm so tired. *Emotionally* tired. All this shit with Evan—and then Keith—is too much, and I have no idea what to do or think. All I know is that the deepest parts of me miss Evan Kohl—my heart, my soul. All that cheesy Hallmark shit.

But he's so fucking unavailable, it's not even funny. Even if he's telling the world he loves me, it's just another manipulation. I mean, fuck, didn't Sam even say he was interviewing for another mistress? How can you declare on a televised interview that you love someone while also vetting the next woman you are planning to fuck regularly under a contract? Something just doesn't add up, but honestly, I'm too tired and too heartbroken to do that math.

Pulling my pillow under my head, I tuck my hands underneath and close my eyes. I school my thoughts into nothing, as I've taken up meditation recently to help me with handling my emotions. A meadow with yellow flowers…something, *anything*, other than Evan Kohl and the destruction he left behind.

I must have drifted off to sleep for a few minutes because I'm jolted awake by a loud knock. Our bedroom window is directly above the front door, so whenever we have a visitor, I can hear it, clear as day.

Scrambling off the bed, I pad over to the window and glance down. I can't see very much, but I open my window and the voices from below drift in. I suck in a breath when I hear Evan's deep baritone. I can't really hear what's being said, but after a few seconds, I hear the door slam shut—probably Avery or Lexi telling him to fuck off, in not so many words. *Good for them.*

Stepping back, Evan curses loudly and turns to stalk down the walkway toward the street. My heart lurches when I see him, even if it's just the back of his head. From any angle, he's beautiful, wearing the same tailored gray suit from earlier in the day, his hair neatly combed. He walks like he owns the world, even after being shut down by one of my roommates. I bet *that* really fucked with him. Evan Kohl never gets shut down. He never gets told *no.*

Well, he's just been told "no" by me. I can't go back to what we had before. I want more. And that, by his own words, is more than he's willing to give. I can't—I *won't* settle for less.

As he reaches the curb where his black Tesla is parked, he stops and turns to look back at the house. My heart stops as his gaze flicks up and collides with mine. For a second, we're suspended in time, our gazes locked. A sexy and, dare I say, hopeful half-smile tugs at the corner of his lips. I feel the sudden urge to call out to him. Beg him to come upstairs, take me in his arms, kiss me, even to fuck me until we're both lost in the bliss of each other's bodies. But I know, if I do that, nothing will ever change.

I'll always want more.

He holds that gaze but doesn't move until he reaches into his pocket and pulls out his phone, probably to call me. Kohl isn't one to lurk beneath a woman's window and yell up to her. I'm assailed with the ridiculous image of him climbing a nonexistent trellis, all Romeo-and-Juliet-like.

Instead he fiddles with his phone screen, then brings the device up to his ear, meeting my gaze again. He's calling me. But though my phone is right beside me on the night table, it doesn't ring, because I've blocked him.

After a moment, he seems to realize I'm not going to answer, and that's when I take a deep breath and force myself into action, though more than half my body seems to be resisting me.

Swallowing hard, I pull the window closed and let the curtains fall back into place, shutting him out. I step back and fall on the bed once more to stare helplessly up at the ceiling.

There's really nothing to say anymore. All I can do is cry.

Chapter 35
On His Knees

THE NEXT DAY, I DRAG MYSELF OUT OF BED AND FORCE myself to take a shower, get dressed and put on some makeup. I have very little desire to leave the room I share with Sam. But if I don't, I'll end up spending the entire day in bed, wallowing in this misery. Keeping myself—and especially my mind—busy will keep me from the endless thought-loop of all things Evan Kohl.

I opt to suspend the job search I'd been engaged in for the past week to replace my barista stint at the coffee shop. But there's a special lecture being held across campus later this morning. I'm tempted to ask one of my classmates to take notes for me, so I can skip it, but decide against it. I have to get out and get back to the life I'd been busy rebuilding in the wake of the breakup. I'd been doing a decent job of it, I thought, until Evan decided to drop his mindfuck bomb on a nationally televised interview yesterday.

Fucking asshole move. But he'd been successful in tying me in even more knots than before. It hadn't been enough to just see him across campus while I'd been walking close to Keith. Or to have him text me asking for—no, almost *demanding*—I meet him for coffee. He'd had to declare to an interviewer, and subsequently, the world, that he was still in love with me, calling me by name. Without any thought of what that violation of my privacy might do to my life.

So far, it had brought a crowd as I left campus last night, along with some phone calls from the press, which my roommates had kindly handled. But given the several sheets of messages piled by the house's landline, there are quite a few.

And now, after having been turned away at my front door, Evan is well aware that I want nothing to do with him, blocked his number and shut him out—quite literally. I hoped he'd drop this and move on. But Evan wasn't that kind of man. Once he'd decided on something, he pursued that outcome relentlessly.

Wasn't that how the entire arrangement between us had come about? Had he taken my previous rejections as final before, this would never have even gotten started. So of course, I suspected this wasn't the end. I would just need to hold my ground.

Taking no chances with possible photographers lying in wait for me at the house, I slip out the back door and down the alleyway, taking the long way around toward campus. I have no idea if anyone is waiting to snap my picture to publish in a gossip blog or tabloid.

As I walk into the lecture hall, I realize I should have left five minutes earlier, because the room is already packed to the brim. I scan the crowd and spot an empty seat, way, way, *way* in the back. Perfect.

Readjusting my backpack on my shoulder, I climb the many steps to the third row from the top, and make my way toward the middle of the row and the one empty seat. I can feel everyone's eyes on me, and it's so unsettling. Pictures of me have been circulating campus social media groups, everyone desperate to know more about the woman who stole the space billionaire's heart.

The minute I reach my seat, I plop down, place my backpack at my feet and lean back in the chair. I spare a glance at the clock on the wall. Five minutes until the lecture begins.

Reaching down, I unzip the front pocket of my backpack and pull out my phone. There are no messages, no missed calls, and I feel a pang of disappointment. Not sure what I was expecting. I blocked Evan on my phone, after all.

Pushing out a breath, I check my email. Then I immediately wish I hadn't. Somehow, the media got hold of my email address and my inbox is flooded with interview requests.

My God.

Now I'm paranoid, wondering if someone's going to try to snap a photo of me here, in class, to give to the media or share on social. I keep my eyes down and refuse to meet the speculative stares darting my way.

Someone walks up to the podium, introduces the special lecturer, and we all settle in for what's going to be a one-hour discussion on the current and near-future developments in the field of artificial intelligence.

By fifteen minutes in, I'm already zoning out, my mind focusing on Evan, replaying those words he stated in the interview over and over again. *She is...beautiful, extraordinary. I'm in love with her. But I've been an arse and I'm afraid I've pushed her away forever.*

I'm deep in my thoughts, when the door to the lecture hall bursts open. We all shift in our seats as a man strides into the room, all power and confidence. He's instantly recognizable. Half the room gasps, but I'm frozen in shock.

Oh, *shit.*

It's Evan Kohl.

My heart crawls into my throat as I sink lower into my chair. What the fuck is he doing here? God forbid I've inadvertently walked into another one of his talks.

But just as that question flits across my mind, the microphone catches his voice, and I hear him utter my name to the speaker. The speaker shakes his head, shrugging at him before Evan edges him to the side, and addresses the class from the podium.

"I'm looking for Madeline Swanson. I was told she would be here."

Oh, my GOD! *Ground, open up please. Swallow me now.*

Collectively, the entire class turns to look at me. No one utters a word, but they don't have to. Evan's eyes climb the tiered seating, following the direction of their attention until his gaze catches on me, and a slow smile spreads across his lips. He has me within his sights—a hunter honing in on his prey, like that hungry wolf I'd once compared him to.

But he doesn't come to me. Instead, he places both hands on the podium, and leans into the microphone. Several people are standing now, their phones held up, capturing the scene that's about to play out. Others, I see, are snapping photos and getting pictures from their seats. It's already a shitshow.

"Madeline, I've come here to ask for your forgiveness. After pushing you away, I know—" His voice is thick with emotion, and he pauses briefly before continuing, "I know I don't deserve it. I know I don't deserve *you.* But this last month without you has taught me something—I don't want to spend another night without you beside me. I don't want to face another day without you in it."

Pain is written all over his face, and my chest literally hurts seeing it. I want to fly down the stairs and fall into his arms, but I'm so shocked, all I can do is blink away the tears that are threatening to fall.

He leaves the podium and approaches the stairs. Taking the steps two at a time, he finally comes to the end of the row where I'm sitting. After a moment's hesitation, he holds his hand out to me. "Please say you forgive me, Madeline," he says in a low voice.

My gaze drifts. Cameras all around me are capturing this moment—some may even be live on the internet as we speak. Almost certainly, this will be viral in minutes and damned if I want this, a pivotal moment in my life, captured for everyone to see. All my words, everything.

No.

Just no. Even here, while purportedly baring his soul, he is taking away my choices. I stand and face him, arms folded, shoulders squared.

I swallow convulsively and clear my throat. "I'm in a lecture that you've just interrupted, and I've made it clear I don't want to talk to you." My heart is beating so hard that I can feel it in my toes, in my wrists, at my temples.

There are whispers all around us, murmurings of surprise, some of disapproval at my answer.

He clenches his teeth. "All I want is a chance to be heard. To tell you—"

"Stop!" I choke out. He's not fucking giving up, and I just need him to go away or at least stop drawing everyone's attention to us. This is insane. "I'll—I'll speak to you after this. After the lecture. *In private.* But you have to wait until then."

His gaze hardens on me, and I can tell he's at war over what to do. After a long tense second, and then two, his fists clenching and unclenching at his sides, he finally nods in acquiescence. "After this, then. I'll wait outside." There are sighs of disappointment that I won't be satisfying the voyeuristic curiosity of my fellow students.

He turns to go and the breath I'd been holding since I spoke leaks from me as I slump to my seat in relief. After an awkward silence during which Evan reaches the floor and apologizes to the speaker, he's gone and the lecture resumes.

But the class is full of whispers, and quite frankly, I have zero idea what the lecture is about. My mind just keeps replaying, over and over again, what happened. I don't dare look at my phone, but I keep seeing the screen light up with texts though I've silenced the notifications so they won't interrupt the lecture. I stuff it into my backpack to avoid the temptation of looking at it. I don't want to know who's saying what about me out there on the internet.

Once the lecture ends, students start filing out of the classroom, and I tuck my stuff away slowly, procrastinating my departure. I'm dreading speaking to him again and have no idea what I want to say. I'm also making sure those phones are far away from us when we do end up speaking.

Right now I'm fighting an internal World War III. My heart wants to run to him and feel those strong arms close around me, pull me close. My brain is telling me to forget about it and kick him to the curb already.

Even as I step off the stairs and gingerly apologize to the speaker, who's still gathering his notes, I have no idea which way that war is going to end up.

But here I am, about to make a decision in the next few minutes that will affect the rest of my life.

I can see Evan lingering in the hall beyond, past the students, some of whom have stopped to shake his hand. He's gracious, but I can tell he's very distracted, scanning the cluster of students for me. When his eyes land on me, trailing at the back of the crowd, he excuses himself and steps to the side, waiting until I can reach him.

"Madeline—"

"Not here. Come on, there's an empty classroom around here somewhere." Some of the stragglers are still lingering, watching us speculatively, but Evan turns away from them and puts a hand on my shoulder guiding me to walk deeper into the building. As soon as we're out of eyeshot of the other students, I step away so that he's no longer touching me, and his arm slowly drops. His eyes are glued to me, but I look straight ahead.

Just around the corner, there is a small classroom, and I try the door, slipping in before he can say a word. I make sure to stand closest to the door so I don't have to fight my way past him to escape. As he enters after me, I make sure to position myself accordingly.

I slide my backpack off my shoulder and set it on the nearest desk and then turn to him.

"Okay, so obviously you are very determined to say what you need to say to me, but I want your word that once you have said it that you'll back off, stop bothering me and let me stand by my choices."

He swallows visibly before nodding. "Very well."

I lace my fingers together in front of me and wait for him to speak.

"I'm a fucking fool. I was wrong, so wrong about us. We weren't over. We *aren't* over. I—I need you." He hesitates, and my gaze flickers away from his. Deeply uncomfortable at the pain I see there, I squeeze my eyes closed, forcing determination. He sucks in a breath and adds, "I love you, Madeline." My eyes open and we lock gazes as my breath freezes. "Deeply. I've never felt this way about anyone else. Ever."

I let out a breath and shake my head as tears threaten, prickling at the backs of my eyes and throat. "I see through this. You cut things off between us so callously, don't contact me for a month. No word. *Nothing.* Then I hear you're interviewing for a new mistress."

Surprise flashes across his face, and it gives me a little satisfaction to see it. He obviously didn't think I knew about that.

"Yeah," I say bitterly. "I heard all about that."

"Madeline—" He reaches for me, but I flinch, and his hand drops. "I thought I could replace you. I thought another mistress would fill the deep void you left behind. She would help me forget about you. But halfway through interviews, I realized I just couldn't do it. No one can replace you, Madeline. No one. So I called it off."

I swallow, not sure if I believe him. "Okay, so you finally felt a hint of human emotion. Congratulations." I push out a breath. "But I still think its really convenient that you *happen* to see me across campus walking close beside some other guy and suddenly you're all over me. Blowing up my phone, pounding at my door. You have to have me back? *No way.* This is just another in a long series of efforts to control me."

Evan's shaking his head through everything, but rather than looking angry, he looks like he's in pain. His brow's furrowed, his jaw clenched. He's swallowing hard, his hands clenching and unclenching at his sides. But he says nothing.

The tears are pooling at the bottom of my vision, threatening to blind me. "I can't do this. I just can't—" I finally choke out. Hands fisting at my sides, I snatch up my backpack by the strap and turn to leave the room.

In a split second, he's spun and is now in front of me, blocking my way to the door in spite of my careful maneuverings. The tears are about to spill over, and God, I don't want him to see me cry, damnit.

"Evan—"

But before I can say anything else, he does something I never could have imagined, never could have predicted. My lungs suck in gallons of air, jaw dropping in utter shock.

Evan Kohl falls to his knees on the ground in front of me.

CHAPTER 36
FORGIVENESS

I'M STANDING FROZEN IN FRONT OF THE DOORWAY, WISHING desperately I could leave. But Kohl has dropped to his knees, blocking me from exiting the room.

Mercifully, he doesn't reach for me. My heart is racing in my chest, and I don't know what to say.

"Madeline, I'm on my knees and I'm offering you everything…my heart, my soul. My body. All of it."

I bite my lip, considering. "What was your plan, Evan? Stay away until you saw another man show an interest in me?"

He shakes his head. "It has nothing to do with him and everything to do with the fact that I—I thought I was protecting you. You had developed feelings and—"

"It's not like I did that on purpose. I couldn't help it, and I warned you…. The night I signed the contract, I said there was no way that signing a paper would prevent it."

"You were right. It didn't prevent it, for either of us. But I swear, Madeline, I pushed you away so I wouldn't ruin your life, like the others…. You heard the stories. You know. I'm exactly like my father. I ruin women."

I shake my head. "You didn't ruin them. You didn't ruin me."

He glances down at the floor for a second, before hesitating, then slowly stands up. From his full height, he stares down at me, all earnestness shining in his eyes.

"I knew when I first met you. I could feel how strong you were. Your will…and the more you resisted, the more I wanted to break you. The more you defied me, I…" His gaze drops to the ground again, and he shakes his head.

"…The harder you tried," I conclude in a quiet voice.

"I realized that night of the gala, when you admitted your feelings—I realized I'd let you in too close. But I couldn't help it. For the first time in my life, I encountered something I couldn't control. So I did what I've always done, I backed off and fought it with everything in me."

"So what's changed?" I ask, shifting on my feet. "Why are you coming back now?"

He takes a step forward, his body so close now that I can feel the heat radiating off of him. *Fuck.* My number one weakness is definitely Evan Kohl.

With his free hand, he reaches into his jacket pocket and pulls out a folded document, several layers thick. "This is a new contract," he says. "You can change it or add anything you want. Any stipulation, and it's yours."

I glance down at the papers in his hand as he unfolds them and holds them out to me. It's a tempting offer. The thought of Evan Kohl at my mercy, contractually obligated to do anything I want gives me a rush. What would I ask for? Walks along the beach every Sunday at 5 o'clock? Cuddles and Netflix every night between nine and eleven o'clock? Weekends full of alone time and passionate lovemaking?

But who wants to live like that? Who wants love on a contractual basis?

I take a step back, and his hand, holding the papers, drops.

Shaking my head, I take a deep breath. "I don't want that. I don't want you to do something just because you're obligated by a piece of paper. I'm done with contracts. I want *you*—without clauses and stipulations."

The fear in his eyes is real, and I can almost see the gears in that brilliant mind turning, trying to solve this riddle. Trying to figure out how he can keep both me *and* full control of the situation. "A contract would protect both parties from—"

"From *what*, Evan? Love? Heartache? I think we've already proven that's not true."

His jaw tightens, and he fiddles with the papers in his hand, unfolding and refolding them. "It removes uncertainty," he says, his voice thick, and in that moment, I finally understand.

In his world, everything is tightly controlled. Outcomes are written out and finite. But *this*—what we have between us—he *can't* control. He can't foresee the outcome, and that must terrify him.

"Love *is* uncertainty. It's knowing that every day that other person has the freedom to walk away but chooses not to." I hesitate, clearing my throat to say the rest without trembling. "Love *is* trust."

Evan's eyes drop to the papers in his hand, his contract, and I can sense the inner war, like he's deciding what to say that will convince me to come around to his way of thinking. "The one thing I'm certain of is that I can't lose you again," he murmurs finally.

I fold my arms across my chest, squaring my shoulders. "If that's the reason you need me to sign that, then you never had me to begin with."

He visibly swallows, Adam's apple bobbing up and down. The papers crackle in his hands as they tighten their grip. "You won't leave again?" he asks without looking at me.

"You'll just have to trust me," I answer. And that's the truth. I can't promise him anything. "Just as I'll have to do the same for you. All I know is that I love you, and being away from you was the worst four weeks of my life."

He creases the paper in his hand. "I don't know how to do this. I've tried and I don't…"

"There's no manual, no contract. No rules. Just the promises we make to each other." I brave a tentative smile at him. It's shaky and uneven, just like my insides. This isn't just scary for him. My insides are ice cold and jittery.

I know I wanted to push him away, but now I know I want to run into his arms.

"Madeline, if you won't take the contract, then…" With swift movements, he shreds the contract into pieces and shoves them into his jacket and holds out his empty hand. I place mine in it, and his long fingers instantly curl around it. "Take my heart. It's all I have to give."

The lump in my throat is so large I can hardly swallow around it and the back of my throat is stinging with tears. "Evan…I never stopped loving you. And I know you're scared. I'm scared too. There are no guarantees. But I can promise you that I want this. As much as you do."

He tugs my hand and just like that…I'm in his arms again, feeling that powerful hold wrap around me. My body melts against his, and his arms pull me tighter to him. Reaching up, I slide my hand around his neck as I rest my cheek against his shoulder, my eyes closing to savor the feel of him.

"Christ, I thought I'd lost you forever." His voice is quiet, thick with emotion. "The way you shut me out. It was the worst feeling in the world. I don't ever want to go through it again. I couldn't think—I couldn't *breathe* without you, Madeline."

"We're on even footing now, and there's no contract, no guidelines. Just you and me. Trying at a relationship. This will be new territory for us. An adventure."

"Madeline, I promise, with everything in me, I promise I'll do everything I can to make you happy. To keep you here with me."

I lift my head finally, and our eyes lock for a long, breathless moment. He's frozen and I can read that residual terror of losing me on his handsome features. His jaw is still tense.

Rising onto my tiptoes, I tilt my head up and touch my lips to his. At first, the kiss is tentative—like two teens kissing at the front door on their first date. But soon the contact deepens. His mouth opens to mine and we are falling into that familiar zone— that world all our own where we are lost in each other for long moments while our heads move together, mouths open, tongues tangling, breath mingling.

My body fuses to his, and his arms tighten around me. In minutes, I'm flushed with joy and arousal and want nothing more than to be alone with this man and start our new beginning.

A rushed, hoarse whisper from me and he is whisking us out of the building, our hands cinched together. Just outside the building, there's a clump of people waiting with their cameras poised—probably to grab the sequel to that dramatic scene in the lecture hall.

I curse that we didn't take the back way out, but soon, Evan is directing us toward his car—parked illegally nearby. It speaks a lot to his status on this campus that he hasn't already garnered half a dozen tickets or been towed away. He protectively shields me from the cameras as he opens the door for me and closes it after I sink into the buttery leather seat.

And soon we're speeding through the streets of Los Angeles toward the freeway and Exeter House in Malibu. The only time he takes his hand from mine is when he needs to downshift the car.

An hour later, we aren't inside the penthouse suite more than a minute before we're in each other's arms, holding each other and kissing passionately. Minutes later, our clothes are off and we're indulging in each other. I bask in the feel of his warm skin on mine, his hard body moving over my own. The worship of his hands, his mouth, his body. I'd missed this. Not just the ecstasy, but the closeness, the understanding.

The chemistry between us is still off the charts.

Finally, we come up for air, holding each other close, our sweaty skin sticking together. I smile and sigh happily against his chest and he kisses the top of my head, locking his strong arm across my back to hold me to him.

"God, I missed this…right here. Just lying close to you again," he murmurs.

"That's not all you missed, though," I tease.

Amusement rumbles in his big chest. "No, indeed. It's not the only thing I missed. But we have a lot of fun…in more ways than just that. I have to say that after you left, this place was so empty and haunting for me that I barely spent a night here."

I lift my head to look into his eyes, blinking with surprise. "Really?"

"Really. The first few nights, I couldn't sleep. I'd just pace the floor. I thought I was going mad."

I kiss his chest as if in consolation for that past turmoil. "This has been the shittiest month of my life. I was existing, but I wasn't living."

He nods in agreement. "That's a good way to describe it." His large hand comes up to smooth my hair. "I don't ever want us to go through that again. I'll do whatever it takes, Madeline. You are the one for me. The *only* one. I'm quite certain I recognized that when we met but interpreted it on a level of sexual chemistry."

"Well, we *do* have that...in spades. So you weren't wrong."

"We have that, and mind-blowing as it's been, it's so much smaller than everything else we have. I don't just want to fuck you until we fall down exhausted, I want to be with you. I think about telling you something new I heard or saw several times a day. When I come home from working or sit here waiting for someone to arrive, the person I want it to be is you. When I want to go and see the world—and yes, sometimes I do that for fun rather than just for work, but I can't imagine going anywhere, exploring, or on new adventures without you."

"I'll be here, and I'll also go with you wherever you want. I imagine that's going to be easier once I'm done with school, but—"

"Of course, you'll finish school. I can't wait to introduce you to my colleagues as Dr. Madeline Swan, my brilliant, beautiful, amazing and gorgeous girlfriend."

I laugh. "Not sure all those subjective adjectives are necessary."

He smooths my hair again. "They absolutely are."

"Well then, I guess you'll be my stunning, breathtaking, generous and genius boyfriend, Mr. Evan Kohl."

His hand links to mine, and our fingers lace together. He squeezes his fingers around mine, locking them together. "I have no desire to do anything for the next few days but to stay in this bed, make love to you, sleep and eat in order to get more energy to do it again."

My thumb caresses his. "That sounds like heaven. Let's do it. I've also been suffering from a serious case of orgasm-withdrawal. We have a whole month to make up for."

"Damn, then I need to get my strength up, don't I?"

I smile and look up at him again. "We *both* do. I don't plan on coming up for air anytime soon."

There's a glint in his eye that I recognize, the beginning of hot arousal, but also something else glowing from behind it. There's no mistaking what that is either, the way he's looking at me. Pure, strong love. He's looking at me as if I'm the only person in the world, and it's so overwhelming I can hardly speak.

But when I finally do, the only thing I can choke out is a quiet, moved, "I love you."

His reply is almost immediate. With the slight curving of his mouth upward, he cups my cheek. "I love you. Always."

CHAPTER 37
NEW YEAR'S EVE

IT'S BEEN SIX MONTHS SINCE EVAN TOLD ME HE LOVED ME and we shredded the infamous contract. Since then, life has been hectic but amazing. When I'm not in school and Evan isn't working, we spend every minute we can together—plays, charity benefits, glamorous appearances, fancy dinners, and especially quiet nights on the couch, binging Netflix. It's been heavenly.

Blinking open my eyes, my world comes into focus slowly. It's just after 12 p.m. and the light streams through the huge windows of the penthouse suite at Exeter House. Below, the Pacific Ocean sparkles in the sunlight as it thunders against the beach. Turning my head, I see Evan is already awake.

"Good morning, my love," Evan whispers, leaning forward to kiss the tip of my nose. "Are you ready to play hostess this evening?"

I smile at him, brushing the tip of my finger across the prickles on his chin. He loves it when I do wifey things, like decorating or hosting dinner parties. "Not really," I tease.

His gaze falls to my wrist, and he takes it in his hand, kissing the red marks left by the ropes last night. "I wasn't careful enough last night. I left marks on your skin."

I glance at my wrist. The marks are barely visible and were only made because I asked him to cinch the rope tighter. I like the resistance and the feeling of the rope tugging on my skin. So it's more my fault than his, really.

"I think I'll live," I laugh.

With a scowl, he throws back the comforter and climbs out of bed, buck ass naked. I drink in the sight of his perfectly sculpted ass as he walks to the bathroom. When he reappears, he has a towel tied around his waist and a small tube of ointment in his hand.

He sits on the edge of the bed and holds his hand out. "Give me your wrists."

"You're being overprotective, as usual," I say. "My wrists are fine."

"Wrist," he repeats without moving, without even blinking—as always bringing his usual intensity to any situation, big or small.

With a heavy sigh, I give him my right hand. He takes the ointment and puts some in his palm, then rubs it into my skin gently. Then, he takes my other wrist and does the same thing. The subtle scent of eucalyptus and mint fills the air around us.

He punctuates his careful ministrations with a quick kiss on the backs of both my hands before letting them go.

"Thank you," I say. "It already feels better."

I fling the covers off of myself and move to get out of bed, but he reaches over and grabs me by the hips, preventing me from getting up. "No, no," he growls. "We're not getting up quite yet."

"Uh, yes we are. It's already past noon, and I have to take a shower. We have people coming over soon."

It's our first New Year's together, and I wanted to make it special, so I invited all my friends from Caltech and a few of Evan's friends from work. Well, *friends* is a loose term. Evan Kohl doesn't really have *friends* per se. He has business associates that he's friendly with—but we're changing that, slowly but surely, as he learns to open himself up. It's a slow process, but he's trying and I love him for that.

I feel his gaze on me as I walk to my open suitcase and pull out a new pair of panties and a black lace bra.

"I had clothes purchased for you and put in the closet," he reminds me.

"I know, and I appreciate your generosity." I turn around to face him. "But the underwear you chose aren't exactly practical."

Evan made sure the closet was filled with fine silk and delicate lace, which is great for the bedroom. Not so great for everyday life.

"I don't know why you're still living out of your suitcase," he says. "I ask you every week to move in with me."

During the week, I still share a room with Sam. It's just easier if I have classes because the trek from Malibu to Pasadena is at least an hour one way, on a *good* traffic day, which is extremely rare in Los Angeles. Losing more than two hours a day on just the commute isn't something I can accept.

"When I graduate, we can re-examine the living arrangements. For now, though, my place in Pasadena is way more convenient during the week." I punctuate my statement with a gentle smile to soften the rejection.

He nods slowly, and I can see that beautiful mind is trying to think of a solution. Bless him. It's why he's so brilliant at business. He's a problem-solver at heart, brain always in overdrive while thinking up better solutions in business, the science and technology fields, even in our domestic life. "Maybe we should move into Hill House together. That way we can be together during the week."

My brows shoot up. "What about your work?"

He shrugs a shoulder. "It might be possible for me to rearrange a bit."

"Great, you think on that." I wink at him, clutching a bundle of clothing to my chest. "Meanwhile, *I'm* taking a shower."

I head into the palatial, marble-covered bathroom and turn on the shower. Once the water is hot, I step inside, relishing the feel of the hot water as it glides over me. I'm shampooing my hair when I hear the shower door open. I peek my eyes open briefly to spy a naked Evan stepping inside. His cock brushes against my ass as I rub the shampoo into my hair.

"You fucking tease," I laugh. "Can't I take a shower in peace?"

"No," he says with that sexy accented baritone. "And it would please me if you rinsed that out, then got down on your knees."

"Oh, would it?" I laugh. "And *why* would I do that?"

He cups my breast in his large hand, brushing his thumb over my nipple. "Consider it a New Year's gift."

After a kiss and a rinse, I do just that.

Once our shower is over, I busy myself preparing for our guests to arrive while Evan deals with the caterers who have just flooded into the penthouse. I'm actually really excited about tonight, because it's the first time in a while I'll get to see everyone. I've been so busy with school, and Evan, that I haven't had time for much else.

Around four o'clock, people start arriving. Sam is first, of course, because she's been dying for an excuse to get inside an Exeter House suite.

"Hey, babe," she says, walking in with an armful of gifts. "Where do you want these?"

It's New Year's Eve, but it's also our Friends-mas. We tried getting together before the holidays to exchange gifts, but too many people were traveling to see family and it just didn't work out. Thankfully, everyone could make New Year's Eve work.

"Just put them under the tree," I say. "I left it up so we could do Friends-mas properly."

She places them under the tree, then looks around the living room, taking in the lavish decor. "You have your own elevator! This penthouse is *incredible*. Exeter House really lives up to its reputation. The money in this place is so fucking unreal."

"Yeah, I guess it's not too shabby," I say, laughing.

The rest of the crew trickles in over the next hour. When Keith arrives, I pull him into a hug. We're both a little on edge, because in the past, Evan never really approved of my friendship with Keith—for the simple fact that Keith has a dick. But Evan and I are working on that foundation of trust, so this is all a grand experiment.

Evan walks over, and I can tell he's evaluating the situation. "Hey, man," he says, handing Keith a glass of scotch. "Thanks for coming."

Keith looks confused but takes the glass. "Thanks for having me."

Evan nods, clinks glasses with Keith, then moves on to greet the other guests. Keith and I glance at each other, shocked. "Well, it's a start," I laugh.

Keith takes a sip of his scotch. "As long as he doesn't murder me for touching you, we're good."

Lexi arrives a few minutes later, and after she puts her gifts and purse down, I hand her a flute of champagne. "You're late," I tease. "You need to catch up."

She accepts the champagne and takes a sip. "Thanks, babe! I actually can't stay very long, but I wanted to wish everyone a happy New Year." Leaning in, she gives me a hug. "God, you look so fucking happy, Maddy. I'm jealous!"

"I *am* happy," I say, smiling. "But why the fuck are you jealous? You'll find your person, too. Right time, right place and all that."

She smiles coyly, like she's got a secret. "Yeah, well, the right place, right time may have already happened."

Oh, now I'm intrigued. "Do tell!" I say. "Who is he? What does he do? Do you have a picture of him?"

Lexi laughs. "Don't worry, you'll get all the details soon enough. You might already know him, actually. He's a prospective Exeter House member."

"Ohhhh, what's his name?" I ask.

Lexi waves me off with a laugh. "I don't want to jinx it. I'll tell you when I tell you."

"Okay, okay. I'll be patient," I laugh. "But I'm happy for you."

"Thank you," she says. "I'm sorry, but I've got to run. Let's do coffee next week when you're back in Pasadena."

"Sounds great," I say. "Let's do it."

We all live in the same house, but we're like passing ships in the night, especially since I'm only there to sleep and go to school these days. Our schedules are so varied, we hardly see each other. Lexi and I are long overdue for a catching-up sesh.

Lexi says hello and goodbye to everyone, then with an air-kiss and a wave, she heads out.

After an amazing four-course dinner, we all sit around the Christmas tree, drinking, telling war stories about Caltech. Just as Keith is illustrating his story about a particularly nasty encounter with one of the aerospace professors, there's a knock at the door.

Evan, ever the impeccable host, gets up to answer the door. A handsome, six-foot-something guy is standing in the doorway. A strand of wavy dark hair falls across his forehead, and he combs it back into place with his fingers.

Evan invites the newcomer in, and they move to the living room, where we're all sitting. He looks very familiar to me, and when he's introduced, I realize why.

"Everyone," Evan says. "This is Mr. Ashford Grayson. He's a fellow Exeter House member. He lives just down the hall."

I remember him now...the guy who came out of the mysterious locked black door in the lower levels of Exeter House and helpfully showed me to the elevator when I was lost.

We all murmur our greetings as Evan and Mr. Grayson talk briefly, just out of earshot. I watch the two men, amazed at how similar they are. Both handsome, youngish, and confident. Both rich. *Shit.* Is Exeter House just a watering hole for hot, insanely successful men?

Sam leans in and whispers to me, "Holy shit, Maddy. You've been holding out. Who the hell is this tall drink of water?"

"No idea," I whisper back. "I only met him once, and it was really brief."

Cassie sidles up next to Sam and me. "Oh, my fucking GAWD, Maddy! Hook me up with that one. He looks like he'd be really fun in the bedroom."

"Shhhhhh." I wave at Cassie discreetly. "He'll hear you."

Cassie laughs. "I hope he does."

Sam rolls her eyes. "Who are you kidding, Cassie? You're as straight-laced as they come. A man would have to provide his entire stock portfolio before you'd even consider opening those thighs."

Sam is so frank but it's all in good fun, and thankfully, Cassie knows that.

"Oh, my God, Sam! How dare you," Cassie laughs. "I resemble that remark."

"Yeah, you do," Sam responds.

Evan and Mr. Grayson finish up their conversation, and both men turn toward all of us, sitting in the living room.

"Please excuse the intrusion," Mr. Grayson says, scanning the room. He holds up a bottle of scotch he brought in with him. "I just wanted to stop by and offer my wishes for a Happy New Year."

"Thanks for stopping by, man," Evan says, accepting the bottle.

"Good night, everyone," Mr. Grayson says, before leaving.

"Wow, Evan, you need to invite your sexy neighbors over more often," Sam says. "Is he single?"

Evan laughs. "Ash is single, but he's always got a woman, if you know what I mean."

Sam and Cassie laugh, then say in unison, "Oh, yeah!"

After dinner, the caterers pass around flutes of champagne, and once we all have one in hand, Evan taps on his glass with a spoon to get everyone's attention.

"Friends, I would like to thank you for joining Madeline and me tonight. It means a lot to have you all here." He reaches over and pulls me close against his body, one arm hooked around my waist. "Christmas is a time of warmth and gratitude, and I can speak for Madeline when I say we are thankful for each and every one of you. And as we look ahead to the future, I've realized"—he turns slightly to look down at me—"who I want to share that future with."

And then he does the most shocking thing—he releases me, and one of the waitstaff hands him a small box, then Evan gets down on one knee in front of me. In front of everyone. A collective gasp fills the room.

What...the...?

I glance down at him, mouth hanging open in complete disbelief. "Evan, what is this?"

"For a long time, I didn't think I needed anyone. But the last year has shown me just how much I need you. I can't breathe without you. Madeline Swanson—" He opens the small box and presents it to me. "Will you marry me?"

The ring is stunning and leaves me breathless. The band is a series of infinity symbols intertwined with diamonds, with a *huge*, glittering rock in the center. An obvious custom design. It must have cost a fortune, easily more than I've ever made in my life. I still have a hard time imagining that kind of wealth.

The room is so quiet all I can hear is the beating of my own heart. Six months ago, this wouldn't have been possible—Evan humbling himself in front of *anyone*, let alone a room filled with friends and colleagues. It just shows how much he's grown and opened up.

I smile down at him, my heart bursting with love for this man. "Yes." The word escapes with a breathy sigh. "Yes, I will marry you, Mr. Kohl."

The room erupts into cheers, but all I see is Evan and the relief that washes over his handsome face. He rises to his feet and slips the ring onto my finger, then pulls me into a deep, passionate kiss.

Then, breaking the kiss, he presses his forehead against mine. "I don't know what I would have done if you'd said no," he whispers.

I laugh a little. "I know exactly what you would have done. You would have pursued me relentlessly until I gave in."

His lips twist into a devilish grin. "You know me so well, Madeline."

"Yes, I do," I say with a smile. "And I love you more than you will ever know."

CHAPTER 38
LEXI

I CAN'T BREATHE.

I have no idea what just happened, but it feels like I'm in an alternate reality. Like I'm somewhere outside myself, watching this happen to someone else.

In the dim light of the hotel room, I toss my dress on quickly and fumble around the unfamiliar room for my purse. I hear a voice calling out to me, but it sounds far away, and I honestly can't even respond, so I don't.

This isn't real. It can't be.

I stumble out of the exclusive Exeter House suite number 403 and rush barefoot down the hallway, purse and shoes gathered in my arms, clutched tightly so I don't drop them. My feet slide along the slick marble floors as I make a beeline for the elevator. Crushing the *up* button, I glance over my shoulder to make sure no one is following me.

Especially not *him.*

But I'm alone in the dark hallway, thank *God.*

Fuck. Fuck. Fuck.

I'm trying to wrap my head around what just happened, but I can't think straight. My heart is hammering so hard against my ribs, it feels like my entire body is vibrating. And my lungs feel tight, like I can't draw in a full breath. Lord. I'm going to pass out, right here in the middle of the hallway, facefirst into a plush rug.

A ping, and the elevator slides open. My salvation.

Thank you, sweet baby Jesus.

I rush inside and frantically push the *close door* button, then immediately select the penthouse, where I know Maddy is staying with her fiance, Evan. Or at least I hope they'd made it back up to their room by now. We were all just downstairs for hours at the elegant restaurant Isca, enjoying their elaborate and very expensive engagement party.

They are definitely still in the building, but will they be back in their penthouse yet? What will I do if they aren't there yet?

Oh, my God, *please be there.*

The penthouse button lights up briefly, then switches off. I push the button again and again and again, but the same thing happens. *Damn.* I have no special code or pass key to get me to the members-only part of Exeter House. With a frustrated sigh, I press a button to head down to the lobby instead.

God, I hope *he* didn't think to come down here too. That would be beyond awkward. Halfway down to the ground floor, after digging through my tiny clutch, I discover that my phone isn't there. My mind is racing as I try to think through the blurry cocktail of alcohol and adrenaline currently zinging through my veins. The last time I used it, I was sitting at the bar downing drinks to get my courage up.

Shit. I must have left it there. After hopping to pull on my shoes and zipping my dress back up, I rush back to the bar, which has hardly anyone there and a different bartender. I check all around where I'd been sitting just an hour before and there's nothing, so I ask the new bartender who directs me to the front desk.

Without missing a beat, I turn and race to the front desk in my slippery heels. The receptionist glances up at me, and her smile immediately melts into a look of concern. "Good evening, miss. Is everything all right?"

I clutch the edge of the white marble countertop, struggling to catch my breath while trying to keep myself from falling over. "Yes, um, was there a cell phone found in the bar? Sometime in the last hour?"

The woman peels her eyes away from what must be the spectacle of my smeared makeup and sweaty visage, clothing askew. *Don't think about it, Lex, she'll never see you again.*

"I'm sorry, miss. No one's found a phone but if you leave your name and contact information, we can reach out to you if it's found."

I swallow. *Damnit.* I'm panicking—without that phone, I can't call a friend for a ride, or get an Uber, or…. I'm screwed.

Huh. In more ways than one…

The woman is waiting for my info, which I give to her and then I swallow and summon up my courage. "Can—can you please ring"—I pause, fighting through the panic to remember Evan's last name—"Mr. Evan Kohl, please."

The woman brushes a strand of dark hair behind her ear and glances at the clock on the wall behind me. "It's after midnight. Are you sure you wouldn't like to leave a message instead?"

I shake my head. "No, nope. Definitely not. It's *urgent. Massively* urgent. Please ring her—uh, I mean *him*—now, thank you." I try not to sound panicked, but given the circumstances, that's not even close to possible.

"O-okay." She picks up the phone and dials a number. She seems to be avoiding my gaze as she listens to the ring tone and waits for an answer. For me, that wait is agonizing, and I tap my foot, glancing around the lobby like someone is going to jump out at me.

"Yes, this is the front desk," the woman says into the receiver. "I have a—" She pauses and glances up at me expectantly.

"Lexi Anderson," I supply.

"Lexi Anderson here for you." The woman nods, smiles, and says, "Yes, thank you." Then she hangs up. She waves to a uniformed bellboy, who is standing on the other side of the lobby. "Thomas, can you please escort Ms. Anderson up to Mr. Kohl's suite?"

"Yes, of course," Thomas says.

Inside the elevator, Thomas uses a special key card key to access the penthouse. I'd figured something like that would be needed, despite the panicked button pushing from earlier. I clench my teeth and hug my own arms to me as the elevator climbs to the top floor. The doors slide open to reveal Evan's gorgeous silver-veined, white marble entryway.

Maddy is waiting for me, swathed in a white silk robe, her brows pinched in concern. "Lexi! Oh, my God, is everything okay?"

As soon as I step off the elevator, I dissolve into a puddle of tears in her arms. "I-I didn't know. I had no idea. I went into the room, and he was there. It was dark, and…" Just the memory has me sobbing even harder, unable to finish the sentence.

Evan walks into the foyer, wearing pajama bottoms and nothing else. His hair is tussled, eyes red, like he just woke up from a dead sleep. "Is that Lexi?" His critical gaze slides over me. "What happened?"

I just shake my head, unable to get all the words out. I trust Maddy implicitly, but even admitting what just happened to *her* is difficult, never mind her intimidating partner, a near-stranger to me, like Evan.

"Evan," Maddy chides. "Just give us a minute."

He doesn't budge, eyes narrowing as he looks me over. "Something has obviously happened. Let me call security." He's all power and control.

"*No!*" I practically lunge at him. "I mean, um, no, thank you. It's really not that kind of issue."

While holding me in her arms, Maddy twists to look at Evan. "Can you make us some tea, please? I think I have some lemon ginger in the cupboard."

With a dubious look, he nods and walks off toward the kitchen, which is on the other side of the penthouse, far out of earshot.

"Come on," Maddy whispers, guiding me to the sofa. I sit down, and she plops down next to me, taking my hands in hers. "Sorry about that. He's a natural problem-solver so he slips into that mode easily."

I have nothing to say in response so I merely nod.

She peers at me. "Now tell me, what happened? Whatever it is, we can work through it."

Her warm hands are wrapped around mine, lending me strength. I take a minute to compose myself, breathing deeply. Every possible explanation that's passing through my brain right now sounds downright ridiculous.

"Well, um…so you know how I came to your engagement party tonight with David?" She nods, while I sniff loudly and continue, "Well, I had this plan that we'd, um, finally seal the deal with our relationship tonight. You know, take it to the next level? But we got separated during the party, and I had to wait around for a bit. Then, he had a note delivered to me, asking me to meet him in the room he'd taken here for the night…"

"Okayyy…" Maddy says, her voice soothing and nonjudgmental. I dread telling her the next bit, because I know that understanding tone will quickly shift to abject horror and probably harsh judgment.

I swallow and gather all my courage. "So I go to his room obviously. But when I get there, he's already in bed with the lights off. I figure why not take advantage of the room and the ambiance and…so I decide I'm going to be sexy and adventurous. I take off all my clothes and slip into bed. We immediately start fucking—" I choke on a sob.

"Okay. That all sounds perfectly reasonable to me," Maddy says, trying to comfort me.

I shake my head again. "I'm not finished yet.… So it's happening and it's going really well, until halfway through, I realize it's *not* David. I must have gone to the wrong room, and…" I swallow. "I had no idea it wasn't David while he was *literally* inside me."

Maddy pulls back, that abject horror I knew was coming, written all over her face. "*What?*"

"Yeah," I choke out. "I fucked a complete stranger." I shake my head, fresh tears falling now. "And what's worse…it was absolutely amazing."

Evelyn has been telling stories in her head for as long as she can remember. She lives on the west coast with her family, and a menagerie of pets. She loves lattes, all things Disney, gaming, and writing dark, wildly sexy stories that give readers all the feels.

Sign up for news and updates:
evelynaustinbooks.wixsite.com/my-site/newsletter

www.ingramcontent.com/pod-product-compliance
Lightning Source LLC
Chambersburg PA
CBHW050803190726
48285CB00005B/1773